MW00459726

Two Funerals and a Wedding

a domestic bliss mystery (#8)

LESLIE CAINE

This is a work of fiction. Names, characters, places, and incidents are either products of the writer's imagination or are used fictitiously and are not to be construed as real. Any resemblance to actual events, locales, organizations, or persons, living or dead, is entirely coincidental.

Two Funerals and a Wedding
Copyright © 2014 by Leslie Caine
ISBN: 9781503058699
ALL RIGHTS RESERVED.

No part of this work may be used, reproduced, or transmitted in any form or by any means, electronic or mechanical, without prior permission in writing from the publisher, except in the case of brief quotations embodied in critical articles or reviews.

NYLA Publishing
350 7th Avenue, Suite 2003, NY 10001, New York.
http://www.nyliterary.com

To all of my fabulous friends in the coffee group at St. John's Episcopal Church in Boulder, Colorado. You mean the world to me!

1

"Do you ever get a feeling of impending doom, Erin?" Aunt Bea asked me with a sigh.

This was hardly a time for me to be gloomy. I was marrying the man of my dreams, Steve Sullivan, two weeks from Saturday. He was also my business partner in our interior design company, and Aunt Bea was one of our clients. She and I were currently doing a walkthrough of the new, enormous wine cellar that I'd designed for her.

"I do *now*. Are you trying to tell me you don't like what I've done with this space?" I joked. Or at least, I certainly *hoped* I was joking. She had declined my offer to allow my highly skilled crew to help her stock the shelves, so the unopened wine boxes were now marring the ambience. The overall effect was like trying to enjoy a glorious ocean beach when your lounge chair is completely surrounded by garish-colored tents and huge umbrellas.

"Not at all, my dear. I'm thoroughly enthralled with it. I'm so glad you convinced me to add an extension to the basement. Those goldenrod and maroon colors on the plaster walls are so warm and rich, you can almost taste them. The vines on the columns. The marble-top table. My basement could be a five-star restaurant in India."

"Excellent. That's precisely what I was aiming for." Although it would have felt better if her vocal tones hadn't been so flat. As an interior designer, I pride myself on being able to ascertain my clients' unique tastes, then refine them so that we create a space in which their guests exclaim: "I love it! This room is so *you!*" Identifying Bea's tastes had been a snap; her aim was to make visitors feel as though they'd entered a palace in India the instant they'd stepped inside her front door. Which was more than a little jarring, considering that this was a moderately sized, nondescript beige-with-white-trim two-story house in the foothills of the Colorado Rockies. Throughout her entire house, every room had a gold-and-burgundy color palate, along with numerous white-marble surfaces and pillars. Sitar music played on a nonstop loop from small speakers in every room (except for this one, thank heavens). The aroma of cinnamon and saffron perpetually wafted through the air, even though she hated to cook and had most of her meals delivered.

If I ever managed to convince Aunt Bea to let me redo her home, I would steer her toward subtlety—the less-is-more tenet of design that my affiliation with Steve Sullivan had helped *me* to refine. My biggest accomplishment so far was to convince her to let the wine cellar be her house's singular sound-system-free zone. Not wanting to state bluntly that her interminable Ravi Shankar music was discussed whenever anyone as much as mentioned her house, I had resorted to flowery language. I told her, "A fine glass of wine generates its own symphony." (Yes, my cloying statement was over the top, but I'm passionate about my career and will use every means available to get the best results.)

"I can't figure out what's gotten into me lately," she continued. "I just feel so anxious and pessimistic."

She truly did seem uneasy and kept fidgeting with her hair, which she wore in a bun. She was one of those lucky older women whose hair had turned snow white. She had a rather Buddha-like body, yet she seemed comfortable with her weight and moved gracefully, despite her gold, scepter-like cane that seemed to be more of a fashion statement than a crutch. Maybe she was suffering from arthritic pain, or depression. I decided not to risk insulting her by asking. Instead, I merely nodded and made a sympathetic noise.

She shuddered as if trying to shake off her mood like a wet dog ridding water from its fur. "I can't even tell you how greatly I'm looking forward to your nuptials."

"Not as much as I am," I said, beaming despite Aunt Bea's somber mood. It always made me smile whenever someone brought up the subject of my impending wedding to Steve Sullivan. "But let's get back to business for a minute. Do you like the spacing between shelves?"

She nodded. "They look perfect."

As Bea and I stepped around wine crates and inched along the rows of empty shelving, we discussed the minute details of the first-rate craftsmanship. This project had been pricey, yet Aunt Bea hadn't batted an eye. In the twenty years since Bea's husband had deserted her, she had made a fortune as a wine distributor, traveling extensively and eventually selling her home in Denver and moving to Napa. Last winter, she'd moved here to Crestview, Colorado, and had bought this house, tucked among the aspen and blue spruce in the foothills of the Rockies.

Back when she'd lived in Denver, Bea had become an honorary "aunt" to my adorable soon-to-be husband and his sisters. She was also an old friend of my beloved land-lady and housemate, Audrey Munroe. Audrey called her "Aunt Bea," too, despite their being roughly the same age. Audrey's explanation had been: "It's a nickname. Her actual name is Barbara Elizabeth Quince, but she preferred 'Beth' to 'Elizabeth' or 'Barbara,' which made her initials B.B.Q." Audrey never got around to explaining how she went from Beth to Aunt Bea, and I never asked. Conversations with Audrey are like Aunt Bea's bottles of Cabernet. They're absolutely delightful, provided it's past the noon hour when you open one, and you restrain yourself from overindulg-ing in them. I loved the woman dearly. Audrey was walking me down the aisle, a concept that never failed to make me smile; as if, for all of our disagreements, Audrey could *ever* "give me away."

The moment we finished our walkthrough, Aunt Bea said she'd like to sit at the table for a minute before we went back upstairs. We claimed our customary seats at the four-top table in her cozy, faux "Indian restaurant," just outside the carved oak door to her wine cellar.

"What is our Mister Sullivan up to today?" she asked.

"He's working on the design of the new restaurant on Maple Street."

"Steve's designing 'Parsley and Sage'?" she asked, with a grimace. "That figures. I'm sure Drew is taking full advantage of Steve's generosity." She snorted. "I just hope he isn't lead-ing Steve into trouble. It would be just like that self-centered jerk to con Steve into loaning him money, and then repay him with a jar of parsley and sage."

She was referring to Drew Benson, Steve's best man. Hav-ing met in second grade, Drew and Steve were each other's oldest and closest friends, and I felt compelled to defend him.

"Steve says that Drew saved his life when they were horsing around on the roof of a skyscraper in Denver."

"That's true," Aunt Bea said, "but I'm certain it was *Drew's* idea to climb onto that ledge in the first place."

She was not alone in that assumption. I liked all of Steve's friends immensely, but Drew was the type of guy you enjoyed most when he was just a voice on the phone. He'd left Denver and moved to Napa shortly before Steve and I had started dating. Now that he was opening another restaurant here in town, Drew was planning on living here at least six months every year. Unfortunately, Steve seemed to revert to a more boisterous—and boyish—version of himself whenever the two of them were together.

"I never see Steve anymore," Bea said, somewhat echoing my own train of thought.

His absence from Aunt Bea's life was due to his dislike of her. Bea had lived in the same Denver neighborhood where Steve and Drew had grown up. When Steve and I were drawing up our invitations, he had described her as "the loon from the family closet." After working on Aunt Bea's wine cellar for three months now, I had found her to be eccentric but not at all "loon-like." I'd begun to suspect that Steve's troubles with her were mostly due to her animosity toward Drew—for whom Steve had a blind spot in his heart.

"You'll see each other at the party tomorrow night at Parsley and Sage." When she gave me a blank stare, I added, "And at the wedding the Saturday after next."

"Oh, I'll be at both celebrations, Erin. As long as my premonitions turn out to be unfounded and I'm still up and kicking."

"Are you seriously afraid you won't be around in two weeks?" I asked.

Her only answer was a heavy sigh. My worry about her began in earnest.

"Did you have a bad dream last night? Are you feeling under the weather?"

"No, but I should have a talk with that young man of yours. I guess it can wait until tomorrow night. We need to discuss some serious matters. Ask him to carve out some private time for me at the party."

"Okay. I'll do that."

Our eyes met briefly, and I could see real fear there. I got the feeling that she was so scared about her impending death that she wanted to speak with Steve about her will.

"Are you all right, Aunt Bea? Is there anything I can do?"

"Not really, Erin." She was glancing around at the exceptionally well-constructed walls and ceiling as if she expected them to crumble all around us. "But thanks for asking."

"You're not envisioning the wine cellar collapsing, are you?"

"No, but I feel like...we've unearthed something. I think we've unleashed an evil spirit into the world when we constructed the foundation for this cellar."

"*Evil spirit?*" I scoffed. "I doubt we dug deep enough into the Colorado bedrock to reach Hades, Aunt Bea."

She rapped the floor with her cane three times, as if testing her theory to see if cracks—closely followed by demons—would emerge. "You're young and naïve, Erin. There *are* evil spirits. And we coddle them with our alcoholic 'spirits.' Liquor sometimes keeps them at bay, and sometimes sets them loose."

Unsure how to take her bizarre pronouncement, I decided to try to lift her mood by being supportive. "It's true that drinking can bring out the absolute worst in some people. But for most of us occasional drinkers, it simply encourages us to let our hair down a little and have a good time."

She glared at me as if I'd insulted her. "I'm not talking about some innocuous piffle, Erin. I've made a small fortune in this very industry—by selling well-aged alcoholic beverages. I *literally* mean that evil spirits are released when we open something that's been confined for many years...be it in the earth, the trunk of a tree, or an old bottle of wine."

Ah. Here was the "loon" side coming out.

"But you believe that *good* spirits are released, too, don't you?" I asked hopefully. The woman was supplying the wine and champagne for my wedding. Her current indigo mood gave me visions that she would tap on her champagne glass to command everyone's attention, only to announce at our reception: "The evil spirits in this champagne will burn our souls like acid. We are going to suffer for all eternity. Bottoms up!"

"Good forces are always balancing out the evil forces in this world, Erin. That's a comforting thought...until you find yourself the victim of an opposing force. And by the time you get to be my age, you realize how blurred the line between good and evil really is."

Her remarks were unsettling. Was she implying that she'd crossed over to the dark side at some juncture of her life?

Using her cane to steady herself, she rose from her jacquard chair and slowly turned in a full circle, studying our surroundings once more. "Good work, Erin. I'm very pleased. The next time you come here, it will be completely finished. All of my precious bottles will be put where they belong, and the ugly packaging will be out of sight."

"That's precisely what *I* typically say to my *clients*. I wish I could at least *help* you shelve your wine bottles."

She shook her head. "I'm very particular about who touches my personal stock. But I'm giving you your own bottles of excellent vintages for your wedding. I'll also bring some of my premium wine tomorrow night to Audrey's."

"'Audrey's?'" I repeated. "The party is at Parsley and Sage."

"No, it isn't. I meant to mention that to you earlier, but kept getting distracted by this or that. It's at Audrey Munroe's, dear." She patted my arm as if I was a confused child. "You're falling victim to the scatter-brained-bride syndrome. You've got too much on your mind these days."

"That's true, but the party really *is* at Parsley and Sage. Steve, Audrey, and I wrote the invitations together," I explained as we made our way upstairs. "It's one of the bennies that Drew gave Steve for designing his restaurant. He's letting us hold the party there before his grand opening in two weeks."

She began to sort through some mail in a nook of her antique writing desk in her foyer. "The invitation said that your shower was at Audrey's. I have my invitation right here. I got it three or four weeks ago."

She handed me the invitation. The printing and stationery was the same as the cards I'd helped Audrey stuff into envelopes, except for the venue address—and the now-missing 'no gifts' request. Audrey must have redone them all. Our party was indeed being held at Audrey's house.

Stunned and embarrassed, my cheeks felt hot. I stared at the address and turned it over to check the flip side. How had this happened? The party was tomorrow, yet I hadn't been told the party was now taking place at my current, albeit temporary, residence.

"This isn't a complete surprise to you, is it?" she asked. "I spoke to Steve about this a couple of weeks ago. I called him to ask about the location, because I thought there must have been a mistake; you'd mentioned earlier that it was at the restaurant. Audrey and your future husband aren't conspiring to keep the location of your wedding shower a secret, are they?"

"No," I lied. "Of course not."

"I hope I didn't spoil their surprise," she suggested as if she knew I was fibbing.

"No, Aunt Bea. I just…forgot that we'd switched venues."

She searched my eyes, still not buying my story. "That would be an inauspicious way to start a marriage. If he's waited this long to tell you where your own party was."

"It was just a mistake."

"I'm sure. Because your fiancé is too mature to *still* be suffering from Drew's bad influence." She clicked her tongue and shook her head in disgust. "All the trouble those two boys used to get themselves into! By high school, the cops were giving them a scolding every couple of months. Thank goodness *one* of them outgrew all of that nonsense before they got themselves killed."

2

To my annoyance, my parking space at Audrey's house was blocked by a moving van in the alley behind Audrey's house. Two men were carrying out the dining room table, to be replaced tomorrow, no doubt, with the rental chairs and occasional tables from "Gala Rentals." I hoped that Audrey had also taken it on herself to keep Hildi, my black cat, upstairs and out from under the movers' feet.

I marched down the sidewalk, ruminating over having heard for the first time that Steve and Drew had apparently run crosswise with the law as teenagers. My thoughts warred between wishing that Steve had chosen a better "best" man and feeling guilty for harboring such ill will toward Drew Benson. As an African-American teenager, Drew caught the attention of the Denver police more quickly than if he'd been Caucasian. He'd been adopted as an infant by a white couple in Cherry Creek, the affluent neighborhood in Denver where Steve had grown up. I had been adopted myself and had endured schoolyard bullying. With Drew being black and having white parents, his challenges must have been exponentially greater than mine. It was quite possible that Drew was completely worthy of Steve's appreciation and admiration. It was also possible, though, that the guy was a complete jerk, and that Steve was blinded by his loyalty and wonderful childhood memories.

My mood brightened as I entered the elegant foyer that I'd designed for Audrey more than three years ago, when I first moved to Crestview. I had lived in a bedroom of this fabulous old house rent-free, in exchange for redesigning the interior, until six months ago when I moved into Steve's house.

I felt a pang as I heard Audrey's voice. Judging from her: "Higher, lower, no higher…" she was vacillating as she tried to identify the ideal height for the chandelier to a workman in the dining room. I was so lucky to have Audrey Munroe in my life. She had become my de facto mother and my dearest friend. My own adoptive mother had passed away, and my adoptive father had deserted us when I was in first grade.

Even so, as I entered the dining room, I was unwilling to spare her the challenge of eyeballing the best height for the light fixture, which I was able to determine at a glance. "Hi, Audrey."

A former ballerina with the New York City Ballet, she did a partial pirouette as she whirled around to face me. "Erin, there you are. Miguel, this is Erin," she said to the workman who was struggling to connect the links of the heavy Swarovski crystal chandelier.

He and I exchanged greetings.

"Could I have a word with you in the front room?" I asked her.

"Oh, feel free to speak openly. I already warned everyone here that I'd tricked you, so they're expecting you to put me in my place."

"You changed tomorrow night's party location without telling me."

"True. I apologize, Erin. You have so many things on your plate. I didn't want you to lift a finger for party planning, which you would have wound up doing, had you known it was happening right here. Furthermore, we had to do many of the preparations today instead of tomorrow. So I figured that a full day and a half to adjust to the idea would be sufficient."

"Therefore, you've deceived me weeks ago and never told me that you shifted locations."

She looked at me quizzically. "I...think that point has already been established. But, yes. I knew you were going to be peeved, so I procrastinated. But in my defense, you know full well that I *live* for celebrations like this. *You're* planning your wedding. *Steve* is planning the rehearsal dinner. I've been cut out of the loop entirely, yet we agreed that *I* was allowed to give you this party as my gift to you. Holding it in my home with five-star-restaurant-caliber food is friendlier and more comfortable. Plus, it's much easier than having guests haul their gifts to a restaurant and our having to haul them back here afterward."

"We weren't going to *have* 'presents.' We stated on the original invitations that 'your presence would be our present.'"

"Oh, Erin, dear, nobody honors that," she said with a chuckle. "When you have a wedding 'shower' it means to 'shower' you with gifts. Those invitations were just going to confuse everyone."

"But you wasted all of our original invitations," I countered, "and you'd already pledged to go along with me on our having a gift-free wedding shower, in exchange for my taking your advice not to have guests donate to our favorite charities, in lieu of wedding gifts."

She snorted. "Discarding a lousy idea doesn't count as a compromise."

"It *wasn't* a lousy idea."

"Charity donations zap everyone's fun. And wedding guests consider their gifts to essentially be a reimbursement for the considerable expense of the reception."

"But *our* plan would have benefitted needy organizations. Steve and I don't need anything, and we wanted to make our gift to each other to be the wedding reception of our dreams."

"Charity donations in lieu of wedding gifts is appropriate choice for your second or third marriage. Just not your first."

"I have no intention of ever *having* a second marriage."

"Nobody ever does. Outside of Hollywood." She gave me a once-over. "I guess I might as well tell you this now while you're already angry with me. Two weeks ago, I registered you for wedding gifts at the Paprika, with Steve's blessing. I know you wanted to choose that less-pricey department store, but Paprika needs your business more than a national chain does. Furthermore, Paprika needs to be supporting *your* business. Steve agreed with me that it makes good business sense."

She'd consulted with Steve about this? And he hadn't told me? The doorbell chimed. Audrey headed toward the door, leaving me to ponder why I was being left out of the loop at my own wedding.

"Does this look okay?" the workman on the stepladder asked me.

I shook my head. "It's too high, Miguel. Count five links down from the ceiling, and five up from the chandelier. Hook those two links together." Knowing Audrey, she'd promptly run to answer the door precisely because she knew I'd advise him in her stead.

"Speak of the devil," Audrey called out from the front room, without opening the door. "It's Steve." She strode past me, after winking at Miguel. "You can let him in, and you two can sort things out while I go busy myself with some noisy gardening in the back yard."

"Steve and I are *not* going to argue," I called after her. For one thing, Audrey, not Steve, had been driving the locomotive that shifted our party from the restaurant to her house. I opened the door. *What a gorgeous man!* This was the second reason I was so confident that we wouldn't argue; my heart always melted at the sight of him. And the best part was that, the way his gaze locked into mine, I knew he felt the same way about me.

We gave each other a quick kiss as he stepped through the door. This was the tail end of September. The weather was hot and muggy by Colorado standards, which translated to "pleasant" by upstate New York standards, where I'd grown up.

"I missed you today," Steve said, grinning at me. "And every night for the last three weeks."

"I've missed you, too. Which doesn't get you off the hook completely. I just found out about tomorrow night's party. I would have appreciated a heads-up or two. You also should have told me about the registry at Paprika, and that Audrey's now hosting our wedding shower."

"Yeah, my bad. Sorry. I should have kept you up to date." Steve got that distant look in his eyes that I'd been seeing too often this past month; he was worried about something that he was hesitant to share with me. "Parsley and Sage will be lucky to open in a month, let alone in two weeks. No way could we have a party there tomorrow night. And Audrey insisted that *she* be the one to tell you, because it was her idea in the first place."

"I found out from Aunt Bea, not Audrey, and I assumed Audrey was the mastermind. In any case, it's pretty shoddy communication between us."

"I'm sorry, Gilbert." Calling me by my last name was an endearment, and I still felt the magnetic pull of him. "We *did* agree to give Audrey free rein with the shower, and she made some excellent points about our registering for gifts. When she gave me the list of what you'd like at Paprika, I assumed she'd run the change in plans past you. Especially because I agreed with every single selection on the list."

I shook my head in dismay; Steve was describing quintessential Audrey-like behavior. "She made up the registry list without ever mentioning it. *Now* I know why she kept insisting I go with her on her various window-shopping expeditions there."

"Huh. Well, it's nice to know that Audrey's been keeping you company, while I've been forced to ignore you. I've been running around like a chicken with its head chopped off for the last two months."

"Hmm. That reminds me. She asked if I liked a particular cleaver while we were there, and I said yes. *That* probably made it onto our registry."

"I don't think I saw it on the list…but we *did* get a wedding gift today that looked suspiciously like a hatchet."

I laughed.

His eyes sparkled in merriment for a moment, but then his tension returned. "You and I haven't had any time for a personal conversation this entire month." He grimaced. "We need to talk."

His words instantly set my insecurities ablaze. "Okay," I said forcing my voice to sound breezy. I led the way into Audrey's front room and promptly sat on my favorite chair—

a Chippendale with a cross-stitched floral pattern that my mother had created.

Steve didn't close the door behind us, which was a good sign; we could still hear the workers' voices in the kitchen, so this impending conversation couldn't be about anything earthshattering.

He raked his hand through his dark brown hair. He had an errant lock, which hung down on his forehead and was sexy as hell. "Drew's whole business is in jeopardy." His voice was rife with concern. He stood in front of the honey-colored loveseat. "Turns out, he got screwed-over by the former manager at his Napa restaurant. The guy embezzled something like twenty thousand. So, naturally, Drew's checks to his subcontractors have bounced. He's got way too much money invested in opening this new restaurant here to throw in the towel. The whole thing is a train wreck."

Only then did Steve sit down. Meanwhile, my pulse had been rising with Steve's every statement. This was precisely what I had feared would happen from the first time Steve excitedly told me about Drew's expansion of his restaurant business to Colorado. We typically required our customers to pay a percentage upfront to cover our expenses. Against my objections, Steve had waved this policy.

"You can't let Sullivan and Gilbert Designs get tangled up in Drew's debt," I stated. "You're going to have to quit working for him until he can afford to pay you, Steve."

He grimaced and took an uneven breath. "I realize that's what I *should* do, but I just can't leave him high and dry like this."

"You're going to have to force yourself, Steve. I know you credit him with saving your life, but—"

"I don't just *credit* him. He *did* save my life. After *I* dared him to join me out there on a ledge. I don't want to leave him on a financial cliff now."

"What choice do you have? You know better than anyone how easy it is to take your own business from the black to the red."

"*That's* what you got out of what I just told you? That I'm going to put us in financial ruin?"

"No, Steve! That's not at all what I meant." I hesitated. In truth, my remark *had* been intended to remind him that he'd been down this road before and knew better than to travel it a second time. A year or two before we'd met, Sullivan Designs had almost been bankrupted by a con artist who'd lured him into forming a partnership with her. Steve had already admitted to me that Drew had never offered to help him back when he was on the verge of financial collapse. "How would you have handled this if he were any other client?"

He rose and began to pace. "Doesn't matter. He isn't. He's my friend."

"Which is why business and friendships shouldn't be mixed."

"I don't need an 'I told you so,' Erin. I'm already aware I've screwed up everything."

"Not *everything*," I replied, my heart softening as I studied the strain on his handsome features. I stood up and crossed the room toward him, feeling awkward, but unable to remain seated. He was now staring out the window. The slant of sunlight on his white shirt through the lovely paned glass gave me the image of him as the romantic hero in a historical novel. "You're still my favorite man in the entire universe. Furthermore, in spite of the economy, Sullivan and Gilbert Designs has steadily gained new clients. So…we can probably afford to do *some* pro bono work, at least, for Drew."

Sullivan didn't reply, merely raked his hand through his hair once again, which instantly put me back on edge. That gesture of his was often a poker-player's tell that he was holding back something.

"You're not…also loaning Drew money, are you?"

"Not a substantial amount, no. But I spotted him five hundred to pay the plumber. Before you get all critical, bear in mind that I'm trying to help my life-long friend get out of a jam. Which he's gotten into through no fault of his own."

If he's telling you the truth about his dishonest ex-manager, that is. I chose to bite my tongue. "Just remember, Steve, you're already doing a lot for him. He's living here for free for six weeks in our guest room, and he's got the best designer in Colorado working for nothing."

"Second best," he said, giving me a wink.

"You mean behind *me?*" I said, sincerely delighted and surprised.

He chuckled and hugged me, whirling me around in his arms, our minor discord forgotten. "What?!" he asked in mocked horror. "Did you think I'm marrying you just because you're so amazing and so beautiful? And because I love you more than anything in the world? No way! My evil intentions are to exploit your talent!"

"Wow! You really know how to flatter me!"

"Only because *you're* so deserving of compliments, Gilbert."

"So are you, Sullivan. I'm constantly learning more about design from working with you." He smiled at me with so much love in his eyes, my own eyes misted. He kissed me, then held me tightly against his chest. Our bodies fit together perfectly. We were made for each other.

I hesitated, torn. If I kept my mouth shut, maybe things would work themselves out with Drew. Or maybe they'd get even worse, and I'd get so upset that I would erupt in another week or two. Perhaps right before our wedding. The adage: "A stitch in time saves nine" popped into my head. "I really wish I could leave the subject of Drew alone. But...Steve, I'm worried that you're failing to see him as the man that he is today. As opposed to the boy you loved throughout your childhood. Have you double-checked his story about the embezzler?"

Steve released me from his grasp. "Talk about a buzzkill," he grumbled.

"I know. I'm sorry. I just...need to be upfront with you about my doubts about your friend. It's next to impossible to ignore your personal history and see who an old friend truly is *today*."

"Why would I *want* to?"

"That's just it. You obviously *don't* want to. But when it comes to mixing friends and money...you *should*. Today Aunt Bea told me that Drew was—"

"Aunt Bea has never liked him," Steve interrupted. "The woman's a racist!"

I held his gaze, unwilling to dismiss her opinions that easily. "You'd told me that Drew hasn't always been kind to Aunt Bea."

"Yeah, but that was only the one time. When she caught him in the act of making fun of her weight. And we're talking about something that occurred twenty-some years ago. At any rate, yesterday I talked to Lucas LeBlanc, Drew's chef. He backed up Drew's story of the embezzler. So, yeah, I checked it out."

By taking the word of Drew's employee. How dependable does Steve think that is? I closed my eyes for a moment, rather than continue to meet his icy glare. This was not a well-timed conversation. We should have thoroughly sorted out the what-ifs back when Drew first told Steve about his new restaurant and offered him the major design job. We'd discussed the challenges of business partners marrying; we knew that balancing work life and personal life would be difficult at times. Still. I wasn't prepared for these issues to arise right before our wedding, and for our having been placed on this high wire by Steve's best man.

Our gazes locked once again. His remained smoldering, and not in a good way. "We disagree about this one, particular client," I said quietly.

"Exactly. And we agreed back when we merged our businesses that the project leader makes the ultimate decision. Which means *me*."

"Erin? Steve?" Audrey called. "I need your opinions on seating options for the back yard."

Steve turned.

I grabbed his arm. "Make decisions with your head, darling, not your heart."

"I will," he snapped. "I'm not Drew's...or anyone else's... fool."

He didn't exactly jerk his arm free from my grasp, but he strode out the doorway without a glance back.

3

The next day, things felt slightly strained and awkward between us when Steve and I met at the office of our wedding planner, Fitz Parker. We had hired Fitz upon getting a glowing recommendation from Michelle, Steve's youngest sister, who'd gotten married about three years ago.

Despite his Anglo-Saxon name, Fitz appeared to be of Italian descent—olive complexion, black hair, and broad features. He had some of the affectations of being gay, but I'd caught him ogling a couple of women surreptitiously. His occasional effeminate mannerisms and figures of speech struck me as just as big of a put-on as the purple velvet vest that he was currently wearing. My theory was that he felt that sexual ambiguity made both the bride and groom less intimidated by his virile physique.

"Audrey absolutely forbade me to give her a helping hand with planning tonight's bash," Fitz was telling me, "even after I told her I'd do it gratis."

"She loves planning parties," I explained.

"Well, so do I, darling," he replied with a flick of his wrist. "Plus, you've *hired* me to perform that function for you."

"Are you still coming tonight?" I asked.

"Wouldn't miss it for the world," he replied.

"Good," Steve said. He was a man of few words today.

Someone rapped on the door, then immediately opened it. Drew Benson walked in, a self-pleased grin on his chiseled, African-American features. He was a muscular, athletic man with a clean-shaven head.

"Hi, folks," he said.

"Hi, Drew," I replied, confused by his dropping by uninvited. "Did you think we were sampling wedding cakes today?" Truth be told, I was annoyed at his intrusion. He was spending much more time with Steve than I was, and this was the one and only hour that Steve had carved out of his work-day to spend with me on our wedding plans.

Drew chuckled. "No, I realized I had to reveal my surprise gift right this minute, or it'd be too late." He gestured at some-one in the doorway. "Come in, Lucas."

In stepped a short, heavyset balding man, his sandy-col-ored hair in a comb-over that looked foolish compared to Drew and his macho shaved head. Lucas also had a pencil-thin mustache that had gone out of style with David Niven. "Here I am," he said with a hint of a French accent, "at your service. It's my pleasure, as well as Monsieur Benson's, to ensure the bride and groom that they will have the best of weddings."

There was an awkward pause. For my part, I was com-pletely confused.

"Lucas LeBlanc, world-famous chef, is going to be your caterer," Drew announced. "My treat."

"We already hired a caterer," Steve and I said in unison.

"Not anymore," Lucas said, with one hand aloft.

"You guys obviously didn't hear the buzz within the restau-rant-trade circles," Drew explained. "Your would-have-been caterer, Wilson Hommel, is being sued for food poisoning. You're not going to want him serving food at your wedding. I acted swiftly and came to your rescue, before you needed to ask." He glared at Fitz. "*Somebody* had to step up to the plate, eh, Fitzsy?"

Now that it was clear that Drew and Fitz knew each other, I recalled Steve mentioning that Drew and Michelle had once been an item and remained friends. Drew had probably attended Michelle's wedding and could have run into Fitz there.

"Is that true?" I asked Fitz, and in the same breath, added, "Why didn't you tell us?"

"It was an irrelevant incident that could have happened to anyone." He spread his arms. "Chef Hommel and I discussed this at length, and we agreed that there was nothing he could have done to prevent it. Even so, I planned on discussing the matter with you today, and would have advised *not* taking any action until we get the results from the health examiners."

"What difference does it make whose fault it was?" Drew asked. "Regardless of the cause, nobody's going to want to eat his food...and I already saved the day."

"First the location of tonight's wedding shower changes," I grumbled to nobody in particular. "Then we've been registered at a second store. Now we have a different caterer. My wedding is starting to feel like a surprise party."

"And that's the *opposite* of how I'd like you to feel, poor darling," Fitz exclaimed.

"Hey, Erin," Drew said. "The shower snafu's on me. I'm the one who had to move it from my restaurant like we originally wanted. But *now* I saved you from poisoning someone at your wedding." He took a step toward Steve, still seated beside me, and gave him a friendly chuck in the shoulder. "I'm always watching out for my main man."

Steve grinned from ear to ear. "I appreciate it, bro."

"No problem."

Feeling like my ideas for our wedding were being leap-frogged, I barely resisted the temptation to roll my eyes.

"I have prepared for you a menu that I believe will be—" Lucas kissed his fingertips on one hand then spread them as if to release his kiss into the air "—divine." As I watched him, I wondered how my clients would react if I mimicked his theatrical presentation while describing my expectations for an interior design. They'd probably swat me. A bigger concern, though, was that Steve continued to beam at him as if this matter was settled.

"It isn't wise to switch caterers this late in the game," Fitz protested. "Making these decisions is what you're paying *me* to do…to hire the best venders in the business and keep everyone coordinated and working together. A wedding is like a beautiful dance ensemble. You can't just switch lead dancers! The food-poisoning incident wasn't Chef Hommel's fault. One of his staff members had a minor case of hepatitis, and she concealed the fact that she was feeling ill from him and all of her coworkers."

Lucas snorted and eyed Fitz with borderline contempt. "Silly man. This is already out of your hands. I am the best chef in all of California."

"Hardly," Fitz growled. "If you were even in the top *hundred*, I'd have heard of you."

"Chill, dude," Drew retorted, not only matching Fitz's menace, but surpassing it. "If you don't like it, Fitzy, you can refund my friends' money and walk. You're every bit as replaceable as the caterer."

"Come on, Drew! This is our decision, not yours!" I turned to Lucas. "Can you even get a staff together here in Colorado? In ten days' time?"

"But of course. Trust me."

"I can't. I've never even *met* you. You weren't on duty the one and only time Steve and I ate at Drew's restaurant."

"Then trust *me,*" Drew interjected. "I owe you one for not hosting tonight's party. I'd never hire anything but the best for you."

"Remember how delicious the food was that night?" Steve said to me. "Lucas has such a well-trained sous chef and staff, and such great recipes, he doesn't need to always be there. That's all the more reason to trust him as a caterer."

"You said it, man," Drew said. "And this is a big deal for me. Serving our menu from Parsley and Sage to all your guests will be a great boon for my business. Which I'll need, now that my grand opening is delayed."

"It's a win-win, bro," Steve declared. He and Drew fist-bumped.

"Once again, dude, I've saved your lives."

"Not really," I muttered.

"You can say that again," Fitz said, giving me a long look. I knew he could see at a glance that hiring Lucas wasn't my first choice. He shifted his focus to Steve. "This is a huge mistake, in my opinion. But, hey, you *two* are calling the shots."

Steve gave my hand a squeeze, seemingly oblivious.

Why did his speech patterns and bearing seem to regress by ten years whenever his 'bro' was nearby?

"You don't mind, do you, Gilbert?" Steve asked.

"Well, to be honest, I think we're being rash. I'd rather talk to the caterer and then make an informed decision. I don't like having decisions like this sprung on us."

"No worries, Erin," Drew said. "You'll save a bundle on what Mr. Hepatitis Caterer charges. It's Steve's big wedding, too, you know."

"I realize that," I said through gritted teeth.

Steve stood up, only to bend down and whisper in my ear, "Let this go, okay? Lucas is a wonderful chef, whereas our caterer's employee gave someone hepatitis."

"Okay," I said, albeit reluctantly.

"Great. And now I'm even, Steven!" Drew gave him something that was half a hug, half a chest bump.

The phrase "even Steven" sounded to me as if the wedding "gift" from the best man was costing the money Steve had loaned him for the plumber. But, hey, what an awesome bro-in-law Drew will make! I saw a flicker of annoyance cross Steve's features, but he chatted with both men as he showed him out the door.

Fitz's and my gazes met as I turned back around in my chair. "Drew is the type of man who will not live long," he said under his breath.

4

Audrey Munroe was one of the best hostesses I'd ever met. The woman knew the art of making every single guest feel welcome. Simply by coming to her house and making yourself at home, you felt as though you'd paid her an enormous compliment. Her talents were in full bloom at our wedding shower. Two hours into our festivities, the house was packed, and everyone was all smiles. It made my heart soar to see this many people I truly cared for this happy and at ease.

Audrey had even managed to extend her unparalleled hospitality to Lucas LeBlanc, who had come uninvited twenty minutes or so ago—halfway into the festivities—and promptly called attention to himself. Upon his arrival, he announced to Steve and me that he had crashed the party. He then proceeded in his bullhorn of a voice to introduce himself as our wedding caterer and the head chef for the soon-to-open Parsley and Sage in downtown Crestview. "I've brought everyone petite samples of my finest cuisine as an act of atonement. *Oui, oui?*"

Non, non! I thought, annoyed at his presumptuousness.

Ever the gracious host, Audrey replied, "Come in, Lucas. You're ever so welcome, with or without appetizers." Then she teased, "Did you bring a case of champagne as well?"

He replied that he had, thoughtlessly, merely brought his 'Crab Lucas' and his 'Crepes Lucas.' Then four tuxedoed servers with enormous trays entered the house. Each of the servers said, "Compliments of the Parsley and Sage," as they presented their tray to a cluster of partiers. The bite-sized pieces of both the crab and the crepes were melt-on-your-tongue delicious. The catering staff Audrey had hired tactfully hung back, meanwhile, rather than forcing guests to choose between caterers. Then, Lucas and his quartet left, leaving a trail of *bonsoirs*.

Lucas's stunt struck me as self-serving but harmless, and I surmised at once that it could only have been Drew's idea. I scanned the room to get a take on how everyone else felt. Audrey caught my gaze, grinned, and rolled her eyes at me. At the opposite side of the room, Steve and Drew were sharing a boisterous laugh. Our guests seemed to be chatting happily and were clearly enjoying their appetizers à la Lucas. I wondered how our wedding planner, here as a guest, had taken this. He wasn't in my immediate vicinity.

As I tried to squeeze past some guests, Mark Dunning, Steve's sister Michelle's husband, grabbed my upper arm. He still had his mouth full of crepes when he said, "You're not actually going to serve sissy food at your wedding, are you?"

"Sissy food?" I repeated.

"Yeah." He took a swig of beer and swallowed his food. "You know. Girly French food. I want roast beef. Potatoes."

I did my best to maintain a poker face. He had blue eyes and dark hair, and had perhaps once been a nice-looking man, but I disliked him so much that these days I could only notice his pug nose and big belly. Upon our first meeting, which was last Easter, Mark had entrenched himself as my least-favorite future in-law by acting like an arrogant, abrasive bully. Tonight he'd sunk even lower; earlier this evening I'd spotted him stomping his foot in front of my cat's sweet little face and laughing at her reaction. I'd yanked him away and chewed him out, only to have him insist that he was trying to step on a spider, but missed.

"We'll be sure that Lucas serves something for a lumberjack's palate," I replied.

"That's all I ask," Mark said, spreading his arms, sloshing a little beer from his glass in the process. "Just so long as we aren't talking about sawdust."

"I'll keep the no-sawdust suggestion in mind when we fine-tune our menu."

He nodded and turned away. Aunt Bea had given him a start in the liquor distribution business, where he'd done exceedingly well. I hoped for Michelle's sake that he had some redeeming qualities that I'd simply failed to see. Their daughter was only two and the wedding was less than three years ago. As uncharitable and judgmental as this was, I couldn't help but wonder if she'd rushed into marriage because she was pregnant.

After spending a few minutes in an enjoyable conversation with a cluster of friends, I found our wedding planner in the kitchen pantry, gulping a large glass of what smelled like scotch. Although Fitz was here strictly as a guest, he appeared to be seething, which was likely due to our new caterer's stunt.

"Are you hiding out?" I asked.

"I *am*, actually. I shoulda known better than to let that jerk get to me."

"Do you mean Lucas LeBlanc?"

"No, Drew. Drew-be-drew-be-doodoo head." Apparently he was still angry with Drew calling him "Fitzy." He swayed a little on his feet. "I shoulda known better than to let him get to me like this. The guy's an asshole. Everybody knows it. Nobody can actually *say* that, though. Not unless you're black like him. Otherwise you're afraid of being called a bigot."

"He's my future husband's closest friend," I stated.

"Yeah. I s'pose you have to be loyal. True blue. Apologies, Erin. I shoulda pretended to like the asshole for the sake of my job. Maybe I should have taken Drew's advice and walked out this morning."

"You needn't feel that way. Provided you keep your opinion about Drew to yourself until *after* my wedding."

"Not a problem." He raised a palm, as if in an implied vow. "I never drink at weddings. Unlike Drew-be-doodoo. The reason your sissy-in-law is so fond of me? At her wedding, I assigned a member of my staff to keep an eye on Drew, and to steer him away once he got loaded. Prevented the ass—. Prevented the guy from spoiling the night for everybody."

"Drew's been a delightful guest tonight." Even if he hadn't been, I'd have stood up for him to Fitz, who was truly acting unprofessionally by badmouthing a member of the wedding party.

"Maybe so. My guess? He *won't* be delightful in another thirty minutes. An hour, tops."

Fitz was well on his way to drunkenness and was no one to talk. "I came in here to check our coffee supply," I told him, in order to begin a tactful segue. "Would you like a cup?"

"Yes, I would." He set down his glass and took a step back. "I'll drink nothing but coffee, from now on. I promise. The next time you see me, I'll have transformed into an alert drunk. A semi-gay, semi-alert drunk that knows how to keep his mouth shut." He pantomimed zipping his lips.

An hour or so later, Aunt Bea finally arrived. She was dressed in a shimmery gold-and-turquoise muumuu with gold satin slippers. Both of her forearms were bedecked in so many gold bracelets that they were too closely jammed together to jingle when she moved her arms. She'd used a lot of eyeliner in a Cleopatra-esque effect—or perhaps it was raven wings. Either way, I liked the look; it was fun, and I told her so.

"Thank you, Erin," she replied. "This is my chubby, elderly Elizabeth Taylor outfit," she replied, holding her arms out in opposite right-angles in a mock Egyptian-dancer look.

I chuckled. "I'm so glad you came. Audrey was just asking about you a few minutes ago."

"Was she?" Aunt Bea said with a broad smile. "I'll say hi to her as soon—" She broke off as she glared at someone past my shoulder.

I followed her gaze. As Fitz had forewarned, Drew was what my mother would have described as "making a spectacle of himself." He was walking on the three-inch-high marble hearth of the fireplace in the living room, pretending to be on the edge of a cliff.

"Ugh," she growled under her breath. "That man is a horse's ass. Although that's derogatory to horses."

Drew seemed to find his own childish antics humorous. He mocked falling toward an attractive friend of mine, then immediately launched into an animated soliloquy in her direction. The man resembled a windup toy gone bad. Frankly, he didn't strike me as drunk so much as high on uppers.

"Does Drew have a cocaine habit?" I asked Aunt Bea quietly.

She gave me a sarcastic chuckle. "Not a habit. An addiction. He mainlines coke."

That was worse than I'd imagined. "You mean…he *used* to be addicted, right?" I asked hopefully. "Several years ago?"

I was watching him as I spoke. My friend had turned away from Drew. In fact, everyone in the immediate area was drifting away from that side of the room. He launched into a terrible Michael Jackson impersonation of "Thriller." This despite that fact that Sara Bareilles's "Love Song" was currently playing.

"Does that look like a *former* user to you?" Bea asked me.

I turned my back on him and said to Bea, "Let me go find Steve. I think I forgot to tell him you wanted to have a private conversation with him." First, though, I planned on not only *finding* Steve, but on insisting that he call a taxi for Drew and get him out of here. The man needed to wind himself down someplace safe. And someplace that was unoccupied by people I cared about.

With so many distractions—a houseful of our wonderful friends and Steve's family members—it took me a good twenty minutes to make the circuitous route through the house. When I finally found Steve, he whispered in my ear that he'd taken Drew upstairs, and that Drew was meditating so that he could get a grip on himself. "That's good," I said, not mentioning that *my* getting "a grip" on him might have included partial strangulation.

Steve and I wound up chatting at length with his mother and one of his sisters. I was so dearly hoping that, with a couple of glasses of Aunt Bea's world-class cabernet and surrounded by a houseful of delightful people—not counting the world's worst best-man—Steve's mom would relax in my presence. When we'd first met, nearly a year ago, his mother had been warm to me. Ever since we'd announced our engagement, however, the woman wore a phony smile whenever she looked my way. Despite my efforts to return to her good graces, Eleanor Sullivan appeared to be pained by my close proximity to her only son.

Steve's sister wandered off. Deciding to be brave, I went ahead and sent Steve in search of Aunt Bea, while I tried to manage a private conversation of my own with his mother.

"This is a lovely gathering," Eleanor told me for at least the second time tonight.

"Thank you," I said. "I'm just happy to be fortunate enough to marry into *your* lovely family."

She blinked at me, eyebrows raised, her pained smile in place. "Well, you're so lovely to look at."

I'm pretty sure *my* fake smile at that remark was better than hers as I replied, "Thank you, Eleanor." Granted, my vocal intonations were tantamount to drizzling honey onto a thick slice of baloney, but there was no mistaking her implication that my loveliness was only skin deep. Ignoring Steve's mom's frostiness toward me and everything about Michelle's husband, all of the Sullivans truly *were* lovely people.

Her gaze drifted to her other daughter Amelia, who was across the room, chatting with Fitz. For some reason, a look of alarm flashed across Eleanor's face.

Hoping to avoid feeling like a complete fool for trying to engage Eleanor in conversation, I said, "I mentioned to Amelia earlier how stunning her sapphire necklace is. Is that a family heirloom?"

"It's not an heirloom," Eleanor said, still watching her eldest daughter like a hawk. "Aunt Bea gave it to her."

"Amelia offered to let me borrow it for the wedding."

"Michelle wore it for *her* wedding. Bea told both of the girls that they should share it, and that each of them could wear the necklace for her own special occasions."

I wasn't sure how to respond, or why Eleanor seemed so worried that Fitz and Amelia were having what looked like a pleasant conversation. Maybe she wanted me to ask both Michelle's and Amelia's permission to wear the necklace. The jewelry no longer felt worth the effort; I could simply wear blue panties and borrow a friend's nail polish.

"I'm surprised that you invited Fitz Parker," Eleanor remarked.

"You knew that we took Michelle's advice and hired Fitz as our wedding planner, didn't you?" I asked her.

"Yes, but I didn't realize he had anything to do with the shower. I haven't seen him in ages. I had better run some interference." She set her wineglass on a side table.

My first thought was that there must be lingering animosity between Amelia and Fitz from a previous squabble of some sort, but then I reconsidered, knowing about Amelia's struggles with mental health. "Is she having a bad day?" I asked gently before Eleanor could rush away.

"*Every* day is a bad day when you have a psychosis," she snapped. Then she smiled, touched my arm warmly and said, "I'm sorry, Erin. That was uncalled for. What I should have said is, yes, it's been an extremely bad day."

"I'm sorry that—"

"Excuse me," she told me, already walking toward Fitz and Amelia.

Damn. I knew how to fix shoddy interiors, not relationships with future in-laws. Steve, along with our dear, loyal friends, was always assuring me that she'd love me once she got to know me. She was clearly avoiding every opportunity to get to know me, however, so I had no choice but to let our relationship evolve at its own glacial pace.

Fitz caught my gaze and lifted his coffee cup as if in an unspoken toast. Amelia appeared to flinch when she spotted her mother approaching. Curiously, she took a step away from Fitz.

I ventured outside, to visit with some of our guests who'd chosen to be in the back yard where we had four strategically placed outdoor heaters to balance out the nippiness of Colorado's typically brisk night air in late September. It was indeed chilly, but beautiful. A recording of a local jazz ensemble was playing on the audio system. The skies had grown pitch black, except for the sprinkling of starlight. We'd echoed the night sky with strings of small white bulbs along the spruces that bordered the property lines. I joined a small cluster of friends near the heater in a back corner of the yard. My heart was overjoyed with the beauty and rightness of this place and time, and of the union that I was about to enter into. My friends, I noticed, were starting to collect their belongings and to remark about the lateness of the hour.

Just as I began to gush about how honored and happy I was that they'd come, I was surprised to see a flash of turquoise below the street light; Aunt Bea had departed so abruptly that she hadn't even said goodbye to me.

Just then Steve emerged from the house. I could tell from his gait that he was angry. I hoped he was perturbed over Drew's behavior and not by his conversation with Bea. He spotted me and joined us. He made a good show of chatting effortlessly as we wished everyone well.

Several minutes later, we had clearly transitioned into the winding down phase of the party—thanking and saying goodbye to guests.

We soon found ourselves alone on the deck. "What did Aunt Bea want?" I asked.

"To put me in her will."

"Really?"

"On the condition that I boot Drew Benson out of my life."

Uh, oh. That was quite an inappropriate demand, especially for an honorary relative. "You said no?"

"Of course I said no."

I nodded, not wanting to admit to myself that I would be happier, too, if he gave Drew the boot. I decided to ignore all things related to Drew Benson for the rest of the evening. Tomorrow, however, I vowed, I would have a full, open discourse with Steve about my misgivings over his best friend.

I shivered a little, and Steve put his arms around me. Then he nuzzled my neck, and next thing I knew, he was kissing me passionately. Monday at the latest, we would have that discussion about whatever my minor concern was about what's his name.

"There's our lovebirds!" a man called out.

We broke off our kiss and turned toward the house. It was Steve's dad, George, crossing the lawn, his mother and his sister Amelia a step behind. "You're heading home?" I asked. The three of them lived about an hour's drive away. "Audrey was completely sincere when she offered you the use of a guest room, you realize."

"Oh, we don't want to impose," his mom trilled. "George snores."

"I can't be all *that* loud. *I* sleep right through it."

I looked at Amelia, who had her typical bearing of staring into space. "Amelia, I feel like I barely spoke to you tonight. I looked for you a couple of times, but—"

"She and I were upstairs, going through some of your design magazines together," his mother interjected.

"Not *all* of the time," Amelia corrected. Her speech patterns typically had a childlike quality, but now her words were also a bit slurred. "I had a *great* time mingling with your guests. It was a nice party, Erin."

"Let's go, George," his mom said. "It's a long drive. We should have left ages ago. But *he* was having too good of a time."

"*You* were, too. You seemed to be yacking your head off."

Eleanor shot him a glare, but then donned her typical fake smile as she met my gaze. "Thank you for inviting us, Erin," she said to me, then gave Steve a hug and a kiss on the cheek.

Given Amelia's interest in my design magazines, I asked if she would like me to take her to the Design Center in Denver some afternoon next month. "Absolutely," she said. "That would be fun." She glanced back at the house and said, "I hope nobody gets hurt."

"At the party?" I asked, confused.

"Drew and Mark were roughhousing a little," my future mother-in-law explained. "Good night." She took Amelia's arm and ushered her toward the street, waving off the valets that Audrey had hired.

Steve's dad gave me a big hug. "You'll both get used to each other," he said in my ear. He gave Steve a more manly hug, which involved slapping him on the back, then strode after the women. Steve and I dutifully followed them along the path in Audrey's side yard, but we were both taking our time.

Steve pulled me toward his chest the moment we could no longer see them walk away. "Sorry about my parents,"

Steve said quietly. Standing this close, with our arms wrapped around each other, our bodies fit together so perfectly.

"They seemed to be a little unhappy with each other just now. Your mom obviously doesn't care for your choice in brides."

"Sure she does. My mom wants me to be happy. She knows that you make me happy. She was probably just worried about Amelia. She's been having another downward spiral. Dad told me that she's been hearing voices again, that she thinks people are out to kill her."

"That must be so hideous for—"

A thump resounded from inside the house.

"He's having a seizure!" Audrey's voice cried.

"Call nine-one-one!" another voice cried.

Steve and I rushed inside through the front door. Fitz Parker was lying in the middle of the foyer floor, his body flailing in violent convulsions, his eyes rolling back in his head, and his face crimson.

5

"Is anyone here a doctor?" I cried.

Silence. I scanned the worried faces. Jim and Julie were the only doctors we'd invited, as best I could remember, and they'd already left.

I dropped to my knees beside Fitz and, despite my trembling hands, unbuttoned the top buttons of his shirt. His eyes were rolling back and his body was twitching. Steve knelt by Fitz's head on the opposite side of me.

"Erin," Audrey called, holding the phone out to me. "I called nine-one-one. An ambulance is on its way. Come talk to the dispatcher." I had no idea why Audrey had singled me out, but feeling too discombobulated to argue, I rose and accepted the phone.

"This is Erin Gilbert," I said into the phone, allowing Audrey to usher me into the kitchen.

"My name is Thomas. I'd like to give the paramedics as much information as possible. Do you know if Mr. Parker has taken any drugs or has any medical conditions?"

"No, I don't. He had too much to drink tonight, though. But the last time I saw him, he was halfway across the room drinking coffee, and he looked fine. Maybe twenty or thirty minutes ago? I didn't speak to him. So I guess I can't really say for sure if he was okay then or not. He nodded at me and gave me a thumbs up, though."

"Is he wearing any kind of an alert tag? A chain around his neck, or a wrist or ankle bracelet?"

"I don't think so. I loosened his collar, so I know he wasn't wearing a chain. But let me..." My voice faded as I tried to make my way to the foyer. The cluster of guests who remained blocked the doorway. Everyone's faces looked pale and despairing. My heart was pounding so hard, I could hardly breathe.

The sirens were loud and a pair of vehicles had just then pulled up front. Red flashing lights were distorted by the cut glass in the sidelight.

"What happened?" I asked, as I weaved my way through the crowd.

Michelle was sobbing. Audrey turned toward me, her face sheet white. "His heart stopped." I brushed past them. Drew was giving Fitz mouth to mouth. Steve was pumping Fitz's chest to keep his heart going. Mark was kneeling by Fitz's feet, watching the others work.

Someone pounded on the door. "That's the paramedics," I said.

"They're too late," Michelle cried. "They got here too late."

It was almost 11 a.m. when I awoke in a double bed at the Marriott. In my still-half-asleep daze, I barely pieced together the ordeal of the long, dismal night that I'd endured, with three or four hours spent at the police station. Audrey and I had been told that her house was off-limits until the investigators could determine the cause of death. In our zombie-like state, she and I decided to get a hotel room, despite Steve urging us to instead go to our home, and Drew offering to let Audrey use our guest room while he slept on the sofa.

I hoped that the investigators would discover that Fitz's death was from natural causes. His beet-red face, however, had seemed anything but natural. Those horrible images would be burned into my memory banks for some time to come.

There was a knock on the hotel door. Audrey opened the bathroom door a little and said, "Can you get that?"

"Got it," I replied, already in the process of working the safety lock. I opened the door to my friend, Sergeant Linda Delgardio. She was in her uniform, and it was clear from the expression on her face that she was here on business. I was only slightly surprised to see her; we'd spoken last night at the police station and, hoping she'd be my contact person, I'd told her that Audrey and I would be here at the Marriott.

"Hey, Erin," she said. "I wish I'd been able to come to your party last night."

"So do I. Maybe things would have turned out differently. Come on in, Linda."

"Is Audrey here?"

"Trying to make myself presentable," she said as she emerged from the bathroom, "with mixed results. Hi, Linda. Good to see you again."

"You, too. I'm afraid I've got bad news for you. We got the results of the autopsy on the guest who died here at your party. His stomach contents reveal that he ingested cyanide last night."

"Dear God," Audrey said. "How? Are all of our other guests okay?"

"They're all fine."

"Thank goodness for that much," I said, half-heartedly. Even though I knew I was being petty in comparison to a young man's death, I was filled with ungracious anger at the horrendous timing. It was so unfair that this had happened at Steve's and my wedding shower. Our marriage would be forever linked with a murder. I hadn't known Fitz well and wasn't close to him. He'd invited himself to our party, insisting that his attendance at the shower would help with his planning as he gained inside knowledge. Audrey, too, was cheated by having this happen in her home, at a party she was hosting. The best party hostess I knew was forever going to have been the person who hosted the party where someone died.

"Was the poison in something he ate?" Audrey asked. "Or drank?"

"The coroner can't be certain, because the catering staff was washing the glasses and cups continuously. He believes it was probably dissolved in liquid. And, due to time of death and his toxin levels, it was most likely the final thing that he drank."

He'd been drinking Scotch. Then I'd offered him a cup of coffee. My stomach clenched. "Was it in his cup of coffee?" I asked.

"Probably," Linda said. "That would fit with the coroner's findings, and coffee is a strong flavor that can disguise the poison's taste."

"I feel...so...responsible," I muttered. "*I'm* the one who told him he should be drinking coffee."

"Don't blame yourself, Erin," Linda said. "One way or another, a determined killer would have found a way to poison him."

Linda shifted her attention to Audrey. "You're not going to be able to return to your house for another day or two."

Audrey nodded solemnly. "Can we go over to the house and collect some personal items? Such as clothing?"

"Certainly. You'll have to have a police escort with you, though, for the sake of our maintaining chain-of-evidence."

"I suppose it will be hard to uncover much more evidence," Audrey said, "given my over-achieving catering crew last night."

"I can bring you over to your home right now, if you'd like," Linda offered.

"That would be nice," Audrey replied.

Linda grimaced a little. "Afterwards, we're going to need to talk to both of you again at the stationhouse."

I couldn't quite suppress a groan. "Is Detective O'Reilly going to be in charge again?"

"I'm afraid so."

I rubbed my now-aching forehead. "Don't you have any other detectives in the Crestview police department?"

"We do. But he gets automatically assigned to you, now that you've established the unfortunate pattern of knowing the victim."

"Which he always suspects is because *I'm* a serial killer."

"I know better, though," Audrey said.

"We all do," Linda added. "Including O'Reilly. He's just doing his job…in his own slightly abrasive way."

"Thanks, Audrey. And Linda." I sighed. "I can already guarantee you that I didn't see anything suspicious last night."

"Nor did I," Audrey immediately chimed in.

"It might have looked as innocent as someone putting a spoonful of sugar into a cup of coffee. The service staff said several guests had coffee at one point or another."

Over the years, I'd acquired the ability to shut my eyes and visualize how rooms would look after I'd redone them. Now

I shut my eyes and tried to visualize our party guests as they'd been last night, searching my mind's eye for white coffee cups.

"I can only remember seeing two guests for certain with coffee cups. I saw Fitz Parker stirring his cup. And I remember Drew Benson, holding a cup of coffee in his hand…and watching Fitz stir his coffee." I thought about sabotaged sugar or cream. I supposed anyone could have dropped powdered poison into Fitz's cup whenever he'd set it down.

"We do have one possible clue," Linda said. "Do you know if any of your guests was wearing a sapphire necklace?"

"Yes, Amelia Sullivan, Steve's oldest sister, was wearing one," I said. "A large sapphire on a gold chain. Why?"

"We found it in the victim's pocket. The chain had been broken."

6

We were quiet as Linda drove us to Audrey's house in her patrol car. I'd already asked Linda to help me get my cat into her carrier so I could take her home; Hildi stayed where I stayed, and she and I would be back at Steve's and my home tonight. Having chosen the back seat for Audrey's sake, I focused my thoughts on the necklace, as opposed to worrying about acquiring germs from previous down-on-their-luck occupants in this car's seat.

Had Amelia given the necklace to Fitz for some reason, maybe with the instructions that he was to surprise me with it before the wedding? Had she taken it off and left it for me, only to have Fitz pocket it? It was possible that Amelia had fidgeted with it until the chain broke, and that Fitz had pocketed it with good intentions. He might have volunteered to have it fixed, or had found it and meant to return it.

Amelia *should* know the answers, but her brain couldn't always separate fact from fiction. Last night, Eleanor had said that Amelia was having an exceptionally bad day, although she'd seemed subdued but basically fine whenever we'd spoken. I hadn't paid attention to what she'd been drinking. If

Eleanor had seen her daughter holding an alcoholic beverage, that might explain Eleanor's alarm when she'd seen Fitz and Amelia chatting. If she'd been imbibing last night on top of her meds, there might be little chance she knew how her necklace got into Fitz's pocket.

"You don't mind if I look around, do you?" Linda asked as she escorted us inside our house.

"No, go right ahead," Audrey replied. "Erin, could you please go pick out a bottle of wine for me?"

"Sure thing."

"That's not going to interfere with the police investigation, is it?" she called to Linda, who'd donned plastic gloves. "I can take one of my bottles of wine from my cellar with me?"

"Yes, provided it's unopened."

I went downstairs into Audrey's wine cellar and felt such a strong pang, I had to catch my breath. This was such a soul-cheering space. We'd enjoyed many a conversation seated at the French-café style table. With Fitz's death last night, was Audrey ever going to feel secure and tranquil in her own house again? Would we be able to pull off a carefree, joyous wedding despite our wedding planner being murdered at our shower?

I decided then and there that my move back into my home with Steve tonight would have to be temporary. I'd return here whenever Audrey was allowed back into her home, and I'd stay with her until the wedding next Saturday. Despite this tragic situation, I wanted to stick with my original plan of letting Steve have his bachelor pad and me to have my girl time with Audrey before making the formal transition into marriage. Plus, I was certain that Audrey would be jittery for a while at being alone in her house in the aftermath of this dreadful event.

I selected a bottle of Shiraz. When I brought the wine to Audrey in her bedroom, Linda was emerging from the laundry room. "Where did the blood come from that's on this washcloth?" Linda asked us.

"Drew got a nosebleed last night," Audrey said.

"He did?" I asked.

"A pretty bad one. It started to bleed shortly after his inane balancing act on the hearth."

"I saw his antics, too," I said. "I didn't think you were in the room."

"I wasn't. Eleanor Sullivan told me about it. So I sought Drew out to see if I could encourage him to switch to soft drinks, and that's when he got his nosebleed. I brought him upstairs and handed him the washcloth, and got him to sit down and tilt his head back."

"Is there any chance he'd gotten into fisticuffs with Mr. Parker?" Linda asked.

"No, Fitz was on our deck, sipping coffee the whole time," Audrey answered. "In fact, that could have been a good opportunity for the killer to slip the poison into his cup. I heard him ask one of the wait staff for a refill. She'd replied, 'I'll bring out a little pot for you.'"

"Unless she was talking about marijuana," I said.

Both Linda and Audrey scowled at me.

I sometimes made throw-away comments like that, and afterwards I almost always regretted them. Such as that one.

Steve had told me that *he'd* brought Drew upstairs and that Drew was meditating. Drew must have gone upstairs twice. And Eleanor said that she and Amelia were upstairs at some point.

"I hope you're developing an intricate timeline of who was where and when last night," I said to Linda. "It's so difficult to keep track when you've got over fifty guests."

"We're trying to," Linda said. "On the one hand, there were plenty of witnesses. But everyone was consuming alcohol, and only the killer knew that there was any reason to pay attention to others' whereabouts until *after* the victim was poisoned."

"How long after Fitz swallowed the poison until he would have become ill?"

"Five to twenty minutes."

"That lets Lucas LeBlanc, the caterer from the wedding, off the hook," Audrey immediately said to me. "He'd left a full hour ahead of that."

"He's *probably* off the hook," Linda corrected. "As well as all of the guests who left a full half hour before the victim collapsed. It gets fuzzy, though, because we don't know for absolute certain that the cyanide was dissolved in his coffee, as opposed to his consuming something that had been poisoned earlier."

"Did you run background checks on all of the servers at the party?" I asked Linda. "Maybe one of them had a big ax to grind with Fitz."

"We ran a quick check, but nothing's turned up yet."

Disappointed, I nodded. It would have let me feel a tiny bit better about the poor man's death if none of our invited guests was his killer.

An hour later, I remained seated in one of my least favorite places in all of Crestview—an investigation room at the police station. I was also engaged in one of my least-favorite activities: being grilled by Detective O'Reilly, whom I'd learned some years ago was nicknamed "Oh Really" by his fellow officers, due to his ever-cynical statements to witnesses.

"Did anyone at the party have an axe to grind with the victim?" he asked me.

"Not as far as I know. My sister-in-law had raved about him, so that's why we hired him. I don't think anyone outside of Steve's family knew him at all, although Steve's friend, Drew Benson, didn't seem to be fond of him. Like I said, they'd exchanged words about the caterer yesterday morning."

"Did Fitz argue with anyone last night?"

"Not when I was around. Although it's possible he argued a bit with Lucas LeBlanc, when he arrived with his crepes and crab cakes."

"And Mr. Sullivan's family members had gotten to know Fitz two-and-a-half years ago, at his sister's wedding, right?"

"Yes."

"Was there any friction there?"

"No. Or at least, not that I knew about. Again, Michelle highly recommended him." I hesitated, wondering if I should tell the detective about Fitz's and my final conversation. That, too, had been in my previous statement.

"You look as though you have something you want to add."

I wanted to know how Amelia's necklace wound up in Fitz's pocket, but I wasn't sure that O'Reilly would approve of Linda's having told me that. Instead, I said, "It's probably irrelevant, but Fitz claimed that he'd run interference at Michelle and Mark's wedding, because Drew drank too much. Drew and Michelle used to date."

"So Drew and Fitz not only weren't fond of each other, but actively disliked one another?"

"In my opinion, yes."

"Intensely...in your opinion?"

"That depends on your definition. Fitz told me that Drew was an asshole during a private conversation last night. He said that everyone felt the same way about him, but that nobody was willing to speak up because it was politically incorrect, due to Drew's race. Drew was calling Fitz 'Fitzy' at Steve's and my wedding consultation yesterday morning."

O'Reilly leaned back in his chair and stared at me for an uncomfortable length of time. "You don't like these interviews, do you?"

"No, I don't," I snapped. "Can you blame me?"

He smirked at me. "Do I *blame* you?" he scoffed. "That's an interesting question. I never cease to be baffled by how often you've been involved in murders."

"Neither do I, Detective O'Reilly. But I assure you, I'm not to blame for my wedding planner's murder. It was the last thing I would have wanted to happen."

"Glad to hear it. I don't want the job security as a homicide investigator that your living in my home town seems to have given me."

"Are we done here?"

"I suppose so. Let me make sure your fingerprints are still on file. For exclusionary purposes. You understand."

"Not really. Did you find a bottle of cyanide with fingerprints on it?"

"No, but we found a necklace in Mr. Parker's pocket. It was on a thin gold chain that appears to have been severed."

"The chain was *cut*?"

He continued to stare at me, giving no reaction himself to my question. "Are you or Audrey missing some fingernail clippers, by any chance?"

"I don't know. I haven't needed to clip my nails recently."

"Mr. Parker also had a pair of clippers in his pocket. The curvature in the cut of the gold chain matches the clippers perfectly."

"There were probably some nail clippers in both of the upstairs bathrooms in Audrey's house. It would have been easy for anyone at the party to grab them. Including Fitz." But how could he—or another guest—cut the necklace off Amelia's neck without her noticing? I suppose if someone was bold enough to lift the pendant away from her skin on the pretext of studying it, it was possible to covertly clip the chain with the other hand. But the pendant would immediately fall. "Did you talk to Amelia about her necklace apparently being stolen?"

"She claims to not have noticed that it was gone until she got home. Yet she also didn't contact anyone about the theft."

"She sees and interprets things differently than most people do."

"So we gathered. You stated earlier that you'd complimented her necklace when she first arrived, and that she'd offered to let you wear it at your wedding. Did you ever notice that she was no longer wearing her necklace?"

I shook my head. "She was wearing it while she was in the living room. Eleanor Sullivan told me that she and Amelia both went upstairs after that. The next time I saw Amelia was as they were leaving, and she was wearing a coat that was buttoned up."

I paused, thinking that the only way I could envision someone surreptitiously cutting the necklace with nail clippers was if Fitz had done the deed while making out with Amelia. Then again, someone could have claimed a tag in Amelia's dress was showing and distracted her sufficiently to not only cut the delicate chain, but whisk her necklace away without Amelia's knowledge.

I studied O'Reilly's typically smug expression. Now that he'd brought up the necklace himself, there was no harm in my being inquisitive. "What do you make of this, Detective? Do you think Fitz essentially seduced the necklace away from Amelia, or do you think someone framed Amelia by putting her necklace and the clippers in Fitz's pocket? Maybe after he was dead?"

"At this point, we're looking at all of the possibilities. But, yeah. Amelia's high on our list, along with the people who were supposedly ministering to Mr. Parker after he collapsed."

The implied "including you" in his piercing gaze was so obvious that I felt my cheeks grow warm. "I'm not getting into a staring contest with you, Detective. I didn't kill him, and I don't know who did."

7

While I was getting into my car in the police station parking lot, Steve's brother-in-law, Mark Dunning, called my cellphone and asked if he could meet me for coffee. He'd said he was in Crestview for work, which threw me for a moment because he was a liquor distributor and this was a Sunday. Then I remembered he'd once told me that Sundays were good days to talk to bar owners. This was the first time Mark had ever called me, let alone wanted to see me. Logically, this had to have something to do with Fitz's death. But I didn't have any good reason to say no, and maybe I'd get a more favorable opinion of the man when he was drinking coffee instead of alcohol. Yet when I saw his broad features, all I could think of was him teasing my darling cat last night.

Mark was waiting for me at a table. He spotted me as I entered and snapped his fingers at the barista, and ordered a cup of coffee for me. She caught my eye and I smiled and said, "I'll have my usual." This café was near Audrey's and was a favorite hangout of mine. They made a superb chai tea. Its soft, smooth, creamy texture was sheer perfection, as were its flavorful, yet not overwhelming, spices.

I'd designed the interior of this café about two years ago, and I took particular delight in its cozy feel. All of the tables and chairs were hand-selected from antique shops and then refinished to give the space a personalized, homey atmosphere. As I greeted Mark and took a seat in the captain's-style chair across from him, I tried to quash my assumption that this charming setting would not compensate for my decidedly uncharming companion.

"Glad you could make it," Mark said. "I happen to be in Crestview on business and had some time to kill. I'm meeting with some of my major clients in another hour."

He was repeating the information he'd given me over the phone. Curious, I asked, "Are you going to be Parsley and Sage's distributor?"

"No, Drew's got some deal with...a competitor." Judging by his furrowed brow, I'd obviously hit a nerve. "It's just as well. For all we know, he'll never open his doors."

"Actually, things are looking up. He heard through the grapevine that he's getting his liquor license tomorrow." Steve had sent me a text to that effect an hour earlier.

"Really? Huh. Drew bought someone off, then. That would certainly explain the reference to a grapevine."

"What makes you say that?"

He shrugged. "Insider scuttlebutt."

"Meaning what?"

Mark took a slow sip of coffee, eyeing me over his cup all the while, as if for dramatic purposes. He dried his lips with the back of his hand. "Meaning, last I heard, Drew's lawyers were struggling to get him approved for having 'good-standing' business practices." He used air quotes and sarcastic tones to emphasize the term *good standing*. "Not to mention, he had to demonstrate rehabilitation due to his criminal record."

"From when he was just a teenager," I interjected, hoping more than actually knowing for a fact that his arrest record was in the distant past.

"Among other things. Such as his stints in rehab in San Francisco. Coke's an occupational hazard in the restaurant business."

Now Mark had hit a nerve with *me*. My mind leapt into a veritable flash-mob of horrid thoughts: Drew wiping out our bank accounts; Sullivan & Gilbert Designs going bankrupt; Steve and I getting framed and arrested for Fitz's murder; Drew laughing at us at our trial.

Meanwhile, Mark studied our surroundings. "Speaking of restaurants, my wife told me you designed this place. Nice job."

"Thank you," I said weakly.

"Listen, Erin." He scooted closer, leaning as far over the table as his heavyset frame would allow. "I wonder if you can help give me some peace of mind." Apparently his saying "nice job" was supposed to suffice as buttering me up before he asked a favor.

Just then the attractive, dread-locked barista arrived with my chai, and I took the opportunity to chat with her. At the moment, I dearly needed to replenish my own peace of mind before worrying about Mark's.

I took a sip of my chai. Delicious, as always. As soon as the barista was out of earshot, Mark said to me, "So anyways, I heard that your party-planning fag managed to swallow cyanide last night."

I gritted my teeth. "A healthy young man died hour ago. Show some respect!"

Mark spread his arms as if dumbfounded at my reaction. "He told me himself at my wedding that he was gay. It's not like he was ashamed of it."

"You have no right to use derogatory terms to identify people. Fitz's sexual orientation is none of your business. Or mine."

"I sure hope not. It *becomes* everyone else's business if he's spreading AIDS."

"Did you have sex with him?"

He grabbed the ledge of the table and gaped at me. "I'm not a faggot! You don't see me swishing around talking about parties and flowers and frilly lace, do you?"

I rolled my eyes and took a second sip of my beverage, trying to gauge if it was cool enough to chug. "Mark, I am not enjoying this conversation. Furthermore, I'm extremely busy. So let's cut to the chase. What did you want to talk to me about?"

He stared at me for a moment. "Now I get it. This is a touchy subject for you." He held up his palms. "Sorry, Erin. My bad. I forget sometimes that my brother-in-law works in a girly business himself, and that you're marrying the guy. What I'm wondering is…do you know if cyanide causes the runs?"

I quickly lost my appetite for my chai and set down my cup.

"I'm taking Imodium," he continued, "or I never could have survived the drive from Denver. I'm worried 'cuz I was drinking scotch last night, too. Granted, Fitz was sucking down twice as much of it as me, but then, I'm bigger than him. So I'm thinking, maybe I got a batch of poison in my system. Did the police figure out what was poisoned?"

"How did you know what Fitz was drinking? Were you sharing a bottle?"

He shook his head. "We were both standing near the bartender for a while. I mean, I did *talk* to the guy when he was around. It's not like I can't make nice to…gays. *That* isn't offensive, too, is it?"

I ignored the question. He continued, "I'm in the bar-and-restaurant business, so I have to work with them all the time. Besides, Michelle's always had a soft spot for the guy. For Fitz. Whatever you think of the guy's lifestyle, he didn't deserve to have someone bump him off like that. Especially not to be writhing in the floor in pain."

"No, he didn't deserve to die."

"Getting back to my questions, though…was it in the scotch? And did Fitz mention any diarrhea?" He made a hurry-up gesture as if I should be answering him now.

I sighed and took a slow sip of chai. He could have simply Googled the question and spared me. "The police don't know how he ingested the poison. I suggest you make an appointment with your personal physician. I have no idea what Fitz's first symptoms were. All I know is that cyanide poisoning moves quickly. That's how the police knew that he was poisoned during the latter stages of the party."

"Yeah. That much I already knew. But you're probably right. I'll give my doc a call. I figure it had to have been the scotch or the coffee that did in Fitz, right? I sampled a lot of the food, so I'm sure I'd have keeled if that had been spiked with poison."

"So, I take it, you *didn't* drink the coffee?"

"I never drink coffee after one p.m. Keeps me awake. I saw *Drew* messing around with the coffee, though. You know about the sky-high murder rates black people have, right?"

I set my cup down for fear that I would be tempted to fling it at his shirt. "His 'people' are your current neighbors. Drew was raised by a white couple in the same affluent part of town as your wife."

He grimaced. "Please. Don't remind me."

Once again, I wondered what Michelle had been thinking when she chose him to be her spouse. She should have tried to find a good man, like her brother or her father.

"So, did the police tell you if they had any suspects?" he asked. "Anyone in custody?"

"No. Why?"

He gave me another shrug. "I'd like to know if I can feel safe if Michelle still wants to go to your wedding."

"You're planning on skipping our wedding?"

"Not unless *everyone* starts dropping like flies." He glanced at his watch. "Actually, I have some calls to return that I should make in private." He pushed back his chair. "I'm shoving off, too. Just...do us all a big favor, Erin. Talk to Steve. Tell him to get a different best man."

"I am not about to tell Steve—"

Again, he lifted his palms. "Hey, this isn't a skin-color thing. The problem is, you just don't know Drew like *I* know him. The man has a violent temper. My wife is afraid of him. She's afraid of being alone with him."

"Yet she hasn't breathed a word of that to her only brother. Steve would never have him asked him to be his best man if that's really the way that Michelle feels."

"But, I'm telling you, that *is* how she feels. She just scared to admit it. She's in denial. She showed me an old scar she got on her ribcage. From when that no-good piece of—" He broke off, and looked down at his hands. He was wringing the linen napkins so hard that his knuckles were white.

I'd had more than enough of this conversation and took one last sip of my chai. I rose and started to put on my coat.

"I'm warning you, Erin. The guy's dangerous. Even if it's not the color of his skin that makes him so violent, *something* sure does." He waggled his thumb at his chest. "So if you're smart, you better mark Mark's words, Erin. Drew killed Fitz. If you're too color-blind to see that, yeah, you can count out both me and my wife. We're not breaking bread with a killer, and I'm not letting her *near* your wedding."

"She's the groom's sister. She needs to cancel for herself." I whirled on my heel and headed toward the door.

"Fine. I'll tell her to get in touch with you. Your guest list is the least of your problems."

I opened the door.

"Use your pretty little head, girly! You've got a murderer in your wedding party!"

8

I drove a couple of blocks to get out of Mark's sight, then pulled over and called Steve to discuss the conversation I'd just endured. Steve gave Mark's opinions about Drew no credence whatsoever, but he agreed with my assessment that he should talk to Michelle in private about it; both of us felt that Mark was a strong suspect in Fitz's murder, which made us both fearful about his sister's wellbeing.

I remained a little shaken by the time I arrived at Aunt Bea's house to inspect her now-fully-stocked wine cellar. She led me down the stairs. Limping a little, she explained that she'd spent too much time standing up at my party. "I'm so sorry about your wedding planner's death," she told me.

"Me, too. We heard that Fitz's family is holding the funeral the day after tomorrow. Hopefully the police will have the killer under arrest soon. Preferably by the rehearsal dinner. We'll all feel so much more at ease once the killer is behind bars before our next big gathering."

"Is the rehearsal the Friday after next?"

"No, it's that Thursday. We wanted to let everyone have a full day and a half to rest up. It's at the Red Fox. Up the canyon. But, then again," I added with a smile, "judging by experience, it's probably a good idea to check your invitation and not take my word for it."

She blushed. She hadn't been invited. *Damn me and my big mouth!* It should have occurred to me that Steve wouldn't want Aunt Bea there. Still, that was a rude omission, considering Steve's whole family would be there, and she was being so generous to us by supplying the alcohol.

"Didn't Eleanor send you an invitation?" I asked, feeling my own cheeks warm. "You're more than welcome to come, Aunt Bea."

"No, but thank you. It's nice of you to invite me, Erin, but technically, I'm neither family, nor an out-of-town guest. It makes perfect sense that Eleanor didn't send me an invitation."

Especially considering that Eleanor *hadn't actually been in charge of the guest list.* Blaming her had seemed less hurtful than letting Bea know that the fault was with Steve. Not knowing what else to say, I muttered, "Okay, if you truly feel okay about not joining us."

"I do. I might come to pay my respects at the service, though. Even though I barely knew Fitz, it was such a terrible pity for him to die so young."

"I didn't realize you knew him at all."

"I got to know him a little from Michelle's wedding. I supplied the alcohol for that wedding, too. I happened to be in town right while they were in the middle of planning, and Eleanor and Michelle invited me to tag along to some of their appointments."

"Oh." Taking a tag-along to that type of appointment struck me as somewhat unusual. "Do you have a special interest or expertise in weddings?"

"Well, I've been to several weddings in India. They're major events there, lasting forty-eight hours or so."

"So I've heard. I don't know how they manage. I'm stressed enough now with planning for just a couple of hours."

She nodded, but said nothing. I studied Bea's hooded, blue-gray eyes. There was a palpable sorrow in her gaze. Then again, after my hostile conversation with my future brother-in-law, she might have detected some sadness in mine.

A wise saying came to mind: "Everyone you meet is fighting a battle that you know nothing about. Be kind, always." In the context of Fitz's murder, Bea's battle could be serious. She'd said the day before our fateful party that she had a sense of impending doom. Could she have gotten a death threat that she didn't want to tell me about?

"Do you and Fitz ever travel in the same business circles?" I asked.

"No, not really." She sighed, which she'd been doing more and more lately. "Now that you mention it, he could have easily gotten himself into a bad situation with some of his former clients. He told me in private that he got into the wedding business because it was a great way to meet women. He claimed that 'bridesmaids were always ripe for the picking.'"

The phrasing was so distasteful that I couldn't help but grimace. "Yet his choice of clothing and certain affectations were decidedly gay."

She snorted. "All part of his routine. He told me that he used that to his advantage, by whispering in his target's ear: 'Pretending to be gay for the sake of my career finally paid off, the moment I saw you.'"

Again, I grimaced, thinking of how little I would have wanted a Lothario to hit on my bridesmaids. "Did he flirt with Michelle's bridesmaids?"

"Oh, he did much worse than that, I'm afraid," Aunt Bea said with a chuckle. "He bypassed them and scored with the bride."

"Michelle had a…dalliance with him?" I asked, stunned.

"She sure did. It nearly cost her her marriage. So you can imagine how surprised I was to learn that she'd recommended his services to a second member of the Sullivan family."

"So am *I*." *If what Bea was telling me about Michelle and Fitz was true, that is.* I felt more than a little skeptical. Steve disliked Bea, and typically, he and I liked the same people. With the unfortunate exception of Drew Benson.

"Mark, Michelle's husband, became so jealous of Fitz that he all but called off the wedding," Bea continued. "In fact, Fitz truly should have had the decency to decline managing your wedding."

"Are you sure that they had a fling?"

"Quite sure, my dear. Michelle told me about it herself."

I still didn't want to believe her. "I spoke to Mark recently, and he was calling Fitz names…assuming that he was a homosexual."

Bea snorted and put one hand on her ample hip. "I would think he'd be worried that Fitz might have been *bi*sexual. But Mark must have been fibbing to you, for reasons of his own. He knew full well Fitz was straight. And he didn't like him hitting on his wife, whatsoever."

Bea seemed to be hinting that she suspected Mark of murdering Fitz. "I have to admit that I caught Fitz ogling young women a couple of times," I remarked.

"Well, it wasn't really limited to 'young' women. I invited Fitz out one night to talk business over glasses of wine. I wanted to use him as a source for potential customers. He was ogling every single woman's chest as she walked toward our table, and her fanny as she walked away. I was worried he would strain his neck before the evening was through."

Our inspection of the now amply stocked wine cellar didn't take long. Now that so many of the shelves were full, I had merely wanted to make sure that she'd found the shelving space to be precisely what she'd wanted. While I scanned the cabinetry for gaps in seams, uneven shelves, and gaps between bottles, I pondered Mark's and my conversation yet again. He could have been concerned about Fitz giving him AIDS after all, through his relations with his wife. Maybe Mark's jealousy was so far out of control that he'd killed Fitz. If so, that could explain why he was making a point of calling him gay; that would shift everyone away from the jealous-husband motive for murdering Fitz.

I told Aunt Bea that I couldn't find a single fault with anything about the space, and Aunt Bea replied, "Neither can I. It's perfect."

"That's so wonderful to hear! Do you mind my taking photos for my personal records?"

"Yes, I do," she said to my surprise. "I don't want my competition to get a leg up on me. I still want my business to thrive for decades to come." She dropped rather heavily into a chair at the round table near the door. She was a little out of breath. I pulled out the chair beside hers and sat down, willing to act as if we shared some exhaustion.

"What do you think of Mark?" I asked.

She grimaced. "The police should have Mark Dunning as their number one suspect."

Certainly, he was now *my* prime suspect. Steve could be completely right that Mark was trying to set up Drew as the fall guy for a murder that he'd committed himself. Yet I needed to take everything Bea said with a grain of salt, now that she'd managed to alienate Steve's affections so thoroughly. "Tell me something, Bea. Why did you tell Steve you'd put him into your will only if he cut all ties with Drew?"

Once again, she sighed. "I might as well fess up. I was bluffing. I already put Steve and his sisters in my will. Five years ago. And the reason I brought it all up now was due to this feeling that my time left on this earth is drawing to a close. He would be so much happier if he got himself away from Drew's sphere of influence."

"He *is* happy, Bea."

"Of course he is. He's about to get married to *you*, for heaven's sake. What I mean, though, is that he'd be so much better off with Drew out of the picture. Drew belongs in a rehab facility, not a wedding party! The other day, when I was consumed with the feeling that the end was…nigh, I foolishly decided that maybe my last good act on this Earth should be coercing Steve to get away from Drew."

"By threatening to disinherit him?"

She nodded, her face drawn. She suddenly struck me as old and tired. "As a last resort. I intended to merely offer him some advice. But he made it so clear that he didn't believe a single negative word I said about Drew that I lost my temper. I wound up telling that I would disinherit him if he didn't cut ties with Drew immediately."

"Steve is hardly the sort of man who is waiting around to inherit your or anyone else's money. What made you think that he'd agree to something like that in the first place?"

"Like I said, Erin, I lost my temper. He was being dismissive of my well-founded misgivings about Drew. So I fibbed and told Steve that I had only recently decided that I wanted to give him and his sisters the bulk of my estate. And that my fear, where he's concerned, was that having him inherit a good deal of money would only make him a bigger patsy for Drew. Steve snarled back at me that he didn't *want* my money… that I should leave him out of my will, or else he really *would* give it to Drew, just to spite me. I retorted that if he didn't cut all ties with Drew, that's precisely what I'd do…I'd disinherit him. But I didn't mean it, Erin. He and the girls are the closest things to my surviving legacy that I'll ever have."

Her eyes misted, and in that moment, I had a clear vision of how lonely and elderly she was. "I understand," I told her truthfully. "I saw that gorgeous sapphire necklace that you gave Amelia…and Michelle."

"I gave it to *Amelia*, so that she could have something all her own. Amelia has a big soft spot for her sister, the same way Steve has for Drew. Amelia hardly ever wears that necklace."

"She had it on at the party."

Bea widened her eyes in surprise. "Not when *I* saw her, she didn't. I would have noticed. She must have taken it off by the time I arrived."

9

I felt a measure of relief to arrive back at Steve's and my home that evening. "Are you home for good?" Steve asked, with a rather lascivious grin.

"That depends on whenever Audrey returns to her house. She's happy enough at the Marriott, but as soon as the police have finished dusting for prints and so on, then the cleaning crew finishes up, she'll want my company."

"So will *I*," he countered.

I wasn't in a playful or romantic mood and merely added, "She'll be scared to be alone at a murder scene."

Steve scratched his chin. "You got me there. Although Drew's out and about most of the time. He's at our house less often than you might think." He shook his head ruefully. "I'm sure glad he was at the party last night. He didn't hesitate to give Fitz mouth-to-mouth, even though we knew he might've been poisoned."

"True, but then, Drew wasn't exactly sober when he was making that decision. He wasn't using good judgment at any point last night. He was making a lot of our guests uncomfortable while he clowned around."

"Yeah. He got too boisterous. But he was just letting off steam. It's been one hell of a tough month for him."

"Not as tough as *Fitz's.*"

Steve glared at me. "Drew just can't do anything right where you're concerned."

"And he can do no wrong where *you're* concerned. So we're perfectly balanced." I wanted to stop, but I could feel my blood pressure rising. If Aunt Bea was right and Drew was a heavy cocaine user, that could explain both his behavior and his financial woes. Also his nosebleed at Audrey's house. I considered the fact that I'd never seen him with his sleeves rolled up, let alone in a T-shirt. If the love of my life was getting sucked into the vortex of a drug addict, we were heading toward some serious troubles.

"Does Drew ever wear short-sleeve shirts when he's here with just you around?" I asked.

"Yes," Steve snapped, glaring at me. "He *does* have needle marks, if that's what you're driving at. He got hooked when he was younger, but he's clean now."

"Maybe you're wrong about his being clean, Steve. He acted high as a kite last night. Aunt Bea told me that he mainlines cocaine."

"She's exaggerating. That's what she *always* does. She'll say anything to make a better story. Think about it, Erin. She's been living here in Colorado for nine months now. Drew's been in California almost that whole time…up until he moved into our house. Bea and Drew don't like each other, so they avoid each other whenever they can. So you tell me: how could she have any idea whether or not Drew is shooting up with drugs?"

"Maybe she knew all the signs, or she heard about his addiction from a trusted source," I replied. "But even if she's lying through her teeth, isn't her story worth checking out, for Drew's sake?"

"Erin, I'll talk to him about it. I will. Okay? In the meantime, give Drew a break. He's just—"

The outer door banged shut, startling me. Drew Benson strode through the doorway. "Give me a break about what?" he asked. He glanced at Steve, then settled his gaze on me.

"I heard a rumor that you've got a really serious cocaine addiction," I answered.

He gaped at me, straightening his shoulders indignantly. "That's a load of BS! Who told you that?"

"I don't want to make an issue out of who-said-what, Drew. The thing is, I'm worried that it's true. You seemed to be running on high-octane last night, and you had a nosebleed. It's a natural conclusion to draw that you're...heading the wrong way down a one-way street."

"Erin. Get serious. I work hard, and I play hard. Just like your fiancé. Neither one of us has a problem with drugs or alcohol. No matter what some old busybody told you. Okay?"

"Okay by me, bro," Steve said. "Erin?"

Drew had obviously figured out that my news source was Aunt Bea. "No. Sorry, but I'm not convinced. It's pointless to take a drug user's word that he's no longer using drugs."

Neither Steve nor Drew replied. I studied Drew's handsome features. He was wearing a hangdog expression on his face that struck me as false, and it only made me all the more certain he was lying.

"If you'd be willing to go to a lab with me or Steve and can pass a drug analysis test right now, I'll apologize on bended knee. Furthermore, I would be willing to give you a sizable loan to help you open Parsley and Sage as quickly as possible."

Both Steve and Drew exchanged glances as if they were not only stunned, but disgusted with me.

"You want me to pee in a cup for you? Who do you think you are? My mother? Steve's mommy?"

"I'm nobody's mother, Drew. I'm just someone who's unable to take you at your word."

"But you *are* willing to take a nasty old woman's slanderous words about me."

"*She* can't prove their accuracy," I snapped back. "Only *you* can do that."

"Erin, Drew is my friend, not my ward," Steve said. "But, Drew, I know where Erin's coming from. She's just afraid you're spinning out of control. She doesn't want to see you get hurt."

Drew glared at me with fiery eyes. "If you must know, I *can't* take a drug test, Erin. I smoked pot last night. That's *legal* in Colorado. But I refuse to allow that on my permanent record when I'm trying to build a chain of national restaurants! Furthermore, I don't *want* you or Steve to loan me money. I value our friendship too much for that. I'm hurt and offended that you thought you could bribe me into obeying your manipulative garbage!"

"That's enough, Drew!" Steve snapped. "Erin was just trying to err on the side of caution. She'd be the first to tough-love you into a detox center, if it turned out that you needed help."

Drew and I both sighed. For my part, I was counting to ten, which I wish I'd done before making several of my last statements. If I wasn't so certain he was using cocaine, I would understand why Drew—and Steve—were offended by what I'd blurted out. In any case, I'd wrongly put Steve smack in the middle.

"You're right, bro, of course." Drew turned toward me and gave me a sheepish grin. "Sorry, Erin. I've been having a real lousy time for the last few months. My stress level is off the charts."

"*Everyone's* under stress right now. And I *was* trying manipulate you into proving that you don't need help. That's because it's the nature of the beast to deny it if you have an addiction."

"Yeah. I can see that. The thing is, Erin, I'm telling the truth. I haven't used coke in years. And I appreciate that you're strong enough and care enough to ask."

"That's kind of you to say."

Drew threw his arms around me and gave me a big hug. *Now* who was being manipulative? Steve was smiling at us, in obvious relief.

"Have you guys eaten yet?" Drew asked the moment he'd relinquished his grasp.

"No," we answered simultaneously.

"Well, then," Drew replied, rubbing his hands together, and giving us a truly charming smile, "prepare to be gastronomically delighted. Chef LeBlanc isn't the only person who can cook in this town."

I willed myself to let this go, to smile back at him, and to take advantage of this opportunity to get to know Steve's dearest friend a little better. I could manage that much for all of our sakes.

The problem was, I didn't believe him. I believed Aunt Bea. Furthermore, I didn't like Drew and Steve's relationship. In Drew's company, Steve acted less mature and more macho. Plus, there was a maddening element of truth to what Fitz had said about everyone pussyfooting around Drew because of his race. Would I feel this awful about myself for making these assertions if Drew happened to be blond and blue-eyed?

My mind was racing through all sorts of hideous scenarios. Fitz and Drew had known each other, and had held each other in contempt. Had their relationship actually been limited to Drew's being a guest at one wedding reception that Fitz had planned?

As I watched Drew and Steve interact, I tried to gauge if Drew could be a murderer. I couldn't answer my own question.

10

The following day I had a steady stream of wedding-related errands and used our downtown office as a temporary base. That afternoon, Audrey called and said that "we" had gotten the clearance to return to her house. Then she asked when she could expect me. I headed to Steve's and my house to get my darling kitty, plus some items that I needed, most notably: a carefree conversation with the love of my life. He had been at Parsley and Sage the entire day.

Our front door was unlocked, and I was surprised and a little annoyed to find Drew sprawled out on the living room sofa. He lifted a hand in greeting as he continued a flirtatious conversation over his cell phone with some woman. I glanced through all of the doorways to see that, indeed, Steve wasn't home yet. Drew ended his conversation with: "Oh, me, too, babe. Can't wait to see you."

I proceeded into the master bedroom to repack some items of clothing. A couple of minutes later, Drew popped his head through the doorway. "Hi, Beautiful. I'm just taking a little R and R."

I disliked this new name for me, but decided to let it slide. "Do you happen to know when Steve will be home?"

"It's probably going to be a while yet. He's down in Denver, looking at some bar chairs for me. I hope they work out. They're a steal."

Goody for you, I thought, uncharitably. Steve and I had an appointment in less than two hours with Lucas to finalize our menu. I hoped Steve would be able to make it back in time. "How's the situation with your former employee in Napa going?" I asked.

He grimaced. "My lawyer doesn't think we'll be able to recoup anything. Looks like I'm going to have to kiss the money goodbye."

"You're still going to file criminal charges, though, aren't you? You don't want to let someone get off scot free after stealing ten-thousand dollars, do you?" I asked, deliberately halving the amount that Steve told me he'd lost. "Isn't that considered grand theft?"

"Right. I'm hoping the police can throw the jerk in jail."

Drew hadn't corrected my sum. My suspicion that he'd lied about the embezzling former manager was stronger than ever.

"Hey," Drew said, "I just made a run to the liquor store, so you're well-stocked. Can I get you anything to drink before you go? A beer? Glass of wine, maybe?"

"No, thanks." I completed my simple packing job, reeling at the concept that I couldn't trust my future-husband's best friend. And that somebody had just been murdered in our midst. How was this ever going to get resolved? When I glanced at the doorway, I was surprised to see that Drew was still standing there, watching me.

"We're okay, aren't we?" he asked in a flirtatious tone. "You and me? You realize that I wouldn't ever do anything to hurt my main man, right?"

"I know that you sincerely think the world of Steve," I answered carefully.

He studied my eyes, a half smile on his lips. "And yet... there's something that's not sitting right with you. You still think I'm a junkie, don't you?"

"I'm still *afraid* that you are seriously addicted to cocaine, that you mainline it. And that, if so, it will destroy your life and will deeply hurt the man that I love. So...yes. That bothers me greatly."

He shook his head, as if in pity for my lack of understanding. "I'm doing fine, Erin. I'm a nice guy."

"Steve likes you. I like you. I hope everything is wonderful for you. Always."

"Likewise. Back at you." He stepped out of view for a moment, and returned while putting on a dapper-looking black wool jacket. "Well, if you'll excuse me, I have a date. You have some very attractive friends, by the way. I'm taking Emma out tonight. Or, I should say, she's taking me out to show me the town."

"Oh." I was surprised. That was the friend of mine he'd been hitting on during his cliff-walking nonsense on the hearth. She'd seemed uninterested. So. Now Steve's untrustworthy best man was *also* dating a friend of mine. "Emma's great. Have a nice time."

"You have a nice evening, too, Erin. I hope Steve gets home soon." He let himself out.

Frustrated and worried, I took a moment to collect myself. Mark's accusations yesterday about Drew were now haunting me; I kept having terrible visions of Drew poisoning Fitz's coffee.

Hildi trotted into the room, her body English sending the strong message: *Thank goodness* he *finally left!* Unfortunately, it was time for both of us to leave and return to Audrey's. After indulging myself and Hildi by playing catch-the-end-of-the-ribbon with her, I opened the closet door, where she knows she's not supposed to go, which had made my curious kitty obsessed with my closet. Her carrying case door was open and located immediately inside the door. When she started to enter the closet, I whisked her inside the carrier with ease. She was too surprised and offended to protest, other than one low growl. Feline cursing, I was certain.

As I rose and grabbed the strap of my overnight bag, I unexpectedly caught sight of my reflection in the mirror above our dresser. My face was showing signs of my emotional strain; the arcs under my eyes were almost as dark as my brown eyes.

Was I wrong about Drew being an addict? If I was being honest with myself, his having such a big place in Steve's heart was difficult to take, regardless of any worries about his drug use. Could my low opinion of him be strictly the result of jealousy?

I'd soon settled back in at Audrey's. Hildi curled onto my lap, and we were both purring contentedly in our own way. Then Steve called my cellphone to say that a traffic accident had caused a major jam. He would be in Crestview too late to attend our meeting with Lucas LeBlanc, and suggested that I could always call his cell whenever I needed his opinion. That, as I told him, was not going to be helpful whenever my question was: Which of these dishes taste best?

Audrey had overheard my end of the conversation and immediately volunteered to step in for him. Thirty minutes or so later, we were driving in my Sullivan & Gilbert Designs minivan toward Parsley and Sage to meet our new caterer.

"I love being your sidekick," Audrey declared.

"My wedding-reception sidekick?"

"No, your crime-solving sidekick. You're going to help your police friend, Linda, and that stick-up-his-ass Detective O'Reilly to solve Fitz Parker's murder. And I'm going to be your sidekick." She gave me a happy grin.

"A young man is dead. This is hardly fun and games, Audrey."

"And that's a tragedy for his friends and family. But we'll be helping them by figuring out who his killer is."

"My wedding is consuming all of my brain these days, Audrey. I need to figure out a whole new menu for a wedding that's less than two weeks away. I have no intention of playing amateur sleuth."

"But...your talents are needed. *Our* talents, I should say. We'll be able to learn more about Drew Benson's relationship with Fitz by asking Drew's head chef."

The last thing I wanted was to be involved in another criminal case. But Audrey had a point. Focusing on the matter at hand, I replied, "I don't think that he's going to tell us a thing."

"Think positively."

"I positively don't think he'll tell us a thing."

"Whereas *I* intend to use my wit and charm to coax him into spilling the dirt on his employer."

As I pulled into a space in a downtown parking garage, her phrasing stuck with me; it was normally "dishing the dirt" or "spilling the beans." I had an image of Lucas dumping the contents of a flowerpot on Drew's head. Combining my wedding planning with investigating a murder was hardly the stuff of dreams. Of *happy* dreams, that is.

We made the short walk along the Opal Street pedestrian mall, then entered Parsley and Sage. I'd seen Steve's drawings and computer mockups, but there was something so dream-come-true-like about seeing the space with my own eyes.

The kitchen was open so that patrons would be able to see the chefs weaving their culinary magic. The huge ovens with a gleaming cooper hood were in place. I find the reddish-gold hues of copper to be breathtakingly lovely. The pinewood plank bar, finished to a fine sheen, was also gorgeous, perfectly matched with the comfy-looking stools. The tables and chairs were yet to arrive, and none of the all-important finishing touches were in place—no vases and arrangements in the built-in nooks on the paneled walls, no bottles on the shelving behind the bar, no light fixtures in the main dining areas. Even so, I could imagine a large lavender—or perhaps indigo—vase on the top shelf of the bar, harmonizing and setting-off the bar area like a beautiful centerpiece.

After a few luxurious moments, I was able to shift my focus to my fellow human beings. Lucas was saying something to us, and gesturing for us to come toward him. He then called to someone, "Lock the door. My clients have arrived."

The spell that Steve's ingenious design had cast on me was broken. I hated the notion of being locked in a room with Lucas. Behind me, a man was responding to Lucas's instructions. I vaguely recognized him as one of our construction-subcontractor's crew members, and not one of Drew's, let alone Lucas's, employees. We could have thrown the lock ourselves. Even so, the man quickly obliged.

"Chef Lucas," Audrey cooed. She was already slipping into her witty-and-charming-sidekick persona. "This is such an honor to see you in your own environment!"

"The honor is all mine, mademoiselle," he replied with a bow and an enormous grin. He rounded the kitchen half wall only to usher us toward the bar. "We are a work-in-progress, as you can see, so we'll sit at the corner of the bar, *oui*?"

"*Oui, Monsieur*," Audrey happily replied.

Audrey claimed the seat on the corner, positioning herself between us. "Wasn't it so tragic that a guest at our party was poisoned?" she asked, wasting no time delving into the topic of the murder.

"Indeed." He smoothed his thin mustache with his index fingers. "That was so terrible. Have the authorities found a key suspect, do you know?"

"Not yet," I interjected.

"They're honing in on people from Fitz's past," Audrey replied. "Former clients or lovers, competitors, employees, and so forth." She was winging it, and doing a good job, in my estimation.

"That is very logical," Lucas said with a sad nod. His somber, attentive expression struck me as perfectly in keeping with an innocent person's reaction. I wanted to pay strict attention, not because I'd started to hope that we would learn anything, but because I anticipated that Audrey was so eager, she would jump to erroneous conclusions.

"It's ironic that you got the job this weekend due to someone else's caterer giving a guest food poisoning," I said, adopting the in-for-a-penny-in-for-a-pound motto.

"This was a lethal substance in the food or drink, *n'est-ce pas*? It was murder, not sloppy food preparation."

"Right. There's a huge difference," I replied. "It's just that now I worry that my wedding guests will shy away from your food. You were the only chef of the *hors d'oevres* that any of our guests are ever going to remember."

He paled noticeably. "What a terrible thought!"

"Yes, it is," Audrey chimed in. "We should all put our heads together and see if we can identify some clues or theories that may help the police arrest the killer immediately."

"I would of course like to see that very much." He shrugged. "But, alas, I know nothing. I was just...passing through on Friday night, noticing only the guests' delighted faces as they tasted my delicious food."

I had to resist smiling at his wording. His French accent and curious phrasing sometimes struck me as every bit as much of an act as Fitz's sexual orientation had been.

"Yes, but you can get a lot of information from a person's facial expressions," I said. "Did you watch Fitz's face, for instance?"

He snorted. "Now there was a sourpuss for you! His eyes were filled with hatred for me. So foolish. It was bite-sized morsels of delicious food! Such a small...and good...thing to cause him so much ill will. Jealousy is terrible for the digestion."

"What about your boss, Drew Benson?" Audrey asked. "Please don't breathe a word of this to him, but he strikes me as being reckless."

"Reckless? Yes, I suppose so. He is an extreme skier. And he jumps from planes."

"No, I mean that he can act rashly...without considering all the consequences. I can see him feeling so threatened by a competitor that he could take someone's life."

Lucas made no remark.

"But *you* are the one who actually knows the man," Audrey persisted. "I've only met him in the context of Erin's wedding. Do you agree? Have you seen him...throw a tantrum?"

"He gets very angry. He is not always easy to work for."

"The idea for you to bring trays of food to the party must have been his, right?" I asked.

"Yes, of course. He bought all the ingredients, and I prepared them here. The police have already inspected this entire building, searching for traces of poison. They found nothing. It was not my food that contained the cyanide, I assure you. And the food that I served to your party guests never left my sight. It was made from fresh ingredients, prepared by me alone, and brought straight to your house, mademoiselle." He gave a slight bow of his head to Audrey, revealing the bald spot beyond his comb-over.

"Do you think Drew could have killed Fitz?" I asked.

"I do not know. Perhaps so."

"What would his motive have been?" I asked. When Lucas merely furrowed his brow I added, "Did he have a bad relationship with Fitz that made them enemies?"

"I only know that he has mentioned his name before several times, with…how do you say…rancor in his voice. He said that they quarreled about Michelle Sullivan, your fiancé's sister. He did not feel that Mr. Parker treated her well. From what I have heard, they each shared that opinion about the other."

"Neither of them thought that the other was treating Michelle as well as he should?" I prompted.

"They both had been in…how do you say…intimate relations with her."

That echoed what Aunt Bea had told me. Audrey and I exchanged glances.

"When Drew spoke about his anger for Fitz," Lucas went on, "he would say that he wished to tear him limb from limb. I do wonder if the method of poisoning would not be too tame. I believe it is more of a woman's murder weapon of choice, *n'est-ce pas?*"

My mind raced to form a list of suspects. If Bea and now Lucas were right about Fitz having had a physical relationship with Michelle, both Michelle and Mark had a motive. Maybe Fitz had strong-armed Michelle, and perhaps Amelia, into giving his business a boost, in exchange for keeping Michelle's husband in the dark about the affair. Bullying Amelia into giving him her pricey necklace could have been a final payment in a blackmail scheme. Which would also have given Eleanor, Amelia, and Aunt Bea a motive to want the man permanently out of the picture.

11

The next evening, I was in for a big surprise when I got home. Eleanor Sullivan, Steve's mother, was sitting on the back porch, awaiting my return, apparently aware that I typically used the back entrance. She rose while I emerged from my car.

"Hi, Erin. I happened to be in the neighborhood." She gave me a warm smile. "I had to return something to Paprika."

The gift hatchet? I mused to myself. "I'm so glad you could stop over." Although it was strange that she came here instead of our office; Paprika was a mere three blocks from Steve's and my office, much closer than Audrey's house. Come on in."

"I hope I'm not interrupting anything."

"Not as far as I know. Audrey could be busily turning her bathtub into a terrarium again."

Eleanor gave no reaction to my joke and probably hadn't been listening. I held the door for her and she walked inside.

"It was a lovely party." Her eyes widened as if realizing that her assortment of small talk was stale and, in the light of recent events, inappropriate. "Except for what happened to poor Fitz."

In my nervousness about her unexpected visit, I had to fight my impulse to wisecrack about my delight that forty-nine out of our fifty guests were still alive. "Can I get you a cup of tea, or a glass of water? Or wine?"

"No, thanks." She took a seat on one of the stools. "I'll just sit here at the counter. But you go ahead and get yourself something. Or do whatever you'd be doing if I hadn't popped in when I did."

I would probably change my clothes, then I'd get on the phone to confirm this evening's appointment with Suki, Fitz's assistant. Leaving the room or making a phone call hardly felt appropriate with Eleanor here. "I guess if you weren't here, I'd be sitting at the counter, all by myself." I sat on the stool beside her. "Is something troubling you, Eleanor?"

She nodded, her eyes averted. "I'm sorry I've been so distant toward you. I *want* to welcome you into my family with open arms. I really do. I know it doesn't seem like it, but I truly like you. And I'm glad you and my son have found each other. Truly. But I've been undergoing a lot of stress. It's so difficult to see your only son get married."

"I can only imagine." Although, truth be told, I couldn't muster much sympathy for her. Steve had lived an hour away for more than a decade now, whereas Michelle's house was in the same housing development, and Amelia still occupied her childhood bedroom.

"I feel responsible for this disaster…for Fitz's death. We never should have been so adamant about your hiring him as your planner. We'd simply wanted to give him a head start, now that he relocated his business to Crestview. But if it weren't for our recommendation, none of this would have happened."

"You had no way of knowing that there was extremely ill will between him and someone that I invited to the party, though...right?"

"No, no. Of course not." She sighed and, one again, averted her eyes. "Although, to be honest, we all knew that Mark didn't care for Fitz."

"Oh?" I was playing dumb. Audrey would have been proud. "Why not?"

"Personality clash, mostly. Sometimes Fitz could be a little pushy."

"How so?"

"He was just a little too eager to be...he'd flatter people too much and try to make himself in charge. I guess that made Mark feel territorial toward my daughter." She rolled her eyes. "Mark has old-fashioned ideas about a husband's role as master of the family."

"So he found Fitz threatening?" I prodded.

"Yes, I think that's exactly what it was."

"I have to say that, in retrospect, you didn't seem all that eager to socialize with Fitz yourself. And you weren't comfortable with Amelia talking to him. Was there some kind of a problem between the two of them?"

"No, no. But if I had to do it all over again, I never would have recommended him. I'm so very, very sorry for ever having even mentioned his name."

"Actually, it was *Michelle* who recommended him so highly. I don't recall you and me ever having a conversation about him."

She winced. "Indirectly, we did. Through Michelle. I'm the one who insisted to Michelle that she tell you all about how great Fitz was."

And you did all of that just to give the guy a head start, out of the goodness of your heart? That seemed unlikely. "It was strange that he wound up taking Amelia's valuable necklace."

She furrowed her brow. "It's hard to say for certain how that happened. My hunch, though, is that Fitz praised it to the sky, and Amelia gave it to him. She does things like that frequently…tries to buy friendship…and that's why I interrupted their conversation. Fitz is a player, more than happy to take advantage of a situation for his own gain. Amelia's emotional reactions are so volatile and unpredictable."

"Yet…according to Detective O'Reilly, someone used nail clippers to cut through the chain, and a pair of clippers were found in Fitz's pocket."

"That's what the detective told me, too." She rose, her lips pursed as if she had no intention of shedding any light on the puzzling contents of Fitz's pockets.

"Was Fitz ever alone with Amelia? Upstairs?"

Her eyes flashed in anger. I couldn't tell if the reaction was fueled by bitterness at the memory, or resentment at my asking the question. "Just for a few minutes. But I need to hit the road now before the traffic starts to build up. All I really came to say, Erin, was that I'm sorry I've been so distant toward you."

"I…have a feeling that there's something you're not telling me."

"No, no, just my long overdue welcome to the family." She gave me an awkward hug. "Let me know if there's anything I can do to help with the wedding. Things must be in a state of chaos under the circumstances."

"Not chaos. Just a bit more hectic. I'm going to be working with an associate of Fitz's now. But he had taken careful notes."

"Oh, good. Well, tell Steve I was here and said hi. Audrey, too. She's such a lovely person." She let herself out the door.

What an odd conversation. Why would she visit me, ostensibly to be more open with me, only to be so cryptic? She must truly feel guilty about her role in Fitz Parker's being our wedding planner. She was so unwilling to discuss why the gold chain might have been cut that I wondered if she felt that was incriminating evidence toward one of her daughters, for some reason.

I picked up my phone and weighed the notion of calling Steve to ask about his mother's relationship with Fitz Parker. I reconsidered, unable to picture myself telling him that his mother seemed to me to believe that she needed to shield Amelia and/or Michelle from the police investigators' eyes.

All I really knew was that Mark, Michelle, Eleanor, and Aunt Bea, plus Drew and maybe Lucas, had experienced some unfortunate interactions with Fitz. I could pass that information along to Detective O'Reilly if anything more noteworthy occurred. I decided to take Eleanor's advice—to go about doing the things that I would have done if she'd never dropped by.

Audrey arrived home shortly before Suki, Fitz's associate, arrived, and she joined us for our appointment. At first, I wondered if it was Audrey's presence that was making Suki so flustered. Partway through the meeting, after I'd had to periodically reassure Suki that everything would be fine, I realized that I didn't believe my own words. Furthermore, we'd reversed roles. When I shot an exasperated glance in Audrey's direction, Audrey reached over the table and patted the young woman's trembling hand. "Where exactly are the 'extensive notes' that Mr. Parker kept for you, my dear?"

"Umm…that's just the thing. I don't actually have them. They're in his private file. For some reason, yours was the only client file he didn't give me the software authorization to open." Her gaze shifted to me, then back to Audrey.

"That can't possibly be all that difficult to resolve," Audrey exclaimed. "I'm sure a computer expert could open that file as easily as your average refrigerator."

"Maybe so, but the police took Fitz's computer and told me I'd be interfering with a police investigation if I accessed any of his private files. I don't want to get in trouble with an officer."

"Was this Detective O'Reilly?" I asked.

"Yes. He…asked me a lot of questions about you. It's made me feel a little…uncomfortable. I hate to have…."

She pursed her lips and suddenly rose, packing all of her papers into her briefcase in a flurry of motion. "I'm sorry to have wasted your time tonight. I'm afraid that Parker's Party Planning is not going to be able to continue to work on your wedding. We'll talk later about returning your deposits and whatnot."

"The wedding is in eleven days!" I cried, rising as well. "I can't get a new wedding planner on that short notice! Even if I could, without Fitz's notes, I might as well not have a planner."

"Maybe you could talk to Detective O'Reilly about giving you Fitz's notes," Suki said as she showed herself out. "I'm sure you'll have a beautiful wedding."

She closed the door behind her.

Audrey and I both stared after her, then turned to face each other. I was trying to think of something funny to say.

Unfortunately, all that came to mind was: *My wedding has turned into a Cable TV reality-show disaster.*

"That little girl is going to have to work pretty darned hard from here on out to get a nice testimonial from me," Audrey quipped.

"Really? *I* thought she was the Mary Poppins of party planners." I sat down again and sank my head into my hands.

"It's okay, Erin. I'll step in and fill the gaps."

"She was probably scared to death to be here, thinking she'll be next. And that I'm Detective O'Reilly's prime suspect."

"That reminds me. Was someone here earlier?"

I lacked the energy to ask how the mention of Detective O'Reilly had sparked that question, but I did, at least, manage to sit up straight again. "Yes, Eleanor stopped by."

"The middle stool at the kitchen counter was off-center, and you and I tend to take the seats to either side of that one. Was it a good visit, I hope?" Audrey was well versed on how strained my relationship was with my future mother-in-law.

"No, it was strange. She was here to ease her guilt for telling Michelle to recommend Fitz Parker to me."

"That *is* a little strange. But then, the death of someone we know brings up all sorts of old wounds and unprocessed emotions." She paused for just a second or two, then said, "We need to talk to Lucas again."

"We do?"

"Yes. Immediately, and in person."

"Why? We just spoke with him last night."

"Lucas left the premises long before Fitz was poisoned. That means he's our least-likely suspect, *and* he has worked closely with Drew for the last couple of years. He told me over the phone this afternoon that Drew has loose lips when he drinks."

"Meaning that he dribbles his liquids?" I teased. After a pause, I added, "I'm assuming that *you* called *him*?"

"Of course. Lucas might have the scoop on how Drew truly felt about the members of the Sullivan family."

"Audrey, none of that is relevant. They're my future in-laws. All that matters is how the Sullivans and Drew felt about Fitz Parker."

"Right. And *Drew* could have been gossiping about the Sullivans' opinion of Fitz to *Lucas*."

"That's remotely possible, but—"

Audrey had already swept up the phone and was dialing. "Hello, Lucas! How's my favorite chef?" Audrey said into the phone, holding up a palm to signal that I should stop talking.

Hildi started wrapping herself around my ankles. Needing a cuddle myself, I picked her up. Apparently, whether I liked it or not, Audrey had unleashed the hounds. I stared into Hildi's gorgeous gold-flicked eyes. "I hope we don't find ourselves chased up a tree," I told Hildi, who touched her nose to mine.

12

Lucas fidgeted with his napkin, reminding me of my conversation with Mark. I wondered if napkin mangling was a reliable method to detect guilt. Probably not.

Audrey had persuaded Lucas to stop by for a home-cooked meal, which she'd thrown together—broiled lamb, steamed green beans, and seasoned pasta. We had finished the delicious food, but not Audrey's pricey bottle of *Chatuneff de Paup*; she had pulled all of the stops for this unlikely-to-amount-to-anything fishing expedition of hers.

"Have you met the groom's sister, Michelle Dunning?" Audrey asked Lucas. "I believe she came out to visit Drew in Napa a couple of years ago."

I attempted to kick Audrey under the table, but only succeeded in kicking her chair leg. Michelle might well have mentioned a trip to Napa during a conversation with Audrey at our party, but I wanted her off this conversation. My stomach was already in knots. If by some hideous chance, a member of Steve's immediate family *had* actually committed the murder, I didn't want Audrey or me to get involved. I wanted to marry the love of my life a week from Saturday, and to leave for Europe, all blissfully unaware of the murderer's identity.

"Yes, I met Michelle. She is a beautiful young woman," Lucas replied. "She was traveling with her not-so-beautiful husband, and they all had dinner at my restaurant."

All? "The three of them? Mark, Michelle, and Drew?" Audrey asked, clearly as surprised as I was.

Lucas furrowed his brow and didn't answer. We sat there in silence.

"Did they bring their daughter, Zoey?" I asked.

"No, it is not a family-style restaurant," he answered. His gaze shifted from me to Audrey. He patted his plastered down comb-over as if to ensure that his baldness was still in doubt. "My apologies, mademoiselle, but I have had time to rethink our conversation at Parsley and Sage."

"About possible murder suspects?" Audrey asked, batting her eyes at him.

"Yes, and I don't think you should continue to ask anyone any questions. I believe you are making a lobster of yourself, just as the chef has brought the water to a boil. *N'est pas?*"

"You're worried about my safety?" Audrey asked. "That's sweet! But you needn't worry. One of the pleasures of being both petite and above a certain age, which we'll call forty, is that people consider me harmless, and overlook me."

"*Which* people?" I asked. There were few people in this world harder to overlook than Audrey Munroe.

"Nobody would dream of seeing me as a threat," Audrey told Lucas, raising her voice a little as if to drown out mine.

Lucas touched his mustache, as if to reassure himself that it was still there. "I would think a killer would find even the meekest of witnesses a threat. My worry, mademoiselle, is that

Drew would know it came from me, if he was asked about his relations with Michelle. I do not wish to lose my job."

"I see," Audrey said.

"Michelle's past relationships with Mr. Parker and Mr. Benson are not a clue. The police don't need to know. Yes?"

"I'm sure the police already know," Audrey said. She turned to me. "Don't you agree, Erin?"

"Well, I—"

"Steve and his whole family know that Drew and Michelle were once a couple," Audrey continued. "Michelle's crush on Fitz Parker was an open secret, as well."

"You should still not tell," Lucas said, shaking his head. "I do not want to mislead. It would look like I am perhaps hiding something from the police myself."

"It's too late," Audrey said. "I already told Detective O'Reilly everything you'd said."

I couldn't help but raise my eyebrows in surprise at Audrey's fib. She hadn't said a word to O'Reilly; we'd discarded the idea of speaking to the detective while we were making tonight's dinner.

"I regret that you did that," Lucas growled.

I began to worry a little. The line was reminiscent of something from an old movie—or two—uttered right before the bad guy lunges at the innocent female. "You won't lose your job, Lucas," I said.

"And what do you know of the matter?" Lucas snapped. "Drew does not respect your opinion. You are just an obstacle in his path."

I was taken aback and instantly felt hurt. "Between him and Steve, you mean?" I asked.

Lucas nodded. "He does not have to work at keeping Steve...how do you say...in his corner. That makes Steve an invaluable asset. Until now. *Now* you are filling Steve's head with such things as the truth that Drew so often does not *do* the right thing, but rather the easy thing."

"Wow. You summed that up perfectly," I muttered.

Lucas dropped his napkin on the table and rose. "No sense in talking on. We agree about what can and cannot be done."

"Even if Mark were to fire you," Audrey protested, "you'll be in steady demand for catering. You'd always be able to make a great living here in Crestview from catering, if that's what you'd like to do."

Lucas drained his wineglass in two gulps.

"That is true. It is not the specter of being fired that worries me. I am not merely his chef. I'm a fifty-fifty partner. *I* am the one who bailed him out in California. If 'Parsley and Sage, Colorado,' goes under, so do I."

13

The next morning, Amelia Sullivan called me and asked if I'd take her to the Denver Design Center today. If the request had come from anyone else, I would have declined and suggested a date next month, when Steve and I were back from our honeymoon. Amelia, however, was so emotionally fragile that I didn't have the heart to decline. My understanding, at least, of her situation was that the medications she took to quiet the voices in her head also slowed her reactions and cratered her word-retrieval skills. The upshot is that she's and attractive, intelligent woman in her late thirties who appears to be mentally challenged.

The Denver Design Center is like a super elegant, high-end mall for interior designers and decorators that, other than their annual open house, is closed to the general public. I enjoyed Amelia's company immensely. Her childlike demeanor in the Design Center matched mine perfectly; visiting the DDC always made me feel like a kid in a candy shop.

I'd set a time limit of ninety minutes for us to window shop, which now felt like needing to leave a movie at the half-way point. I mollified myself by exercising an escape clause;

I hadn't stated that we'd leave the *premises* in ninety minutes. We lingered over cups of coffee at the tables in a hallway with a wonderful view of upholstery fabric in the window of one of my favorite shops.

We'd reached a natural conclusion to our conversation praising the magical ambience of the DDC. I was just on the verge of asking Amelia about her hobbies and career aspirations when she said, "I know how terrible this sounds, but I'm glad Fitz Parker is dead."

Stunned into momentary silence, I soon managed to blather, "You can't possibly mean that, Amelia. Even if you disliked him, he had a right to live out his life to its natural conclusion. We all do."

"You don't understand, Erin. He's not a good man. He pretended to like me. He pretended that I was someone special."

My thoughts flashed back to the party, and Eleanor's angst at the sight of Amelia and Fitz chatting in a corner. Amelia never drank alcohol, due to how soporific the effect would be when combined with her meds. Had Fitz badgered her into having a drink with him?

I used my mantra that I employ in tense situations: *Confidence and optimism.* Right now, I needed to muster plenty of the latter.

"At my party, you mean?"

"No. I already knew what he was like. He flirted with all of us. After the wedding."

"You're talking about Michelle's wedding, two years ago?"

She nodded.

If Fitz gave her a drink, then took sexual advantage of her, that would be rape. One of my future in-laws could have decided that poisoning him was justifiable homicide. The poisoning had to have been premeditated, but maybe plying women with alcohol was part of Fitz's modus operandi.

"When you say *flirting*, you mean…." I didn't know how to complete the sentence for Amelia's sake. My tendency was to talk to her like I would anyone else, but now, ironically, I lacked the confidence.

"There was no inappropriate touching," Amelia said, sparing me from coming up with my own phrasing. "When it came to *me*, that is."

Ah. She'd known about Michelle and Fitz's affair.

"Maybe you can explain something that's been puzzling me, Amelia. I don't understand why, when it's clear that Fitz was such a shameless flirt at weddings, Michelle recommended him so highly. She truly made it sound like I'd offend her if we hired anybody else."

"Michelle was under his thumb. She thought that was the only way she could keep him from talking about the affair."

"To Mark?"

She shook her head. "To Daddy."

"But…would that really have upset your father all that much? That his daughter had had an affair?"

She shook her head. "Fitz wasn't having an affair with *Michelle*. That's just what Michelle told Aunt Bea in order to cover up the truth. Aunt Bea is a Queen Bee of gossip."

"I'm not following, Amelia."

"Michelle was trying to protect our mom. Daddy went over to Michelle's house, looking for my mom, while Mark was away on a business trip. He saw Fitz, sneaking out of the house."

"Oh, my God. Fitz was having an affair with *your mother*?"

Amelia nodded. "Fitz Parker was a bad person. He ruined my mom and dad's marriage, and he ruined Michelle and Mark's marriage."

It struck me as unlikely that Fitz had anything to do with Michelle's marital troubles, although I understood her rationale regarding her parents. Fitz and Eleanor were an odd pairing. Eleanor was at least twenty-five years older than Fitz. No *wonder* she had tried to keep Amelia and Fitz separated at the party. With Amelia's childlike persona, I'm sure Eleanor wanted to shield her from her former lover. Which assumed the affair had *ended*. And that it wasn't a figment of Amelia's imagination.

A shiver ran up my spine at the very thought of Steve's mom turning out to be guilty of poisoning Fitz. Not that the consequences were any easier to imagine if Amelia or Michelle had committed the crime.

Setting aside my own troublesome concerns, I didn't want to encourage Amelia's black-and-white thinking. "There's an old saying, Amelia. 'It takes two to tango.' Have you heard that before?"

"You mean that my mom is also to blame."

"No. I mean that two consenting adults are just that... they're consenting adults. When you look at a marriage that's lasted more than thirty years, such as your parents' marriage, they've experienced countless ups and downs. Who knows what compromises they've each made? In my opinion, it's never fair to judge other people's marriages." I paused, realizing I was being somewhat prissy. "Not that I'm anyone to talk. I blamed my father for leaving my mother and me. Truth be told, I still *do* blame him."

Was I *also* guilty of leaping to conclusions just now? Maybe Michelle had concocted one story for Amelia and their father, and another for her husband. Steve had once told me that I should always take Michelle's statements with a grain of salt because she had a flair for the dramatic. Furthermore, I could

never know what Amelia's inner life was like. If she had somehow gotten her hands on cyanide, maybe she could have killed
Fitz because she believed she would be saving her family.

"Do you know who killed Fitz?" I asked.

"No, do you?"

"No." Although Michelle's husband was still the top name
on my list. Now followed, unfortunately, by Steve's mother,
Eleanor. "Did Fitz steal your sapphire necklace?"

"I don't remember. My memories are all fuzzy. I had a
glass of champagne, even though I knew better. Mom went
downstairs to get me a cup of coffee. I was talking to Fitz. He
was playing with my hair, and my necklace. I told him I was
giving it to you for your wedding. It might have broken. Or
maybe I gave it to him to give to you. I just remember my
mom got mad. She was going to tell Stevie about Fitz. I told
her not to. And Michelle was mad, too."

"About your necklace? And Fitz?" Fearing that anger over
Fitz stealing the necklace led to the murder, my heart was all
but beating out of my chest.

"Michelle's always mad about the necklace. She doesn't
think I should have it when I never go anywhere fancy. I'm
always stuck at home. But I want to get my own place. Daddy
and Mommy are going to help me find a place after the wedding."

"Are they? That's great," I said, though my thoughts were
still racing. I regretted getting coffee. My nerves were horribly
on edge.

"Stevie didn't do it, did he?" Amelia asked.

"*No*, that much I know. Neither he nor I killed Fitz. Did
you really think he might have?"

She nodded. "He told me when we were kids that he'd do
anything to protect me." She chuckled. "I told him he was my

kid brother. And I'd always protect *him*. That's why I was eager to get together with you, alone, before the wedding."

"To…protect him from me?" I asked, still anxious.

She laughed again. "No, to make sure I didn't ever *have* to protect him from you. Now I know that I don't." She reached over and gave my hand a squeeze. "I can tell that you're a really good person. You're always going to be good to my little brother."

"Absolutely." Her statement made me uncomfortable. As much as I liked Amelia, if I was being honest with myself, it wasn't the best scenario to have a mentally ill woman as your husband's self-appointed guardian angel.

"I still hope to be able to let you borrow my blue-gem necklace," Amelia said in a non sequitur. "The police have it."

"They told me that Fitz had it in one of his pockets. Along with a pair of nail clippers."

"Oh! I remember now!" Amelia suddenly cried. "It broke again. I tried to fix it, using some nail clippers."

"Nail clippers?"

"I didn't have any pliers, and I tried to squeeze the link back together."

"So did Fitz take it to fix the chain for you?"

"That's what he *said*. I didn't want him to, though. He would have sold it and tried to claim that I'd never given it to him. I can tell when people are trying to take advantage of me."

I didn't know what to say. Or even what she meant. Did she tell him she didn't want him to "fix" her necklace? She was staring past my shoulder, a wistful expression on her face.

"It had a really delicate chain. Aunt Bea said that's why she bought it for me. The bright-blue stone reminded her of my bright-blue eyes, and the delicate gold chain reminded her of my delicate nature." Her expression changed to an ominous glare. "Not that my nature is all that delicate. I think she meant 'fragile.' She thinks my mental illness makes me helpless. A lot of people think that way. But I'm not. I can take care of myself."

14

After dropping Amelia off at home, I drove straight to the Crestview police station. My hands were still shaking. I didn't know what, if any, impact anything Amelia had said to me could have on the investigation, but it felt like my civic duty to report what I'd heard about a murder-victim's contentious relationships. Plus what she'd said about squeezing a link back together with nail clippers. My fear was that if I waited even an hour to tell the police, I would talk myself out of reporting the information; the last thing I wanted to discover was that any of my future in-laws were guilty of murder.

I caught Detective O'Reilly in his usual foul mood. He came out to meet me in the lobby and greeted me by saying that we should skip the usual formalities and go straight to an interrogation room.

"Here to confess?" he asked with a sneer as we took our seats.

"No, I'm here to redesign the room," I fired back. "You should go with a water-boarding motif."

"Thanks, but I'll pass."

"Really? I could get you a great price on a thumbscrew."

He laced his fingers and sighed. "Okay, Miss Gilbert. What brings you here on this lovely autumn day?"

"Two things. The first is, I need you to give me Fitz Parker's notes for my wedding. His associate, Suki Kramer, said she was blocked from seeing them, and I need to know the status of all the vendors he subcontracted to."

O'Reilly was staring at me with a blank face, so I continued, "Once I have his notes, we can still hold our wedding ceremony as planned."

"That file is evidence. We haven't completed examining it."

"You can keep the physical file itself. I'm just asking for a read-only copy. Or a printout."

One corner of his lips raised in a smirk. "You're still going through with the wedding?"

"Yes," I replied with unmasked annoyance. "Audrey Munroe volunteered to take over the party-planning duties. *Assuming* she can work from Fitz's notes."

He snorted a little, but nodded. "I'll see what I can do. What's the second thing?"

"Fitz Parker apparently had an affair with Eleanor Sullivan, Steve's mother. I was told that by Amelia Sullivan...who might not be considered a reliable witness."

"I've talked to Amelia," O'Reilly snapped. "She is *definitely* not a reliable witness. Did anyone who *isn't* on anti-psychotic medications back up that story?"

"Not as far as I know." I paused. As dismissive as he was to my every word, there was little point in sharing Amelia's story about trying to fix the chain with clippers. "Bea Quince said that Fitz had had an affair with Michelle, whereas Amelia told me Michelle was covering up for their mom when she told Bea that she was the one who had the affair."

O'Reilly muttered under his breath that this whole thing sounded like a soap opera. "Did *Michelle* say anything to you about her relationship with Mr. Parker?" he asked. "Or about her mother's relationship with him?"

"No, I haven't spoken with Michelle since the party." Which reminded me; I wondered if Steve had spoken to her yet about the uncomfortable conversation I'd had with her husband at the coffee shop on Sunday. "Amelia's story of what had happened between her mother and Fitz struck me as plausible. She said that Michelle stumbled onto Fitz and their mother when Michelle came home unexpectedly. If Amelia's story is accurate, it would explain why Michelle recommended that we hire Fitz so avidly, yet ignored him completely at the party. She could have learned in the meantime about his relationship with her mother."

"From what I could see, Michelle Dunning seemed to be extremely distraught after Fitz's death," Detective O'Reilly pointed out.

"True. She was crying pretty hard."

"Yet you believe that was…what? All an act? That she was pretending to be heartbroken over the man who'd slept with her married mother?"

That was an excellent point. Michelle's tears had seemed very real to me. I could feel my cheeks growing warm. "I guess when you put it that way, the story sounds a bit feeble. Never mind my second reason for coming here. Please get me a… harmless copy of Fitz Parker's notes."

"Wait here. I'll be back in a couple of minutes."

He left, closing the door behind him. I stared at the one-way glass mirror, wondering if anyone was on the other side, chuckling at me. If O'Reilly were to drop my name while asking Eleanor about this, I could forget sharing any national holidays with Steve's family.

My own family consisted of my adoptive dad and Jessie, my teenage half-sister. After a ten-year span of only occasional phone conversations, I'd seen them twice since moving to Crestview three years ago. They were flying into Colorado the night before the wedding and flying back to California right after the reception. Although we'd made considerable strides in the past couple of years, we had an emotionally distant relationship. In truth, a large number of friends and even clients had become closer to me than my own family members were.

The longer I sat in this stark, lifeless room, the worse I felt. I might have just now alienated the only family I had. Steve would hate me forever for not telling him about Amelia's statements first. Maybe by coming straight to the police, I'd lost my one chance at happiness. Even now, I would rather hammer a nail through my hand than tell Steve that his sister claimed his mother had been sleeping with Fitz Parker.

Detective O'Reilly returned to the room. The moment my eyes met his, the brusque, indifferent expression left his face. "Are you okay, Erin?"

I shook my head. "All I wanted to do was make sure that I wasn't hiding anything from you that might help you solve this murder. But Steve's mother hasn't exactly welcomed me with open arms. If she learns that I'm the one who told you this rumor about her having a fling with the victim, she'll never forgive me. I don't know if Steve will forgive me, either."

"No worries, Erin," O'Reilly said kindly, as he reclaimed his seat. "We don't reveal our sources when we investigate. She's never going to know you were here. And if that fiancé of yours can't forgive you for doing the right thing...for reporting a contentious relationship someone had with the victim, then the guy doesn't deserve you."

I was touched by his kind words. Then I realized he might not mean a single thing he'd said. "But detectives play witnesses off one another all the time."

"On TV. And sometimes when we're trying to force a confession out of two perpetrators. That is not what we're dealing with at the moment. We're *not* going to take your mother- and sister-in-law into custody and force them to admit whether or not they had sex with Mr. Parker. We're trying to unmask a murderer, not a philanderer."

"Okay." Although, if the philandering had motivated the murder, I would have to testify in the trial. Audrey was right; it was extremely important to my peace of mind that my future in-laws were exonerated before our wedding.

He peered at me for several seconds. "Feel better now?"

"A little, I guess."

He handed me three pages of printed notes from a file with the header: *Gilbert-Sullivan Wedding.* I read the top sheet. Right below his own name, Fitz had typed as a subheading: "I Am the Very Model of a Modern Major General." Under the "Groom" heading, he'd written "Poor Wandering One." The "Bride" category was sub-headed: "I am a Maiden Cold and Stately."

Surprised and annoyed by Fitz Parker's unprofessional behavior by joking about Steve's and my names in his computer records, I flipped through the pages. Under "Flowers" was: "Little Buttercups! Ha ha!" followed by our actual choice of florists and floral arrangements.

For groomsmen was: "My Gallant Crew," and Bridesmaids was: "Three Little Maids from School." (I had to laugh at that one.)

"He…had a little fun with the Gilbert-and-Sullivan theme," O'Reilly said. He gave me a wry smile, then said, "A policeman's lot is not a happy one."

I'd only been home for a couple of hours when someone knocked on Audrey's front door. To my surprise and, frankly, my alarm, it was Steve's mother once again. Amelia must have fessed up about our conversation at the DDC.

I decided that this was not a good time to joke that we had to stop meeting like this. "Eleanor. This is a surprise. Come on in."

"Thank you." She glanced around. "Is Audrey home?"

"No, she's taping one of her shows. I assume you know about her local show: *Domestic Bliss*?" The show itself had lost viewers and had recently become a weekly show that aired only at five a.m. on Tuesdays.

"Actually, I asked because I'd hoped to have a private conversation with you." She proceeded into the front room, and I realized a moment later that I was expected to follow her. She took a seat on the sofa, and I sat in my favorite chair, as she said, "I've been chatting with Amelia. I had no idea you were taking her to lunch today. You should have asked me to join you. Amelia hasn't been doing well lately in strange places."

"We didn't go to lunch. I wanted to get to know her better, so at the party, I invited her to let me take her into the Denver Design Center. You were standing right beside her at the time. This morning, she called and asked me if we could go today. I didn't see the harm."

She pursed her lips. I got the impression that she was seething with anger but doing her best to maintain a reasonably calm façade. "But now you *do* see the harm, *don't* you? Tell me precisely what she told you."

Our gazes locked. I hated the feeling that I was about to be schooled for being disobedient, when I'd done nothing wrong. I reminded myself, however, that she was seeing this from her own perspective—as a mother of a mentally-ill person who, like all of us, was caught up in the whirl of a murder investigation. She deserved my honesty. "She told me that you and Fitz Parker had an affair…at Michelle's house when Mark was out of town. And that George had seen him leaving her house, so Michelle took the fall."

"That's what she told me she said, too." Eleanor balled her fists in her lap and stared at them. "What else did she say?"

"That Fitz was a bad man who'd ruined your marriage and Michelle's, and that she was glad he had died."

Eleanor grimaced, then looked me straight in the eyes. "You haven't told Steve any of this, have you?"

"Not yet." *Just the police.*

She clasped her hands as if in prayer. "Promise me you won't tell him."

"I can't make that promise, Eleanor. I understand, of course, why you don't want your son to know. But he's going to be my husband soon. I don't want to keep secrets of this magnitude from him."

Eleanor paled. I decided on the spot that I didn't want to keep *my* actions a secret from Steve's mother, either.

"The stakes couldn't be any higher for me," I continued. "A man died in this very house. I felt duty-bound to tell Detective O'Reilly what Amelia said. He assured me that they'd keep it on the down-low, and I can assure *you* that he was extremely skeptical about Amelia's claims."

She got up, as if too anxious to sit still. Reminiscent of her son, she strode toward the window. She turned and stared at me with her hands balled into fists. "My past relationship with Fitz Parker has nothing whatsoever to do with his death!"

"How can you be sure of that?" I asked. "Maybe he made a habit of breaking up marriages. Maybe the killer was a past irate spouse."

"There weren't any 'past irate spouses' at your shower! But the police will think George and Mark *were* irate spouses, now that you've made it clear that other members of our family knew our secret. The police will assume one of us is guilty! You've betrayed your own family!" She had tears in her eyes, and was shaking with rage.

My stomach was in knots. "I did the only thing I could do, Eleanor. It's our civic duty *not* to keep secrets from the police when they're investigating a crime. The police shouldn't have been learning about this from me in the first place."

"I *have* told them, Erin! I told Detective O'Reilly. I begged him to keep it quiet. All that you did by telling him was to make it look like Amelia's guilty. She wouldn't hurt a fly!"

"I was just trying to do the right thing," I said, now feeling truly miserable.

Eleanor closed her eyes for a moment, visibly trying to regain her composure. "Michelle and I wanted to let this blow over. We didn't want to wreck Steve's and your wedding." She sighed and gave me a long, sorrowful look. "None of this is your fault, Erin. I'm sorry. I'm just blaming the messenger… and I'm overly protective of Amelia. Every word she said is true. I don't know how she found out, but she did. So now *I* need the chance to tell my husband and son the truth."

Had I only *assumed* Amelia had told me that she'd heard it from Michelle? I was certain that I remembered Aunt Bea telling me that she'd heard about Fitz and Michelle sleeping together from Michelle. My head was spinning so badly now that I couldn't remember our conversation verbatim, even though less than two hours had passed. "Did you ask her how she knew about it?"

"Of course. She wouldn't say."

"Maybe Fitz told her at the party," I suggested.

"Maybe. Unless it was Michelle, who could have told her last week, or clear back when it happened. It's impossible to know how Amelia's mind works."

"My guess would be that Aunt Bea told her. She seems to know everyone's business, and to be willing to share it." *Aunt Bea might have told* me *one story and Amelia another one.*

"Not where Amelia's concerned." Eleanor dropped back down onto the sofa. "She's as protective of my daughter as I am. Aunt Bea still thinks of her as a child. So Bea would never discuss a matter of this nature with Amelia. Bea would have been giving me an earful for my terrible parenting within seconds flat if she knew that Amelia knew anything about this."

"Does Mark know?"

Eleanor shook her head with widened eyes, as if banishing the harrowing idea of that possibility actually occurring. "We've managed to keep him in the dark. I would never have…used her house, Erin, if I'd had any idea my children would find out."

She sank her head into her hands, as miserable as I'd ever seen anyone. "George and I had a terrible fight that night. I'd gone to Michelle's house, but she wasn't home. She'd told me earlier that she was on the fence about going with Mark to California. And when I couldn't get Michelle on the phone, I unfortunately assumed she was in the air; she never turns off her phone. But as it turns out, she'd taken Zoey to the sitter's house and gone to the movies. I had no way of knowing that, Erin. I was too heartbroken to think straight. And too enraged. I called Fitz, and…asked him to come to Michelle's house and keep me company. I wanted to avenge what my husband had done to me. George had had an affair with his secretary, of all people. The worst cliché in the book! And, well, let's just say that Fitz was more than happy to oblige."

"I just feel—"

Eleanor was clearly on a roll, and continued, "Michelle came home and caught Fitz and me in bed in the guest room. It was the worst moment of my life. Needless to say, Michelle was so horrified that all I could do was apologize profusely, and head directly to a hotel. Which is precisely where George found me, an hour or so later. We talked things out, and he promised to never betray me again. As it turns out, *George* had come to Michelle's house looking for me…and saw Fitz leaving. I'd deliberately put my car in Michelle's garage when I'd arrived, so that George couldn't spot it out front. A couple of weeks after I slept with Fitz, George told me about seeing Fitz slinking away…and that Fitz and Michelle were obviously having an affair. I didn't have the guts or the decency to set him straight."

I didn't know what to say. Finally, I murmured, "I'm so sorry."

She released a heavy sigh. Otherwise, we sat in silence for quite a while.

"I guess it's only right that I felt so obliged to confess all of this to you," she finally said, her voice low and indescribably sad. "Now you know precisely what kind of mother-in-law you're getting." A teardrop slid down her cheek. "Now you know why you shouldn't feel like you need to impress me. Maybe you can even begin to understand why I've been so… lifeless with regards to your wedding plans." She met my gaze with her tearful eyes. "I want to be able to celebrate for both of you, Erin. I really do. But it's been such a gut-wrenching déjà vu for me, all this time."

"I can see that, and I can imagine how intensely painful it was to have Fitz involved in your son's wedding. But...I just don't understand *why*. Why did you let Michelle convince me to hire Fitz Parker as my wedding planner?"

Bearing a facial expression reminiscent of her son when he was horribly stressed, she massaged her temples. "We both started to get blackmailed, Erin. By Fitz. He told us that he had to play hardball. That business was down, he couldn't establish himself in Crestview, and he needed us to get your wedding."

Yeesh! "How did he even *know* that we were planning to get married?"

"That engagement notice that you two put in the Crestview paper."

"Oh, right. I'd forgotten. *We* didn't put it in the newspaper; Audrey did. She thought it would be great free publicity for Sullivan and Gilbert Designs."

Ignoring my attempt at a segue toward a less-painful topic, Eleanor muttered, "I put my own happiness above my own children's happiness. Michelle's. Steve's. And now, as it turns out, Amelia's. All so that George wouldn't find out that I'd vindictively slept with another man."

"Don't be so hard on yourself. You didn't know things would turn out like this, Eleanor. I can see why you assumed that no harm was done if George never found out it was you, not your daughter. I've read advice from therapists who say that the spouse who strays is being selfish by confessing to the affair. That sparing your husband's feelings is more important than unburdening your guilt."

"But I allowed him to believe that his *daughter* was having an affair."

"Did that make George think less of her?"

"Actually, no. If anything, he was relieved. He was hoping that she'd leave Mark. She only married him because he'd gotten her pregnant."

"So there's a *second* reason why it made sense not to tell George the truth…as long as *Mark* wasn't led to believe Michelle was being unfaithful."

Eleanor nodded a little. She seemed to be a little less distraught. "The last thing I ever imagined would happen was that he'd be murdered at your wedding shower. I'm sure he only came to the party to try to hit on your bridal party."

"I think the important point here is that Fitz blackmailed both you and Michelle over *his* bad behavior. For all we know, that was how he earned most of his money"

"You think he could have blackmailed other people as well?" Eleanor asked.

"Yes, and I think that, regardless of his agreement with the two of you, he could have told Drew Benson. Or Mark."

"Michelle and I talked about the possibility that he'd claim to Mark that he'd slept with *her*. That's the biggest reason we gave into his threat. We agreed that our best option was to simply convince you that Fitz Parker was the best wedding coordinator in Crestview, and that it would mean so much to us if you'd hire him."

"Do you think Amelia or Michelle gave him the necklace as a final payment?"

She shook her head. "I don't know. It's possible, I guess. The thought did occur to me."

"Have you discussed any of this with Michelle?"

"Not yet. I came straight here after talking to Amelia. I'm just trying to…stop the damage. I've already told George. He's livid with me. But he knows it's in the past. He'll get over it." She searched my eyes. "But, Erin…I want to tell Steve myself. After you're back from your honeymoon. Please, let me do that, Erin."

"I just don't think that's feasible, Eleanor. Waiting that long, with a murder investigation going on, and so many people involved. The whole thing is tied to our wedding. Can't you please talk to him *now*? He should be getting home any minute."

She grimaced, but said nothing. A few seconds later, she replied, "I want to go talk to Michelle. As soon as I can. I'm not comfortable with any of this. Amelia's with her. I'm sure they're hashing through all of this now, in their own way. They seem to have their own language. They've always been so close." She smiled a little. "Amelia's great with Zoey, my granddaughter. She rarely babysits without George or me there, too, though. Amelia's always worried that she'll have a bad day, right when she's alone with the two-year-old."

"Amelia's afraid she might unintentionally hurt her?"

"Or scare her to death by saying something bizarre. Or by doing something outlandish. Or fall asleep when she shouldn't. The meds can be really intensely soporific."

All told, Mark was surely the police's prime suspect. "Is Mark a good father?"

"He really is. That's his one saving grace. And he's certainly been an excellent provider, thanks to Aunt Bea getting him the job."

"And Aunt Bea doesn't know that you...." I let my voice trail off.

"No, and once again, please, please don't tell her."

"I won't. That much I can promise you."

"Thank you so much, Erin. If you're coming to the service in Denver tomorrow, I'll tell Steve the truth afterward. I can see why you wouldn't want to burdened with all of this for any longer than that. George, I'm quite certain, won't be there. Nor will Amelia."

"Thank you."

"Obviously, it's the very least I can do."

"This will be all right, at some point, Eleanor. We'll all get through this. You'll see."

"I suppose so."

She pulled me into a hug, then let herself out. I stood still for several minutes, trying to make sense of this. I had to make such a big adjustment to past conversations and ongoing assumptions. It all began to make sense, though—Eleanor's stand-offish behavior. The general lack of joy that I'd detected from Eleanor and Michelle.

What a sleazebag Fitz had been! To think that he'd complained to me about Drew's behavior. *Now* I understood why Drew had been so rude to him and eager to get his own chef to take the place of Fitz's. That concept, at least, was an enormous relief. Maybe I'd misjudged Drew, after all.

15

The skies were appropriately gray for Fitz's funeral in Denver the following morning. Audrey, Bea, and I had carpooled in Audrey's car; Steve had driven separately and was coming from an antique store on Broadway in Denver.

To my surprise, Drew arrived right behind Steve, obviously having followed Steve's car into the parking lot. He must have joined up with Steve at the store, but it was odd that he'd go way out of his way to attend the service of someone he openly disliked and had only a slim connection with. He was speaking on his cellphone while he and Steve approached, side by side. Audrey and Bea had gone inside and were saving Steve's and my seats. Drew grinned at me and nodded in greeting, then lowered his phone and said, "This could take a while. Go on in, and I'll see you afterward."

Steve took my hand, and we found our seats between Audrey and Aunt Bea. I was anxious to get the service over and done with. Eleanor's promise to hold off on telling Steve about her relationship with Fitz had put me into a box. I'd had a miserable time trying not to talk about it last night during our phone conversation. The more effort I put into steering us away from the subject, the harder it was to think about anything else to say. If Eleanor couldn't go through with telling him today, I would have to tell him myself.

I looked around and spotted Eleanor. George was there, too, right by Eleanor's side. I felt both relief for her sake that he was being supportive of his wife, and fear that his presence would mean she couldn't be alone with Steve for a private conversation.

Drew entered and was coming toward us until he caught sight of Aunt Bea in the aisle seat of our row. He took a seat a couple of rows behind her. I kept an eye out for Michelle, and finally saw her sneak into the very back of the room. She was wearing a large-brimmed hat and sunglasses. The sight sent a chill up my spine. Her outfit struck me as what an abused woman trying to hide her bruises might wear.

The proceedings began. Fitz had an older brother, who spoke eloquently in his eulogy about what a great guy Fitz was. Their parents were sobbing throughout. Some of Fitz's family still lived in Chicago, but the brother said that they knew Fitz had made Colorado his home ever since he was an eighteen year old freshman. Seeing all of our faces here had let him and his family know that Fitz had been loved, and that he had found his home among us. Apparently so much so that they'd chosen to have the service in Denver instead of Chicago.

For a moment, it appeared that the eulogy was over, but he put his notes away and looked out at us, with tears in his eyes. "To whoever took my brother's life, come forward. Confess. You can never give us Fitz's life back. But you can atone for what you did during this lifetime." He looked straight into my eyes and stared at me for at least half of a minute, not speaking. "Otherwise, you will answer to a higher court for all eternity."

Stunned, I glanced at the pamphlet we'd been handed. The eulogist's name was Jeffrey Parker. It rang no bells. He would only know what I looked like if he'd scanned my business website. Fitz must have told him he was doing our wedding. But he had never mentioned he had a brother, let alone introduced us, so why would his brother stare at me like that?

The stranger seated next to Audrey leaned forward and looked at me, as did her companion. Sullivan squeezed my hand. The couple in front of me, whom I also didn't know, turned and looked at me. I could see heads turning ahead of them as well and my cheeks felt aflame.

As soon as the organist started to play a dirge, I whispered into Steve's ear, "Why was he looking at me?"

"He probably didn't mean to. Don't worry."

The rest of the service passed in an immensely uncomfortable blur, with the perpetual sense that people were trying to sneak little glances at me. Whenever our eyes met, I caught their horrified expressions just before they quickly looked away. I'd never met Fitz's brother and didn't even know he existed. I didn't know any of Fitz's family members, and none of them knew me. I barely knew Fitz. Sullivan *had* to be right. But it sure didn't feel accidental that he'd focused with laser-like intensity on me.

As we started the recessional from the front to the back, I dutifully rose, but Steve grabbed my arm. "Let's just wait here for a little while till the room clears out."

"No. I want to speak to Fitz's brother in case there's a misunderstanding. I also want to speak to Michelle before she runs off." I glanced in the direction where George and Eleanor had been seated. They'd already left the room. So much for getting her and Steve alone together.

Steve relented and stood up, as well, but said with his lips barely moving, "My gut says you need to let this go, Gilbert."

"Guts have low IQs. The man glared at me with pure hatred in his eyes. I can't leave him with the false impression that I had anything to do with killing his brother."

"Steve's right," Audrey said. "He was probably slightly cross-eyed and was actually glaring at *me*, for hosting the party." She linked her arm around mine. "Let's not borrow trouble. Skip the recession line and let's avoid talking to the Parkers. Shall we?"

Audrey obviously didn't believe the man was cross-eyed any more than I did. Even so, I allowed myself to be ushered outside. I took a few deep breaths. The autumnal air was nice and crisp, and the first sight that greeted me was an absolutely splendid maple tree, its leaves varying from yellow orange to a rich dark red. They were right. Anyone who knew me at all knew I was completely innocent. I didn't need to confront a grieving family member to plead my case. I should focus on finding Eleanor, with Steve on my arm, and give her the opportunity to arrange a private conversation with her son, while I drove home with Audrey.

"There she is," I heard a man say. I looked toward the voice. It was the eulogist, Fitz's brother Jeffrey, standing beside a slightly thinner and paler look-alike who could only be a second brother.

"Do I know you, Mr. Parker?" I asked my passive-aggressive accuser, walking toward him.

"No, but I know all about *you*, Miss Gilbert. You have no right to be here."

Drew must have been standing right behind me. He suddenly marched past me and stood directly in front of me, as if I needed a human shield. "Listen, buddy, you're barking up the wrong tree. That's all very understandable. You're grieving. Losing your brother is messing with your head. I can tell you this much, for dead certain. Whatever you *think* you know about Ms. Gilbert, you're way off-base. She'd never kill anyone."

"Oh, yeah? You think you know what I'm all about?" Jeffrey snarled, glaring at Drew.

The other brother grabbed him and said, "C'mon, Jeff. We have to leave this to the police. We can't jump to conclusions and make accusations right and left."

"Fitz *talked* to me about her!" Jeffrey protested. "You don't understand!" Despite his statements, he allowed himself to be led away.

Aunt Bea came around the corner of the funeral home just then. Her bristling demeanor made it clear that she had overheard at least part of the miserable conversation.

"Wait," I said to Jeffrey. "I have no idea what's going on. What did Fitz say that makes you think I'm somehow culpable?"

Jeffrey and his brother continued to walk away without reply.

"I'm glad *one* of you stood up for Erin," Aunt Bea snarled at Steve.

"I was perfectly fine, Bea," I objected. I—"

"Drew just beat me to the punch, is all," Steve snapped back.

I was sure that was true. Neither of us had known that Drew was rushing up behind us.

Bea grabbed my arm. Her face bore that same expression of quiet desperation as when she first told me a week ago that she was feeling doomed. "Far be it from me to interfere," Bea said, "but you and Steve need to rethink your wedding plans. Elope, Erin. Leave early for your European honeymoon. The killer isn't finished."

16

"What makes you think I need to leave town?" I asked. "Are you afraid that I'm next, thanks to what Fitz's brother said just now?"

She shook her head. "The released spirits are at play." Bea thumped her cane on the concrete sidewalk. "I have a sixth sense for these things. This isn't over."

"You can't know that, Aunt Bea," Drew scoffed. "Not unless you know who the killer is, and you're holding out on us."

"I don't know *who* the killer is, but I can feel a horrible malevolence. It's engulfing all of us like a black aura." She glared at Drew.

Drew lifted his palms. "I'm not seeing any auras. Just a lot of clouds up in the sky, which, by the way, are a lot more Caucasian-colored than they are black."

I studied Drew's angry features. Was he accusing Bea of making a racist remark? Or of hinting that he was the killer?

"I'm worried that you're undergoing a bout of depression, Bea," Audrey said. "When we start saying that everything is terrible, that truly *makes* everything terrible."

"You're making light of my sixth sense," Bea said with one last rap of her cane on the concrete. It had made a dull thud for metal, and I noticed then that the bottom of the cane was a thick cork, almost like that of a wine bottle.

"Let's go home," Steve said to me quietly. "The Parkers clearly heard some wild, off-base story from Fitz. This isn't the time to try to resolve it."

"Yeah," I muttered. "I'm going to give Linda Delgardio a call. Maybe Fitz's brother told the police investigators why he's acting like I'm the enemy."

Aunt Bea struggled through a brief coughing fit, then said in a raspy voice, "I'm going to speak up for you to Fitz's parents." She shifted her attention to Audrey. "You're willing to stay for a few minutes with me, aren't you?"

"Certainly," Audrey answered. "I'm not about to hold my tongue when some vicious rumor has all but pushed my Erin out the door."

"That's okay, Audrey," I said. "I don't need anyone to leap to my defense. Steve's right. This isn't the time to protest toward a grieving family. We should all just—"

As I spoke, I turned and spotted Michelle Dunning, which distracted me. She was standing alone on the grass, halfway between this side exit and the front door. She had been crying, and she'd removed her sunglasses in order to dry her eyes. Gingerly. Her cheek was swollen and red, and she had a black eye.

Everyone followed my gaze. Both Steve and Drew cursed and immediately strode toward her. Aunt Bea gasped then promptly growled, "I knew it! Mark's abusing her! I'm going to get that bastard fired if it's the last thing I do!"

I trotted after the men, regretting my decision to wear heels this morning. The heels were aerating the lawn with my every step. From the corner of my eye, I saw Audrey grab Aunt Bea's arm, dissuading her from joining us.

"What happened, Michie?" Steve asked, reverting to a childhood nickname. "How did you get a black eye?"

She put her dark glasses back on. "It was just my typical clumsiness." She gave a sheepish, forced smile. "I was having some insomnia last night. So I went trudging down the stairs, half asleep, wearing Mark's slippers instead of my own. A slipper started to fall off. I tripped and banged my face into the banister."

That was feasible. I had once tripped due to oversized slippers. But the timing was suspicious; her facial bruises appeared just after Fitz's sexual relations with either Michelle or her mother had come into question.

"It's Mark, isn't it," Steve snarled, more a statement than a question. "He did this to you."

"No, Steve," Michelle said firmly. "I'm telling the truth. I fell. That's all. Mark was sound asleep the whole time."

While she was speaking, the breeze blew her hair in her eyes. She stuffed the errant tress behind her ear. She was wearing three-quarter sleeves, pushed up to the elbow. Her left forearm was also covered with bruises.

"What about your arm?" I asked. "Did you hit several edges of steps simultaneously?"

"I…" She tugged at her sleeve to cover up her skin. It looked like someone had gripped her arm far too tightly. "They're pressure bruises from my weight-lifting machines at the gym. I get them every time I start out on a new exercise."

"I'm calling Mark," Steve said, pulling his cellphone from his back pocket. "I want to have a chat with him."

"Steve! Don't!" Michelle looked to either side, clearly checking to see if other people were overhearing. "He'll think

I told you that he hit me. But he didn't. I *fell*. Stay out of this. Please! You'll only make things worse."

"In other words, he *is* battering you!"

"No, he isn't. We're just not getting along well…arguing a lot. I don't want Zoey to pick up on our stress. She's always covering her ears now whenever we raise our voices the least little bit." She scanned our faces. "I probably wouldn't have slipped and fallen if we hadn't been arguing last night, but he *didn't* hit me."

"Don't go home," Drew told her. "Come up to Crestview, and stay with Steve and me."

"Oh, Drew," Michelle said sadly. "That is *never* going to happen. Mark's already jealous of you."

"Then you can take the guest room at Steve and Erin's house," he quickly countered. "I'll move out and stay at a hotel. The important thing is that you get away from Mark. You've got a right to live your life without being abused."

She shook her head. "I can't do that. He's got Zoey with him. I *have* to go home."

"Fine. Get Zoey, and drive straight back here," Steve told her. "I'll wait right here for you, Michie."

She covered her face and shook her head. "No. I'm fine, Steve. You're all jumping to the wrong conclusion. Mark is way too gruff with people, but he is not a wife beater. He has never raised his hand to me. It's just that…he's verbally abusive. And it's getting to me."

Michelle started heading to her car, Steve following. I lagged back, not sure what to think. If she was truly being beaten, she should indeed leave immediately. But, like Michelle, I'd bruised my forearm on weight machines at the gym, and I remembered she'd said she was doing a "brutal" workout routine when she'd first arrived at our wedding shower. Furthermore, if she needed to get away from Mark to protect herself, our house wasn't the best option. It would be wiser to fund her moving into an undisclosed location.

"Just take a brief get-away, then," Steve said. "And bring Zoey."

She got into her car. "Stevie. I'll come stay with you if I ever need to. For any reason. I promise." She closed her door.

We watched her drive away. "Why is she covering for that beast?" Drew asked me.

"Maybe she—"

"She doesn't want Steve to worry about her," Aunt Bea said, now standing beside Audrey, a few feet behind us.

If she hadn't interrupted, I was about to suggest that maybe Michelle was telling the truth.

"She isn't ready to admit the truth to herself," Bea continued. "That's a hard thing to do, and it's so scary, it turns your backbone into jelly." There was an angry, defiant expression on her face.

"You're speaking from experience, aren't you?" I asked.

Aunt Bea nodded. "I've been there myself. The best thing my ex ever did for me was to leave me and take up with a younger woman." She released a sad chuckle. "Compared to being battered by your spouse, moving halfway across the country and starting my own international business was a breeze."

I studied Bea's features, feeling a deep admiration for the woman. Steve put his arm around me. I could feel the tension in his rigid stance. I knew he wanted to be with his sister right now, helping her move out, and insuring her safety—at least for the time being.

"Michelle's situation is worse than mine," Aunt Bea continued. "She's got a toddler. And, this is a secret that I shouldn't be divulging, but she's got another baby on the way. I sure hope her fetus wasn't injured last night."

I closed my eyes for a moment. There was too much on the line now. Michelle needed to get out of there. But we couldn't force her.

"If anything happens to any of the Sullivan girls, I'm partly to blame. *I'm* the one who brought Mark into business with me in the first place. *I* gave that monster his big head start."

"He needed a head start, Aunt Bea," Steve said. "That was the right thing to do for Michelle's sake." I could hear in his voice a reflection of my own new admiration.

"You need to stay away from Mark Dunning for the immediate future, Steve," Bea said, shaking her cane at him. "If you go chasing after him when you're this angry, you're only going to make things worse for your sister. All that will come of it is that Mark will swear out a complaint against *you* with the police."

"She's probably right, sweetie," I added. "This needs to come from Michelle. If she files a formal complaint against him, he'll be arrested and locked up immediately. But if you go storming over there for something that Michelle has denied taking place, it's going to be *you* who'll wind up behind bars."

"You have no proof that Mark even touched her," Audrey said. "Michelle's denying it."

"Exactly," Drew said.

"Okay, okay," Steve said, holding up his hands. "I'll go back to Crestview without saying a word to that bastard brother-in-law of mine."

Drew, Steve, and I started walking toward our cars; Drew's sports coupe was such a bright red, it was easy to spot. "Are you heading straight over to Parsley and Sage?" Steve asked Drew.

"No. I've still got business to take care of in Denver."

"With the restaurant surplus store on Broadway?" Steve asked.

"Yeah," Drew said. "I'm also going to scout out the upscale restaurants downtown. See if I can steal some ideas. See you later."

Steve raked his hand through his hair as we watched Drew drive off. "He's up to something," he told me.

"Like what? You don't think he'd go over to confront Mark by himself, do you?"

"Maybe. But I hope not."

"That might not be such a terrible thing," I said, "as long as Drew keeps his cool. Unlike you, *Drew* doesn't have to try to maintain relations with Mark and Michelle. Plus, it's not as personal to him. Drew can be pretty intimidating, physically. He'll probably be able to give Mark enough of a warning to make him think twice before he mistreats Michelle again."

Steve snorted. "If only that were true. You've never seen how things turn out for Drew—the lone black in a lily-white community. He as much as pokes a finger at Mark, he'll be under arrest for assault."

"In that case, let's not take any chances. Let's call the Denver police, and say that your sister has a black eye that she says she got from a fall, but that we think could be spousal abuse. You could call Drew and warn him that the police could soon be on their way to the Dunning's house."

Steve grimaced but promptly called Drew. I could hear Drew's "Yo, bro," greeting even my ear was at least four feet from Steve's phone.

"Hey, bro. Just don't pull a fast one on me and go to Michelle and Mark's house. Okay? Erin and I have decided to call in a complaint and send the police out there to question Mark."

Drew said something in reply that made Steve chuckle a little despite his dour mood. After a couple of jocular exchanges, he hung up. "He says he doesn't even know her address. He's planning to visit with *Jack Daniels* while he chats up the restaurant staff at the most popular restaurants in Denver."

"It's not even eleven thirty in the morning."

Steve laughed. "That's *precisely* what he said you'd say when I told you that."

"Because it's a valid point," I fired back, annoyed. "He shouldn't be drinking whisky at this hour. Especially when he'll be making an hour-long drive to get back to Crestview."

"He won't be driving drunk," Steve muttered. He got into his car and opened the passenger door for me from the inside.

"Are you sure he won't? He has a substance-abuse problem, Steve."

"And my sister is married to a wife-abuser," he snapped at me. "That takes priority. I can't fix everybody at once."

17

"Didn't you tell me earlier you were going to drive back with Audrey?" Steve asked as we drove away. "Yes, but I want to be with you."

"To keep an eye on me? So that I won't drive off to inform my creep of a brother-in-law that I'll beat the crap out of him if there's ever a next time?"

"We're on the same side, Steve," I said gently. "Don't try to turn this into an argument."

"I'm not—" He paused, mid-shout, and took a slow, deep breath. "Sorry. I'm in a rancid mood. We're talking about this big, cowardly sack of shit, punching my own sister in the face. I can't sit back and let it continue."

I held my tongue for a few seconds, reflecting on how chewed up inside Steve must feel. I grabbed my cell phone. "I'm going to call the police now."

"Maybe we'd better wait." He raked his hair back. "That might just inflame both Mark and Michelle. I don't want to get them entrenched into being on the same side. With us as the enemy."

"Okay. I see your point." His face was fixed into a stony glare. "It's possible that she's telling the truth when she says she fell."

"A one-in-a-thousand chance, maybe."

"I agree that the odds are slim," I replied gently. "Mark might merely be verbally abusive, like she says. You could maybe call a social worker first and tell them everything Michelle said, and discuss your concerns…let them help you to evaluate the situation and decide what the next step is."

"Yeah. That's a good idea. I'll do that once we're back in Crestview, and I'm feeling more level-headed."

"Good." I cued up Linda's number on my cell phone. "I'm going to call Linda Delgardio right now, though."

"Why?"

"To ask if she has any idea why one of Fitz's brothers leapt to the conclusion that I killed him."

"Don't say anything about Drew and Michelle yet," he reiterated.

"I won't." I hesitated. "Aunt Bea gave Mark his start just a couple of years ago. She could pressure him by persuading his boss to put him on notice."

"I don't want to deal with Aunt Bea any more. For all we know, *she* could have poisoned Fitz for reasons of her own."

"What possible motive would a seventy-something-year-old woman have to poison a thirty-something wedding planner?"

"Beats me. But she's the only guest who knew Fitz *and* is capable of murder. Not counting my god-damned brother-in-law."

And possibly your best man. I saw the anguish on Steve's features and felt for him. There truly was no connection between Fitz and our other guests except through his sister's wedding.

If only the police could exonerate his immediate family members!

I remembered then that Steve's mother hadn't had the opportunity to tell him about herself and Fitz. My spirits sank a little lower. I really wanted to get this secret off my chest as soon as possible. "Your mother mentioned that she wanted to talk to you. She's probably at the reception in the church hall. You could call her and talk with her now while we're still in Denver...in case it's important, and she needs to speak with you face-to-face. I can always take the bus back to Crestview."

"Really not a good time for me to chat with my mother," Steve grumbled, "with all that's going on."

"True."

Was Bea right? Should we cancel the wedding and elope? Would that help Steve?

Frustrated, I stared out the window and watched the familiar scenery pass. Things seemed to be falling apart all around me. After repeating my confidence-and-optimism mantra a couple of times, I dialed Linda's cell phone. She answered. We exchanged some chitchat, then I told her about Fitz's brother's pointed hostility toward me.

"I just heard about that myself a few minutes ago," Linda replied. "One of O'Reilly's subordinates called from the memorial service, and I overheard his side of the conversation. Did the older Parker brother all but point a finger at you?"

"Yes. It made me want to fall through the floor. Do you have any idea what's going on with him?"

"I've got a pretty good idea, yeah. But I'm not at liberty to tell you. O'Reilly likes to keep a lid on everything. Including misunderstandings among a victim's family members. Such as the powerful emotions that can arise during misinterpretations of email exchanges. That type of thing."

"In other words, Fitz sent an email to his brother about me that was derogatory?"

"I can see how you might come to that conclusion, all on your own," Linda said. "Especially when you consider what you had already observed about the victim's personality and how he treated women."

"Meaning that he treated us all like sexual objects?"

"Yes. That would be a good observation of yours."

Linda was obviously trying hard not to disobey some directive that Detective O'Reilly had made about sharing evidence with me. "So, I gather that Fitz exaggerated his sexual conquests to his brother?" I was getting steamed in spite of myself. The man was dead. It was not as if I could take him to task for lying about me. "And he *lied* and claimed we had more going on between us than the strictly business relationship we actually had?"

"What the hell?" Steve said under his breath, obviously getting angry along with me at Fitz.

"If Fitz told his brother something like that," Linda said, "it could certainly lead to erroneous conclusions about your relationship with him."

"Yeah. It sure could." My mind was filled with possible slanderous things he could have said, that he'd been fighting off my advances; that he was such a wonderful lover that I was now crazy jealous of him. "Thanks, Linda."

"Other than the horrible awkwardness at the memorial service, is everything all right?" Linda asked.

I looked at Steve. "Fitz was an A-one jerk," he said. I patted his knee, and left my hand there.

"I guess so," I replied to Linda. "Memorial services are never cheery for anyone. But Audrey's being a dear and volunteered to take over for Fitz as my planner." I gave Steve's knee a squeeze and, once again, found myself smiling in spite of myself. "*And* I have a wedding to my fabulous love of my life coming up next Saturday."

"Yes, you do," Linda said. "Things are going to improve rapidly from here on. I absolutely can't wait to see you walk down that aisle."

"Neither can I."

Linda and I said our goodbyes, and I hung up.

Steve's face still looked anything but happy. I couldn't help but wonder what his take had been on Aunt Bea's directive that we elope. "Are you souring on the idea of the wedding ceremony?" I asked.

"Not really." He sighed. "Maybe a little. Between our planner getting poisoned and Michelle getting beaten.... We certainly seem more than a little snake bit."

"True. But that's kind of our story. How we met in the first place. Our careers have been pockmarked by homicides and homicidal clients. Why should our wedding be any different?"

Chuckling, he said, "Good point. Plus, we would upset a lot of other people's plans if we canceled our wedding and eloped."

"True. It would be too late for the venue and vendors to reschedule. They'd lose money. And so many people are flying in." I had to swallow a lump in my throat. This was supposed to be the wedding of our dreams. Was it too much to ask that we could get married and not have anyone involved with the ceremony be killed?

After a couple of minutes of silence, I asked, "Do you need my help at the Parsley and Sage?"

"No. You're on vacation this week. Remember? Besides, it's all under control."

"I meant to tell you…I met with Lucas there, at the Parsley and Sage, yesterday. It's wonderful. I loved it, Steve. The space is looking really sharp. Cutting-edge sharp."

"Thanks. Drew's pleased."

"Where did he get the money to keep moving forward like this?"

"I don't know. He said he cashed in on an old debt."

"That's…fortunate," I said, thinking how dubious it sounded.

"*Fortunate* is one way to describe it," Steve muttered. "It's a little sketchy."

He was giving me an opening! "Drew is obviously a truly great friend of yours, Steve. I can see why you care so much about him. And I'm glad he's the best man in our wedding. I really am. But I'm worried about him."

"So am I," Steve muttered. "He's developed some new and bothersome behavioral habits. I hate when he widens his eyes and tilts his head back, with this little smile on his face. He seems to be…high. It's like he's someplace else. Listening to his own music."

"Was he acting that way this morning?"

"A little," Steve said, his brow furrowed. Clearly he was worried about his best-friend's well-being, in addition to his sister's.

My thoughts raced. Maybe Drew truly *was* going to confront Mark. And maybe he was currently all revved up on cocaine. "Steve? The more I think about it, the more I wish we'd made absolutely sure that Drew wasn't on his way to Mark's house."

After a brief hesitation, Steve said, "Me, too."

"I think I'll call Drew and get him to come back to Crestview."

I dialed. The message kicked on. "No answer," I told Steve as I listened to Drew's message. "Drew, hi, it's Erin. Call Steve or me as soon as you get a moment. Okay? We're worried. Thanks." I hung up.

Neither of us spoke. The tension in the silence was palpable. "He's probably in a noisy bar right now and couldn't hear his phone," Steve finally said. "Or should I turn around?"

"We're almost in Crestview. And we don't even know where he is. Let's just head to the office. You can call Michelle. Or do you think *I* should call her right now?"

"I don't know." Steve groaned. "Damn it! I had no idea she was pregnant. And now that I know what Mark's like.... If we get the police out there, I keep picturing her in a knock-down, drag-out with Mark the instant they leave. But...yeah, I want to call her myself. I'd kind of like to be alone when I talk to her. But maybe you should—" He pounded the steering wheel with the heel of his hand. "I wish we'd talked to my parents at the service. They live right nearby. Maybe I should drop you off and turn around."

I hated the idea of letting Steve head to his sister's house alone into a horrible domestic situation. "Michelle asked us to stay away. And Drew was lucid and told us that he wasn't going to their house. We shouldn't barge in where we're not needed."

Steve said nothing.

Was I being sensible, or cowardly? Was I using sound judgment, or selfishly protecting my own interests by not getting involved?

All I knew for certain was that I was frightened. If I kept thinking about Drew, Mark, and Michelle, I was going to get physically ill.

18

Fifteen minutes or so later, I was waiting anxiously in our office for Steve to return. Having wanted privacy, he'd remained by the car on the phone, while I'd entered our office alone. I pulled out a file of table maps for the reception, as well as itineraries and everyone's arrival schedules that Audrey had asked me to review. I couldn't concentrate.

Steve was opening the door. I breathed a sigh of relief when he smiled at me.

"Michelle says everything's fine," he told me. "No sign of Drew. Unless he got there just now. She's out buying groceries with Zoey. She obviously couldn't talk with her daughter right there."

"Well, good, but…where's Drew? Did you call him?"

"He's still not answering. But he makes friends easily. He's probably chatting up some bartender in Denver, getting the goods on how to draw in customers."

"Is ignoring his cellphone unusual for him?"

"Only when he's on a date. Could have bumped into a female bartender. Or restaurant manager. Regardless, there's not a whole lot I can do, 'til he calls me. Michelle and Zoey are obviously safe for now. It feels like cooler heads have pre-vailed."

Thank God. Drew would turn up soon enough, probably with a woman on his arm. Hopefully sober.

Steve gave me a quick kiss, obviously even more relieved than I was. "How's the paperwork going?" he asked.

"I haven't really started. Mostly I'm just happy to do busy-work because I want to avoid going to Audrey's. She wants to go over the wedding plans with me item by item, and I'm not up for it just yet."

"I'm the groom. I can split the workload with you."

"That's sweet of you to offer."

"Where do you want me to start?" he asked. "Table assign-ments at the wedding? I actually had a good idea for that. We could seat everyone alphabetically so that nobody takes their assignment personally."

"Including us?"

"Sure." He grinned. "Why not?"

"So *I'll* sit with my dad and half-sister, whom I barely know, along with the other Fs, Gs, and Hs, while you sit with the Sullivans?"

He laughed. "It's a sacrifice, but it's both practical and equalitarian."

"Hmm. You've taught me something just now, darling. *This* is why brides do all the wedding planning."

Steve laughed again.

"Let's split the office duties instead of wedding tasks, all right?" I suggested.

"Sure thing."

We delved into some of our accounts that we'd allowed to lapse this last month. It was so nice to be talking about clients and assignments rather than Drew and his restaurant.

Also wonderful was that, freed from his guy-pal persona with Drew, Steve was his usual charming, considerate self again. We balanced our budget in less than an hour, and moved onto the happy topic of prospective contracts when we returned from our honeymoon the end of the month.

The door flew open suddenly. Mark barged inside. His furious glare went from me to Steve and back. He stood arms akimbo, the door reverberating behind him. "Sullivan," he growled, "I need your help. Now."

"Why?" Steve asked.

"Your so-called best man is in the back of my car. He passed out on my front porch. He's drunk as a skunk."

"How?" Steve asked. "He told me he didn't even know your address. And that if he *had*, he'd have gone over there to ask you how the hell Michelle got a black eye."

"I don't know how he got there, but he did. And Michelle warned me about how you and Drew wrongly accused me this morning! My wife tripped and fell down the stairs!"

"I've heard the way you yell at her. She had a nasty shiner. What else am I supposed to think?"

"That she lost her balance and fell! Just like she told you!"

"I don't believe her. Or you," Steve growled.

"Fine. *Don't.* But I still need your help getting Drew-boy out of my back seat. He passed out on my front porch."

"Is his car still in your driveway?" Steve asked.

"I don't know where the hell his car is. He tried to take a swing at me, and fell on his face. I tried to tell him the truth. That she fell. Drew refused to listen to me...or to leave till he talked to her. So I locked the door, and went about my business. I assumed he'd left. But I checked a while later, and he'd passed out. Apparently just being sloshed out of his gourd wasn't enough for his standards. He shot himself up with drugs, as well. I found the needle on the porch."

Steve cursed. His expression quickly changed to panic. "Where's your car?" Steve cried. He shoved Mark out of the way.

"Hang a left," Mark called as the door was shutting behind Steve. "It's the silver Mercedes."

"Are you sure he gave *himself* an injection?" I asked as I brushed past Mark to head outside.

"Like I said. There was an empty syringe on the porch. I doubt it was a measles vaccine."

Steve had opened the backseat door of Mark's car and was already ministering to Drew. "He's not breathing! Erin, call nine-one-one!"

"My cell phone is—"

"Use mine," Mark said. Still a step or two behind me on the sidewalk, he made the call then handed me the phone.

"We've got to get him out where there's more room," Steve said. "He overdosed! Why the hell didn't you call nine-one-one when you found him?" he hollered at Mark.

The dispatcher answered while Steve and Mark dragged Drew's lifeless body out of the car. I had to cover my ear while Mark and Steve yelled at each other.

"We need medical help at Ninth and Opal in Crestview," I said into my phone. "A friend, Drew Benton, stopped breathing after maybe drinking, and possibly shooting up with a drug. Back when he was in Denver. The owner of the house where Drew was found unconscious drove him to our office."

As I spoke, they laid Drew flat on the sidewalk. His face was pasty. I had to look away. "Two men are administering CPR now...the man who drove Drew up here to us, along with my fiancé."

"EMTs are on their way," the female dispatcher told me. "How long has he been unconscious?"

"Mark." I held the phone near his mouth; he was giving Drew chest compressions. "How long has he been out?"

"A minute?" Mark answered. "He was still breathing when I got out of the car. I thought he'd just passed out again."

"Did you hear that?" I asked into the phone. Feeling woozy, I leaned against the car. My heart was racing. I couldn't believe any of this was really happening. "I shouldn't have interrupted. They're trying to keep him alive."

"Tell me your name," she instructed.

I answered and gave her Drew's name again, along with Mark's and Steve's. The minutes dragged by despite the dispatcher making a point of keeping me talking. Steve was looking grim yet determined to keep up the CPR.

I felt too numb and hopeless for any relief to register when the paramedics arrived. I clung to Steve's chest as we both tried not to cry. They took Drew away, continuing the resuscitation, which I doubt any of us believed was helping. A police car with two officers had arrived just seconds after and was directing traffic and trying to encourage the dozen or so pedestrians that had collected to be on their way.

"He probably choked on his own vomit," Mark said to me. "It's not like this is my fault. I had no way to know that he was this far gone."

Every muscle in Steve's body seemed to tighten. "If you know what's good for you, shut up," Steve growled. "Don't say another word." I pulled away from Steve and tried to position myself between him and Mark.

"Is there a problem here?" the closest officer said, striding purposefully toward us.

"No, officer," Mark replied, just as Steve was saying, "Yes."

"We have reason to suspect that this man beat up my sister Michelle. He's her husband," Steve continued.

"Steve—" I said, hoping something I could say would help keep him from losing his temper.

"What?!" Mark cried, simultaneously. "That is not the case, officer. I did not beat my wife! I was fast asleep last night. I awoke to a bang…a thud coming from the stairway. And my wife cussing and crying that she'd smacked into the banister." He pulled out his cellphone. "I'll call her right now. You can ask her yourself."

True to his word, Mark pressed the couple of buttons and handed the phone to the officer. A few moments later, the officer was saying into the phone, "Mrs. Dunning? This is Officer Kirkwood. I'm with your husband in Crestview."

There was a pause as Michelle spoke. I hated seeing Steve in such pain, and didn't know what to do to help. I felt like curling myself into a ball, right where I stood on the sidewalk.

"No, he's fine," the officer said to Michelle's question. "He had a passenger in his car who had to be taken to the emergency room." He paused and said, "Yes, that's right. All I can tell you at this time is that he needs emergency treatment. But I need *you* to tell me how you sustained facial bruises yesterday."

"Let me talk to my sister," Steve said.

The officer was covering his free ear and turned away from Steve. After saying "I see," three times, he said, "No, that will suffice. Thank you, Ms. Dunning." He handed the phone back to Mark.

"Are you and Zoey okay?" Mark promptly asked his wife.

"She's simply protecting her husband," Steve declared. "She doesn't want him to get thrown in jail."

"I haven't done a single thing wrong!" Mark shouted at Steve, while hanging up on his wife.

"You found an empty syringe next to Drew and you didn't call for help!" Steve shouted back. "How do we know it was Drew's and not yours? That you didn't shoot him full of poison?!"

The officer, I realized, pressed a button on his handheld radio that I suspected was recording this conversation. He said nothing to stop the argument between Mark and Steve.

Mark faced the officer. "I don't know what was in the syringe, but Drew brought it and used it on himself. He was already drunk when he knocked on the door. It was another ten or fifteen minutes 'til I went out again and found him asleep and drugged out. He'd crashed on the Adirondack chair in the far corner of the front porch. But I shook him and he woke right up. Said he wanted to go back to Crestview. So I drove him."

"Where is this syringe now?" the officer asked Mark.

"It's in my glove box. I have a two-year old daughter. I didn't want her to find it."

"So now your fingerprints are all over it," Steve said. "That's convenient."

"No, they aren't. I used a handkerchief to pick it up. The handkerchief was Drew's, too. He'd dropped that on my porch, too."

Officer Kirkwood motioned to his partner. "Can we look inside your glove compartment? We're going to need to collect those items as evidence."

"No problem." He glowered at Steve. "They'll probably be chock full of Drew's germs and fingerprints, since they belonged to him." He shifted his attention back to the policemen. "Like I was saying, Drew was muttering incoherently, pretty much the whole time I was driving."

"What was he saying?" Officer Kirkwood asked.

"Stupid nonsense about this guy that works for him... Lucas Somebody-or-other, and needing to talk to my wife, Michelle. And her crazy sister, Amelia. And by 'crazy,' I mean *literally*. She's loony tunes."

"Maybe he wanted to warn my sisters about you," Steve grumbled, clearly having a hard time keeping his emotions in check.

I started crying from anger at Mark and empathy for the love of my life. I felt like such a helpless fool. I wanted to insist that we be allowed to leave, but it was worth enduring this conference with the police if our presence encouraged Mark to incriminate himself.

"He didn't even know who I was," Mark whined. "He called me Fitz a couple of times." He snorted. "The guy passes out on my porch, I'm giving him a ride home in my car, and he can't remember me."

"You *didn't* take him home," I pointed out. "He was living in Steve's and my guest room, but you drove him to our office."

"Oh, that's right. Hadn't thought about that. I just automatically brought him here, figuring that's where you'd be." He looked at the policemen. "I'd like to go home now."

"That won't be possible, sir," Officer Kirkwood replied. "We're going to need to interview you as a witness."

"My wife is upset and needs me," Mark replied. "I did the decent thing. I got Drew back in Crestview to where he's staying. Instead of kicking him off my porch, like most people would have done." He headed down the sidewalk with his phone on his ear.

"You can't let him go home," Steve said. "I'm afraid for my sister's well-being."

"Denver's out of my jurisdiction. I can have you file a report and have him held in custody until we get the DPD to talk to your sister in person. But I have to tell you, she was pretty convincing that you overreacted to an accidental injury she'd sustained."

"She's a good actress. She's been acting happy with the creep she married for almost three years." His eyes were looking wild. I had never seen this expression on his face. He was losing control. "I want him arrested," Steve said, pointing at Mark. "He treats my sister like dirt, and he either poisoned my best friend outright, or he allowed him to die by not seeking medical attention."

"Steve, Drew could still pull through," I said. "There's still reason to be hopeful."

Steve hadn't answered his phone when I called him a half an hour after he insisted that I leave. Nor my second call ten minutes after that. Nor a half hour after the second call. I was sitting on my bed at Audrey's place and holding my phone, trying to decide if I should try to reach him a fourth time. He called me. I answered, "Hi!"

"We're going to have to cancel the wedding," Steve said. "I'm sorry."

"What do you mean? Why?"

"He's dead, Erin. My best friend is dead. They said it was an overdose. Cocaine. I should have listened to you. Maybe then he'd still be alive."

19

That night, it took me over half an hour to cry myself out. My tears were driven by my empathy for Steve, but also by my guilt at not liking Drew very much.

During our three-year relationship, Steve and I had experienced more than our fair share of atrocious luck. I'd seen Steve through some bad times, as he had for me. At what I'd thought was his nadir, Steve had been under Detective O'Reilly's all-encompassing cloud of suspicion when the woman who'd broken his heart and stolen all of his money came back into town.

Now, however, he was totally inconsolable. I had told him that I was going to move back to our home and would be there in a few minutes. He'd insisted that he wanted to be alone. His wishes had made me all the sadder.

When I'd pulled myself together enough to go downstairs and tell Audrey, she slumped into the nearest chair. "We were just talking to Drew this morning at the service," she said. "What happened? Did he die of an overdose?"

"Yes. Or at least, that's what one of the ER doctors said it was. They won't know for certain until the autopsy results are back from the lab."

"How's Steve handling this?"

I tried to swallow the lump in my throat. "He was so upset at first that he wanted to cancel our wedding."

"*Cancel it?*" Audrey repeated in horror.

I nodded. "He wants us to just get married by a justice at the courthouse. I think I convinced him to wait another day or two before making the final decision."

"Can't we just postpone the wedding for a month or so?"

"Not really," I said, still having to battle to keep my voice even. I felt annoyed at my emotions. I'd already had enough time to think this all through, and, I thought, to accept Steve's decision, whichever way he went. All I cared about now was that we got married. And that we could get through all of this unbearable sadness together.

"It's too short notice for the venue to reschedule," I explained. "We'd have to forfeit our deposits. And the earliest we can rebook our venue is three months, so we'd be booking in the off-season, during mid-January. We'd rather have a simple civil-service ceremony, followed by a quiet reception, attended by just a few friends and family members."

"Okay. We'll make this work. We can have the ceremony here, keep the caterers, keep the guest list the same, and—"

"That's just it, Audrey. Steve doesn't want a big wedding and reception, now that his best friend is dead. Especially now that he's blaming himself for the death."

"Why is he blaming himself?"

"Steve didn't believe me when I warned him that Drew seemed to be high on coke at the wedding shower. As it turned out, the coroner discovered lots of fresh needle marks on his body, including between his toes. The guy at the morgue showed them to Steve. Now he has an awful image in his head to remind him forever that he should have acted sooner and gotten help."

"Steve is wrong to blame himself. Drew was solely responsible for his own bad decisions, and nothing—"

"Be that as it may, Audrey, that's how Steve feels right now, and I understand and respect that."

She pursed her lips. We were silent for several seconds. Part of me just felt numb. Separate from the pain I felt for Steve having to endure the loss of his good friend, I felt guilty for grieving the loss of the wedding of my dreams. I had another, deeper, underlying fear—that Steve was going to change his mind about marrying me. Maybe he should, considering how wrapped up I was in a stupid ceremony. I should be thinking exclusively about poor Drew.

"I'm sorry for his loss," Audrey said. "I hope he changes his mind about the wedding. Even if we're simply talking about the size of your guest list. The two of you deserve and should have a big, official send off, witnessed by all of us who want to celebrate the start of your marriage."

"We can't always get what we want and deserve," I said quietly. "Life isn't always fair."

"True." Audrey rose and gave me a hug. "At least, in the big picture, you two have found each other. And you'll still be getting married a week from today. That's all that really matters."

"Precisely," I said, and I'd never said a truer word. Even so, it was lucky that Audrey couldn't see my face. I *didn't* deserve Steve. I'd let him down. Maybe he'd realize that I wasn't worthy of being his soul mate.

We released our embrace, and Audrey turned and walked away. "Besides," she said cheerfully over her shoulder, "I'll throw you a surprise reception on your first anniversary that will knock your socks off."

"It's nice to know we have that option," I told her honestly. "Although, what I really want is to have the police find the murderer and get a full confession, and Steve to decide that we should have our wedding just like we'd planned."

"Do the police think there could have been foul play in Drew's death?" Audrey asked.

"I'm not sure. I doubt it. Drew was fine when he left the memorial service. Nobody knew he was going to Michelle's house. Except for Mark and Michelle, everyone we know who was in the vicinity was still at the service."

"Well, that isn't counting Aunt Bea. Or Steve's parents. They both left maybe five minutes after you did. And George said that it was only a ten-minute drive to their house."

"Wasn't Aunt Bea with you?"

"Not the entire time, no. She told Eleanor and George about Michelle's black eye and Michelle's explanation. Right after the Sullivans left, Aunt Bea left as well for about forty minutes; I kept checking my watch. She told me she'd left a sympathy card for Fitz's family in my car and needed my keys. When she returned, she said she realized she'd left it at home and had to go to a store to replace it."

"That's...odd."

"You're being too gracious, Erin. It's not just *odd*. It's *suspicious*. The Crestview police investigations are working on Fitz's poisoning, but if it turns out that Drew was also poisoned, that apparently took place at Michelle's house. The Denver Police will have to investigate, starting from scratch. Who knows how well the two departments will work together. If they get territorial and are unwilling to share evidence and witness statements, these murders might never get solved."

"Or maybe *Drew's* murder—if it wasn't an accidental overdose—will get solved quickly with a large, experienced homicide division in charge. Which in turn means that Steve and I might be able to get married without an albatross flying directly overhead."

"That's just wishful thinking," Audrey said. "You and I were witnesses. We have insiders' knowledge of everyone's relationships. You've got a deadline of wanting to have your wedding without bodyguards and police officers on active duty. All things considered, I think the best thing we can do right now is to solve the cases ourselves."

"Audrey. We can't simply decide to solve the murders on our own! We'd only be lousing up the police's investigations. So, no. We are not going to pair up to solve crimes like Sherlock Holmes and Dr. Watson."

"Would you rather pair up like Scooby Doo and his nerdy owner?"

"No," I said, somewhat testily, "I'd rather let the police do their thing, while I'm being supportive of my fiancé in his time of need."

"Which can start with your calling Eleanor and George to let them know about their son's boyhood friend's passing."

"Fine. I can do that." I turned and started up the stairs for the privacy of my bedroom.

"We'll go talk to Aunt Bea tomorrow," Audrey called after me.

Audrey was slipping into her demanding-mother role, which made me a little uncomfortable. She had made a good point, though, when she said that I needed to call Steve's parents. With Drew's parents having passed away a few years ago and Steve so despondent, they might otherwise not hear about it until tonight's newscast.

Needing to regain my equanimity, I sat on my bed, soaking in the serenity of this room. I'd chosen a lavender tint for the wall paint that was only noticeable due to its contrast with the white trim and my delicate, cream-colored curtains. The bedroom had a softness to even the case-furniture pieces; my dresser front featured a gentle curve, as did the end tables. My color palate was serene in its white-flower-petal hues, but I'd used burnt-orange and sage-green accents sparingly—a glass vase, the painted mirror frame, a small pillow. I loved this room. And I prayed that I would be moving out of it next Saturday.

After a minute or two of breathing in my peaceful surroundings, I dialed the Sullivans' house. Belatedly, I remembered while already listening to the ring tone that Amelia lived there, too, and that, with the death occurring on Michelle's porch in the immediate neighborhood, it was very unlikely that they hadn't already heard my sad news.

Steve's mother answered.

"Hi, Eleanor. It's Erin."

"Oh, Erin. The police just left a minute ago. How's Steve handling this? He didn't answer his phone. Is he all right?"

Indeed, I was not delivering news. "He's really upset. He wants to be alone. I feel like I need to honor that."

There was a pause. "I suppose that's true. But I wish you wouldn't, Erin. I'd feel better knowing his loved one was there with him."

Once again, my eyes filled with tears, mostly out of gratitude for Eleanor's affirming the action that I longed to take. "Maybe I'll go over to the house and tell him I'll sleep on the sofa and stay out his way."

"That sounds like a much better idea."

"It does to me, too. Thank you for supporting me."

"Don't mention it, Erin." Another pause. "You...didn't talk to him about me yet, did you?"

"No, but...I have to soon. At some point."

"If he'll answer his phone, I can arrange to talk with him tomorrow. Just…not tonight, Erin. Please."

"I won't say a word about you and Fitz tonight. Under any circumstances." Even though I wanted to be both respectful and mindful that investigating suspicious deaths was the job of the police, I also dearly wanted to know how Drew had wound up on Mark and Michelle's porch. "Audrey said that you and George left the service shortly after I did. Did you happen to see Drew, or his car, in your neighborhood?"

"No, and Bea told us about Michelle's black eye, so we drove directly there. We didn't see Drew's car. But the police told us his car was parked around the corner, so it's possible we just didn't notice it there."

"That would explain why Mark told us he'd never seen Drew's car. Drew must have initially parked where he could keep an eye on the comings and goings of the house, without being spotted."

"Oh, yes. That makes sense," Eleanor replied. "He was probably waiting to speak to Mark alone, without Zoey, or maybe to Michelle."

"According to Mark, Drew was drunk, and tried to confront Mark, but wanted to speak with Michelle in person before he left. Mark just went back inside and locked the door."

"Oh, dear. How dreadful."

"Did you talk to Michelle when you and George arrived at her house?"

"She wasn't home yet. Mark answered the door, all smiles, holding Zoey and saying she'd just gotten up from her nap. I did what any grandmother would do. Zoey reached for me, and I took her, and insisted that we take her to our house to brighten our day, after the heaviness of the funeral service.

And…that's precisely what Zoey did, for the short time she was here."

I honestly didn't know *what any grandmother would do* when confronted with the possibility that her daughter was being abused. "Michelle picked her up from you to go grocery shopping?"

"Yes. Well, no, after she'd returned from the store."

"That's a little odd. Steve called her as soon as we got back to Crestview, and she'd told him she got Zoey from Mark, and that she and Zoey were shopping."

"That's what I meant," Eleanor said. "Michelle went to two stores. When she picked up Zoey, she said that she was taking Zoey to her favorite store, and that she'd seen Mark. She reassured us that everything was reasonably okay. But then, a little while later, she called to tell us about the call from the Crestview police, and she was badly shaken. She and Drew were the *It* couple in high school. She was devastated to learn that Drew had OD'ed. Then police came here to interview us and take our statements. It's just been…a nightmare."

"It's been a nightmare here, too." I told myself not to say another word, but I started crying in spite of myself. "Steve wants to cancel the wedding. He doesn't want to get married without his best friend standing beside him."

"Oh, dear. He doesn't mean what he's saying, Erin. Don't let him talk you into that. You're the best thing that ever happened to him. I've been a lousy mother sometimes. I've made mistakes. I think my biggest one was never telling him how concerned we were about Drew Benson's influence."

"You didn't like Drew?"

"Painful as this is to admit, no. I didn't. He was like Eddie Haskell on 'Leave it to Beaver,' a show that was before your time. Drew's poor parents tried hard, and they did the best they could. But he had an attitude all his life that the world owed him...." She stopped. "I shouldn't be speaking ill of the dead."

"I'm so glad you did, Eleanor. I'm relieved to hear you say the same things that I've been thinking for months now."

"We're more alike than either of us realize," Eleanor said with genuine warmth in her voice.

Even while I knew that, if Audrey could hear me, she'd feel triumphant at my hypocrisy about my investigating, I asked, "Have you gotten the chance to ask Michelle if she saw Drew at her house?"

"Yes, I've talked with her on the phone a couple of times today about Drew. She never saw him. She didn't even know he was there until the Crestview police called. She's...really upset. His death hit her hard."

I pictured the scene in my head. It would have been possible to go in and out of their garage without noticing someone slumped on one of the Adirondack chairs on their front porch. And passersby might have assumed he was a Halloween gag—the body in the chair. "Well, I'd better let you go, Eleanor. I'm so sorry about this dreadful news."

"Are you going home to Steve now?"

"Yes."

"Thank you, dear. Bye."

She hung up the phone before I could reply. I felt immensely grateful, though, that Steve's mom and I had truly seemed to get past a barrier in our relationship. I finally believed that she sincerely was happy to have me entering her family. At the same time, I felt a pang of shame that my peace of mind had come at Drew's expense. He hadn't boasted to Steve that he was going to confront Mark, yet he'd gone there to discern for himself if his former girlfriend was safe around her bullying husband. Mark could have poisoned Fitz and injected Drew with a lethal dose of cocaine. If so, Drew's decision to run surveillance had cost Drew his life.

I didn't have time to indulge in speculations about Drew's death and my own culpability for not helping him. I needed to be with Steve. Audrey and I exchanged quick goodbyes. Fifteen minutes later, I arrived and let myself into Steve's and my house. The house was quiet and dimly lit, even though it was only eight-thirty or so. The living room had its typical neat, elegant appearance. Steve's taste was all about clean lines. With my influence, the space had gone from almost Oriental in its absence of clutter and black-and-white furnishings, to a sage and dark brown décor. His leather jacket, though, had been tossed on the sofa. I could picture him coming into the empty house, seeing the door to the guest room that Drew would never again enter. Steve shrugging off his coat too overwhelmed and enervated to hang it in the closet. Heading straight to the bedroom in despair.

I followed the path I knew he'd taken, shedding my own coat and dropping it on top of his. Steve was lying on his stomach on our bed. Although I couldn't see his face, I knew he was awake. I knelt beside him and rubbed his back.

"I couldn't stay away," I told him quietly.

He rolled over and reached for me. Neither of us said another word all night, but we made the truest statements we could possibly make.

The next morning, Steve told me that he wanted to head off on a hiking trail by himself, but that he would still have cellphone access. Knowing he truly did want to be alone, I assured him that he could call me anytime, but that I had plenty of tasks to keep myself busy.

I created an excuse and went to Aunt Bea's house. Although I was loathe to admit it, the admiration I'd felt for her after Fitz's service was now tinged with deep suspicion. I didn't buy her story that she was simply out hunting for a condolence card. That was far too little motivation for her to suddenly use Audrey's car without her knowledge or permission.

We sat over steaming cups of chai tea in her living room, and once again, I was taken in by the curiously comforting sensations of being in India. Aunt Bea seemed to be sincerely shaken by the news of Drew's death. Her hands were trembling as she sipped at her tea, and her eyes looked red and weary.

We spoke solemnly about his death, which she was certain that she could and should have foreseen. Just as I was about to ask the real reason she'd borrowed Audrey's car, she asked me, "How did you get involved in interior design?"

"I went to Parsons School of Design in New York...of 'Project Runway' fame."

"But what made you interested in pursuing that as a career?"

"Most of my childhood, it was just me and my mom, living in a modest apartment in Albany, New York. We didn't have a lot of money, and she used to dream of a time when we could afford a nice house. We'd go to open houses on weekends as our form of entertainment. Even as a little girl, I loved to look at people's beautiful homes. I was drooling over *Architectural Digest* and *Better Homes & Gardens* when my friends were drooling over the latest teenie-bopper stud muffins in Seventeen Magazine."

"Ah. So you were searching for a home of your own in those magazines."

"I suppose so. What drew you to becoming a vintner in India, of all places? Isn't there a big sector of India's population that doesn't drink for religious reasons?"

"Yes, but India is a large, overpopulated county. There are many people who *do* imbibe. Weddings especially are their pull-all-the-stops indulgence, which means that alcoholic beverages can be a lucrative venture."

"But…a considerable percentage of the Indian population lives in dire poverty. Doesn't that reduce your market considerably?"

She shrugged. "I like breaking the mold. Europe, South America, California, and various parts of the US already have so many vineyards. It's a relatively recent market in India. I like being able to leave my own footprints. Even if they're merely left in the desert sand."

That was an interesting analogy, though I doubted there were many deserts in India. My thoughts were squarely focused on Drew dying at Mark and Michelle's house. Without any segue, I said, "You gave Mark a head start in the beverage distribution industry, because he married Michelle."

She grimaced. "Yes. And now I intend to get him *out* of the industry for mistreating her."

"Are you one-hundred percent certain he hit her?" I asked.

She shrugged. "I'm certain enough. Ninety-eight percent, we'll say."

"Did you go talk to him after the memorial service? Is that why you borrowed Audrey's car?"

She arched an eyebrow. "I drove to Michelle's to make sure that I hadn't started any trouble by blabbing to Eleanor and George about her black eye. But when I started to drive up, I saw that Eleanor and George were talking with Mark in the doorway, and everyone seemed to be all smiles. So I just kept going." She snorted. "Apparently, Drew was already keeping watch on the house. I thought it was a strange coincidence that there was a red convertible on the next block, but I didn't think it could be Drew's. He'd been adamant about Steve not going over there. Maybe I underestimated him. I just didn't think he really cared about Michelle. Or anybody, other than himself."

"You never talked to Mark or Michelle?"

She shook her head. "I was too embarrassed to let myself get caught trying to help out the Sullivans, one more time. They appreciate it when I actually *do* help, but resent it otherwise. *Then* they call me a busybody and the 'family loon.'"

I hoped I'd managed to keep myself from wincing. I hadn't realized she was aware of Steve's term for her.

"As you know," she continued, "Drew always struck me as arrogant and self-centered. But he was also a true friend to Steve, and he truly cared for Michelle. I wanted him out of my adoptive family's lives, but I would never have wished anything bad on him. I'd have been thrilled if he'd married an Indian princess and moved to Delhi."

My phone rang. It was Steve. I answered immediately. "Hi, darling," he said, but his voice was sad. "I just got a call from a Denver police detective. He wants us both to come down to the stationhouse and let them interview us separately about Drew. I may as well get this over with right away. Want to drive down together?"

"Uh, sure," I said, rising from my seat. "It'll make it a little better to be together for the drive, anyway. Even though they'll separate us during the interrogations. Interviews. Whatever." I'd been through too many of these not to dread the whole thing.

Aunt Bea and I exchanged our goodbyes. I believed her, more or less. Her story left her with a good fifteen to twenty minutes unaccounted for, which might have given her the time to spot Drew skulking around Michelle's house and to wait for Steve's parents to leave with Zoey, but I couldn't really imagine her confronting Drew and injecting him with a lethal dosage of drugs or poison. Why would she?

Although my expectations were extremely low, I'd vastly underestimated just how unpleasant my police interview would be. A uniformed officer took Steve into one room. A middle-aged detective with black hair and a mustache that hadn't been in fashion since the nineties brought me into a separate room. Already familiar with how these things were done, I knew that my best chance of getting any information from him was right at the beginning, when his method was likeliest to be establishing a sense of camaraderie with me. I asked if they were considering Drew's death to be a homicide or an accidental overdose. His reply had been: "Why do you ask?"

Things went downhill from there.

After I'd calmly repeated every aspect of my experiences at the funeral three times and answered every question, I was beginning to get impatient, and told him that I wanted to call an end to the session.

That was the wrong thing to say. The officer glared at me and shut his notebook. "You've been involved in a few murder cases in Crestview the last three years."

"Yes."

"Quite a coincidence, wouldn't you say? All of these murders? All of the victims knowing *you*?"

"Yes. And very unfortunate for my sake."

"No kidding."

"I had nothing to do with Fitz Parker's poisoning. And my fiancé and I were together, driving home to Crestview at the time of Drew's death."

"Even so, don't leave town anytime soon."

"We're going to Europe on our honeymoon next week."

"I don't advise that. You don't want to force me to get an injunction to stop you from leaving the country."

"I didn't kill Drew Benson!"

"For your sake, you'd better be telling the truth. You might have pulled the wool over Detective O'Reilly's eyes, but mine are wide open. And they're looking right at you."

I would have thrown a toddler-esque tantrum on the spot, if I'd thought for a half second that it would help my predicament. This was monumentally unfair. It wasn't bad enough that two key figures in my wedding were murdered within ten days of the wedding? I had to be investigated as a suspect myself?

"I wish you'd focus them on the facts of the investigation instead, and get the killer behind bars." I rose. "We're done here. If you want to speak with me again, I'll be accompanied by my lawyer."

"Just out of curiosity, Ms. Gilbert, what makes you so sure Mr. Benson's death was a homicide?"

"The fact that you're asking about previous already-solved murders, for one thing."

He made a dismissive gesture with his hand. "The memorial service you attended in Denver yesterday was for someone who was poisoned at your house," he countered.

"Yes, but that's within the Crestview police jurisdiction, not Denver's. *That's* why I'm assuming you've determined that Drew's death was a murder."

"By the sounds of it you've turned yourself into quite the little amateur sleuth." He smirked at me. "Do you have any evidence to suspect anyone of killing Mr. Benson?"

"No. I've already told you everything I know."

"I'm curious about your speculations. Any suggestions for where we should look to uncover evidence?"

"I assume you dusted the syringe for prints."

"We did, but we only found one print. Of Mr. Benson's thumb."

That was interesting. The syringe had to have been handled. It should have been rife with fingerprints, unless Drew had been wearing gloves without thumbs. "So someone had made the effort to wipe off all of prints from the syringe, yet wanted you to find a Drew's thumbprint."

The officer held my gaze, but made no remark.

Steve was waiting for me near the front entrance. He put his arm around me as we left. "How did it go?" he asked.

"Miserably, for the most part. All this time I've complained about Detective O'Reilly. But whenever I talk to another detective outside of Crestview, I realize how great he's been."

"I know what you mean," Steve said. "The officer who spoke with me seemed to be pulling at straws. I hope they work with the Crestview police. I don't see this department solving Drew's murder on their own."

"At least they figured out it was murder, thanks to the fingerprints on the syringe. Or, rather, the lack of them."

"Not counting the thumb print," Sullivan added. He'd been given the same information I had. It hit me that the story could have been agreed upon purely for the purposes of interviewing Steve and me. Maybe they suspected we were a Bonnie and Clyde and wanted to see how we'd react.

"I know this is self-absorbed of me, but I'm relieved," Steve said. "I don't know how long it would have taken me to forgive myself if he'd OD'ed. But like Fitz, he was murdered, by someone who targeted him. I wasn't personally responsible."

"Right. You weren't." I was glad I hadn't voiced my doubts about the veracity of the story about a lone thumb print on the syringe.

"So, unless the DPD gets hit by a lightning bolt sent by Thor with the killer's name on it, it looks like the honeymoon's off," Steve said. "Or, rather, delayed."

That sounded promising; going on a honeymoon paled in comparison to the wedding. "Do you want to simply *delay* the wedding and try to reschedule the trip to Europe?"

"No, Erin. I don't want to delay. Will you marry me next Saturday?"

"Yes." I was both so relieved about the wedding and upset about the murder that I started laughing and crying at the same time.

Steve held me tightly and rocked me a little so that we swayed. "Then, after the ceremony, we'll go on our exotic honeymoon. To Sing Sing."

I laughed heartily, mostly out of exhaustion, I think. "Perfect. That's precisely where the CPD and the DPD want to send me anyway. Free transportation."

"Don't worry, darling. I'll slip you a hacksaw in a piece of wedding cake. And I promise we'll break you out of jail before our first anniversary."

"Such a thoughtful husband I'll have."

"Forever and always."

20

As we left the station house in Denver, I decided that it was time to face the ticking time bomb; I convinced Steve to drop in on his parents. I was awash in a sea of conflicting emotions as we pulled into the driveway. I didn't know how he would handle hearing that his mother had had an affair with a man thirty years her junior. Not to mention that she'd gotten us to hire him in order to keep him quiet about it.

Both she and George were home. George answered the door, and he and Steve shook hands, which seemed quaint and charming to me. "Gilbert and Sullivan are here," George called over his shoulder. Eleanor quickly appeared, drying her hands on a dishtowel. She gave me an intense look, which struck me as tinged with fear. She then surprised Steve by giving him a lengthy hug.

"Mom? Are you okay?" he asked.

"Not really. No." Keeping a grip on his arm, she said, "We need to talk. In private."

I saw George wince but doubted that Steve noticed. George touched my arm. "Let me show you the vegetable garden," he said. "You can give me your opinion on the onions."

"The onions?"

"That's okay, George," Eleanor said. "You can stay inside if you'd like. I want Steve to walk with me for a while. Erin, you don't mind, do you?"

"No, no," I replied with false levity. "Take your time. I'll busy myself opining on onions. Giving my op-onion, as it were." I was blathering out of nervousness. I felt complicit and worried, still a little afraid that no matter what Steve said or did to show that my fears were baseless, he'd find out that I was unworthy of him. Now here I was, dropping him off unknowing into an emotional minefield. Was that wrong? Should I have defied his mother's wishes and told him? Where was my Dear Abby app to guide my behavior during a love relationship? I very much doubted I was the only human being who'd ever felt this clueless before getting married.

There was a palpable silence when Steve and Eleanor left George and me standing in the foyer. "Do you have any actual interest in onions, Erin?" George asked.

"Well, I'm not sure how to quantify my interest in onions. The subject is a little outside of my typical arena of expertise, but that makes it a topic I could stand to learn about."

George gave me a big smile. I could see so much of Steve in him that I'd felt a kinship the first time we met. That hadn't changed, despite my knowledge that he'd cheated on his wife. "Well, then, let's go take a look."

He put on a well-used-looking fisherman's hat and led me out the front door. "The garden's 'round back, but we might as well take the long way."

"Why onions, in particular?" I asked. "They aren't the only vegetable you're growing, are they?"

"No, but that was the first thing I ever planted. It's silly, really. My growing onions came about from a kid's song, about a lonely petunia in an onion patch. Eleanor had an entire section of a flower bed dedicated to petunias."

"So you planted an onion among them?" I guessed.

"Yes, indeed. A few years later, I took to planting different types of onion plants. Now I have twenty varieties of onions."

We chatted about his plants as we entered the back yard. Someone slid the door open and called, "Hi, Erin." It was Amelia, closely followed by Michelle.

"Hi," I greeted them.

"When did you get here?" George asked Michelle.

"Oh, twenty, thirty minutes ago. I've been talking to Amelia. You were in the shower."

"I was?"

"Mom said you were." Michelle shifted her gaze to me. "Erin, do you have some time to talk about the wedding and whatnot?"

"Um, sure. But first your father is showing me his onion garden."

We continued on, with Amelia and Michelle taking seats on the back porch to wait for me. George, I'm sure, gave me the Cliff Notes version of his onion tour. Admittedly, I've seen more interesting gardens, but I sincerely enjoy someone showing me their hobbies or passions, regardless of the subject matter. It's delightful to see someone's face light up as they're talking about a special interest, or how precise and efficient a person's movements can be when they've practiced a particular craft.

"Sorry, Dad," Amelia said when he'd shown me the last plant. "I'm going to steal Erin away from you. You don't mind, though, right," she said with no hint of her statement being a question.

"Steve's here, too," I said as I walked back inside with his sisters, while George remained in the garden to "putter around" for a while. "He's taking a walk with your mother."

"We know," Michelle said.

"We saw them leave through the window," Amelia explained. She led the way to her bedroom and shut the door. I had a brief flashback to my preteen sleep-over days. "Are we really going to talk about the wedding?" she asked her sister.

"No. That was just an excuse for Dad's sake," Michelle said.

I studied her bruised eye, which was still puffy and tender looking. It did look a lot better, though, which I told her.

"I'm wearing yellow makeup. It balances out the purple so it hides the bruises better."

"She knows all sorts of tricks like that," Amelia said.

"Not tricks to cover bruises," Michelle hastened to add. "But how to hide blemishes and how to make your eyes look better. Makeup tricks." Michelle and Amelia took seats on her bed. I sat in a rocking chair in the corner.

"What's up?" I asked.

"We're scared," Amelia answered.

"Neither of us has been able to sleep since we heard about Drew," Michelle added.

"I didn't get much sleep, either," I told them. I tried not to look around the room in an obvious attempt to appraise the space. There was always something childlike in a room within one's parents' house. Amelia was quite childlike to begin with, and this room was no exception. She'd painted it a dark royal blue, which seemed a little incongruous with her forest green drapes. It was far too dark of a room. I could almost feel the lightness being sucked away.

"Mark didn't do it," Michelle said looking me straight in the eyes. She appeared agitated. "He didn't kill Fitz, and he didn't kill Drew. Maybe I should have been more adamant, more convincing that my black eye was an accident. I need you to convince Steve of that. He can't continue to treat Mark like the villain in all of this. It will only make my living with Mark that much worse."

"I want to help you, Michelle, but every time you try to convince me that your black eye was an accident, the more I start to suspect the opposite."

She grimaced. "Why? What can I do to change your mind?"

"I don't know, Michelle. Right now, all I can think about is how bad things are for Steve. I just want the police to arrest Drew's killer and let Steve begin to heal from all of this. But... saying things will only be 'that much *worse*' is not a convincing argument. Maybe you should consider leaving him, Michelle."

She shook her head. "He's my husband, and I'm having his baby. And Zoey is just a baby herself."

"You have a loving and supporting family. We'll help you get back on your feet. But for the time being, you might want to just take a breather. Move up to Crestview, and stay and housesit while we're on our honeymoon. Explain to Mark that the stress is getting to all of us, and you just want to let things settle down." The Denver detective words came back to me— that we shouldn't leave the country.

"Thanks, Erin, but that won't be necessary. I'm handling things with Mark just fine. All I need is for everyone to quit treating him like the black sheep."

"Speaking strictly for myself, I do not consider him a black sheep." *More like a black wolf.*

"Is Mom talking to Steve right now?" Amelia asked me.

"Yes, and I doubt it's going well. He probably feels like he's got the weight of the world on his shoulders right about now."

Amelia blushed. "I told Erin the truth about Fitz and Mom," she said to Michelle.

A flash of intense anger passed across Michelle's features, but quickly morphed into a blank expression. "Well, I have to say that I wish my sister hadn't brought you into the family closet so soon. We Sullivans have our share of problems. As I'm sure you've gathered by now."

"It's okay. I love having sisters-in-law nearby," I said. That was true in theory. I had to admit, though, that I liked Amelia more and more, and Michelle less and less as time went on.

I looked at Amelia. "What is *your* take on this, Amelia? Do you want Steve to intervene with Mark?"

"No, I don't. Mark wouldn't hit Michelle. Not unless she hit him first."

"That's not especially reassuring," I said, just as Michelle was snarling, "I've never hit him."

"Yes, you did. You slapped him that one time you were fighting about Drew. He punched you in the stomach."

"That never happened."

"Yes it did!"

"Amelia," Michelle stated, holding her sister's gaze, but keeping her voice gentle, "you're confusing your bad dreams with reality again. It's true that he and I got into an argument in front of you, and that we were really upset. But it was about him spending too much time at a party with his co-worker named *Andrew*, not Drew. I swatted him on the arm, and he pushed me away. That's all. That's what really happened."

"Okay," Amelia muttered, lowering her gaze to the floor.

"Tell her the truth this time," Michelle instructed.

"They did what she said," Amelia told me in a low voice. It was like watching an older sister bully her younger sister.

"I'm having Mark's baby," Michelle said to me. "I'm scared that Aunt Bea is going to be vindictive and will get Mark fired. That can't happen. We can't survive as a family on no income.

You have to persuade her to change her mind, Erin. Please. I'll never ask another favor from you as long as I live. But please, for the sake of Zoey and my unborn child, talk Aunt Bea out of taking any action against Mark. Please."

"I'll talk to her. I can't guarantee any results, but I will talk to her about this and tell her how badly this would affect you."

"Thank you."

I shifted my gaze to Amelia. "How are you holding up with all of this…craziness around you?"

She pursed her lips. "Drew was a good man. Fitz was not."

"Yes," Michelle said. "You're right on both counts." She rose and glanced out the window. "Steve's sitting in your car."

"He is?" I stepped beside her and peered out. I could just see that someone was in the driver's seat from this angle. "I'm going to head out. Bye."

They both said goodbye. I trotted down the stairs and looked for George. I could see through the glass back door that he was still puttering around in his onion patch. I opened the door and called, "Goodbye, George. I'll see you at the rehearsal dinner next Thursday."

"Want me to make up a plate of home-grown onions for the drive home?" George asked with a grin.

"No, but thanks anyway. I wouldn't mind a petunia or two, though."

"Too late in the season for that. I'm confident that you already know what you're missing with the onions. They're best with a T-bone side dish. Drive carefully."

"We will." I went straight to Steve's van and got into the passenger seat.

Steve muttered. "Hey."

"I didn't know till just now that you were back from your walk."

"I've been out here for a little while. I was going to come inside in another minute or two."

"Is your mom in the house right now?"

He shook his head. "She drove to a yoga class." He raked his hand through his hair. "*Now* I have to stop myself from worrying if her instructor is male."

"I got the impression that the interlude with Fitz was a one-time thing. She was hurt, and because she acted out of pain, she made a bad decision."

"Let's talk about it another time. Such as when we're back from Europe. And life stops sucker-punching me."

"I'm sorry."

"Don't apologize. You're the only good thing I've got right now."

A list of other good things in his life popped into my mind, but I decided to let him be sad and angry for now. "I'm ready to head back to Crestview," I said, feeling my cheeks warm in embarrassment.

He started the engine. "This has been a regular barrel full of monkeys. We'll have to drop in on Mom and Dad more often."

I chose not to reply to his obvious sarcasm. I looked up at Amelia's window and saw her watching us. I lifted a hand in a small wave, but she continued to watch me with doleful eyes.

21

"Let's grab some sandwiches and take the rest of the day off and go for a hike in the mountains," I suggested to Steve. We were on I-25, several miles north of Denver, with Steve eerily quiet as he drove us home from his parent's house.

"That's not a good idea. I might mutilate a tree."

"Mutilate a tree?"

"I don't want to take my anger out on you. Or on an innocent squirrel. Hacking a tree into small bits of wood feels like my only option."

"Ah."

We were silent for another few minutes.

"This is my dad's fault, mostly," Steve said. "He was your typical absentee father—off at work while we were growing up. He'd spend twelve hours a day at the office without thinking twice. Coming home after all of us had eaten and were off in our rooms doing homework. Then, come to find out, he was sleeping with his secretary. Having his secret life, while he deserted us...left us to our own devices. Including my mom, while she dealt with Amelia's psychosis. And all the trouble Drew and I kept getting into." He smacked the steering wheel with the heel of his hand so hard that I worried for a moment that the airbag might inflate. "I'm lucky you wanted to marry me in the first place. Now you're dealing with my dysfunctional family, and my blind devotion to my childhood buddy. I hope you haven't changed your mind about marrying me."

"Of course not! Ninety-nine percent of families are dysfunctional. Yours isn't even within the worst quarter of the scale."

Steve smiled a little. "Where did you find a scale of crazy families? Did you rank us according to a questionnaire in a women's magazine?"

"No, it was just a random sampling based on the families I've known. Don't forget that I was given up for adoption as a toddler, and that my adoptive dad divorced my mom and pretty much made himself a stranger."

He glanced at me. "You don't ever worry that I'll do the same thing, do you? Run off and leave you?" he asked gently.

"Sometimes."

"Oh, Erin. I'll never leave you. No matter what happens. If we ever break up, it's going to have to be because you've gotten so fed up, you decide to leave *me*."

"I can't imagine ever doing that. It's not hard to see why you'd leave *me*, though." I paused as Steve navigated us alongside a string of orange pylons for a lane closure. "Maybe this is how the vast majority of couples feel right before their weddings. And I suspect that, as interior designers, we get more glimpses of marriages than most people do. It never bothers me when couples disagree on design decisions. It's more fun sometimes—determining how both of them can be thrilled with the results. But every now and then, with kitchen remodels, there's that particular exchange of one-liners that breaks my heart."

Steve nodded, immediately picking up on my drift. "The wife says: Well, I'm the one who's going to be using the new kitchen. Then the husband says: Well, I'm the one who's going to be *paying* for the new kitchen."

"Exactly. That's the snippet of dialogue that I hear too often, and it always makes me cringe. And I'll bet shortly before their weddings, none of those couples would have dreamed that in another ten years or so, they'd be trying to belittle their spouses over a kitchen remodel. But, really, I think it's their own interior lives that they've misjudged. That the wives weren't anticipating that they'd come to resent doing the lion's share of the household tasks, and the husbands weren't expecting to resent working many more hours outside of the house than their wives, in order to bring in the larger salary."

"Which doesn't justify my father's affair."

"No, it doesn't. All I know for sure is that Eleanor is totally wracked with guilt. She believes she's indirectly caused her family to implode. She seduced Fitz to get back at your dad. For whatever reason, she chose to have her fling at Michelle's house, which just compounded everything. My hunch is that your father feels equally guilty. He seems like a gentle, loving soul to me."

"It's going to be a while before I can forgive him for putting his own desires ahead of his family's needs," Steve grumbled. "You have unusually low expectations for fathers, thanks to yours putting the bar so low."

That was true, I thought. I probably *was* asking too little of George. "Maybe Eleanor so overcompensated with her excellent parenting that he felt superfluous in his own household. It's not for me to say. Things fall apart sometimes. I just think it's best to make all of our relationships as good as they can be. And I think it's just as damaging to a relationship to tear *yourself* down as it is to tear down your partner."

He was silent for a while. "Meaning I need to get a grip on my regret for being so thick-headed about Drew."

"Yes, but, more importantly, *I* need to handle my dad's desertion and know that his actions have no relevance to *your* likeliness to leave me. I hope your parents can put their marriage back together. Not just because they strike me as really good people, but because they raised my favorite person in the entire world."

"I love you so much, Erin Gilbert." We stopped at a light on the south side of Crestview. "You're letting my father off too easy, though."

"What he did to his wife and kids is in the past. Our parents' relationships have nothing to do with yours and mine. We rock!"

"You said it, girlfriend!" Steve replied dramatically, which made me laugh.

I snuggled up to him as best I could while we were both wearing our seatbelts. I hoped the thoughts of the killer weren't tugging at Steve's mind, like they were for mine.

I was loathe to admit it out loud, but one big black mark on his parents was that they could be complicit in murder. It was a ten-minute walk between their house and Michelle's. If they had seen Drew shooting up on their daughter's porch, and he'd babbled about wanting Michelle to move up to Crestview with him, was it inconceivable that they wouldn't have decided to take matters into their own hands? Speed up his course of self-destruction to protect Michelle and Zoey from his influence?

What a hideous thought! Of course they would never have done that! Needing to distract myself, I asked, "What do you want to do about Parsley and Sage?"

"That's not really up to me."

"Didn't you say that you'd received the last shipment of materials and furniture?"

"Yeah. It was all delivered to the restaurant this morning, but I didn't schedule the crew."

"You'd pretty much cleared your schedule to work on it all of next week. And I already cleared mine in advance of the wedding."

He slowly smiled. "We could finish setting it up. Then invite some of Drew's friends over to remember him there, in the place he was so excited about opening."

"Precisely what I was thinking."

I saw him wince and realized that his eyes had filled with tears. "Drew would really have liked that idea," he said.

"Then that's what we'll do." I tried to hide my own tears, but couldn't quite manage the feat.

Steve put his hand on my knee.

"I wasn't as kind to him as I should have been," I said. "I'm sorry. I know how much his friendship meant to you." In fact, maybe their bonding was extra strong with his workaholic father being less of a presence in Steve's life than he could have been.

"You saw his downward spiral, but I couldn't. He was deeply troubled. I just—" He stopped and released a slow sigh. "The killer needs to be brought to justice."

"Yes."

Steve smiled at me. My heart did its typical happy dance, despite everything. We found a parking spot and walked hand-in-hand through the alley to the restaurant, Steve using his key to let us inside through the back. I immediately caught a whiff of a foul odor as I stepped inside.

"Does it smell like gasoline to you?" I asked, hoping my sense of smell was deceiving me.

"Yeah," Steve said. We both sniffed as we walked deeper into the restaurant, trying to identify where the odor was stronger.

My nose led me toward the kitchen. "I'm going to crank up the oven hood," I told Steve. The giant fan began to whirr.

Steve said, "I think it's coming from—" He stopped, looking into the office.

Lucas was kneeling on the floor, facing the opposite wall.

"Lucas!" Steve cried. "What's going on here?"

"This is my own establishment," Lucas said, puffing himself up and squaring his shoulders. "I have a right to do as I wish. What are you doing here?"

"We came over to see if we can finish the work on our own time," I said. "It smells like gasoline."

Steve strode through the office doorway and lifted a gasoline can. "It's empty. You were setting fire to the place," Steve said, his hands fisted.

"No, the can of petrol is for my car. I ran out of gas. I had to walk to the petrol pump. I stopped in to try and use the petrol to clean an ink stain on the chair. I didn't realize that I knocked the can over, with my big fat foot. It spilled everywhere."

"Isn't that your rental car, parked in the private space by the back door?" Steve asked.

"Yes, that is right. I put in enough petrol to make it run. I did that first. Then I came in to eat and spilled the rest. I must leave now. I'm getting a headache. It is probably caused by all the fumes from the petrol."

"Which you spilled on the floor," I said, "throughout the entire restaurant. Especially in the kitchen."

Lucas hung his head. "My excuse is…not so good. I was embarrassed to tell you the truth." He looked at first me, then

Steve, searching our eyes. "I did come here to set fire to the building. I was desperate. This place is going to bankrupt me. I wanted the insurance money. But I changed my mind. I couldn't do it. I couldn't light the match." He held up a cloth. "See? Smell. I was cleaning up the petrol. Look. You see?" He pointed at a mop and bucket in the back corner of the kitchen.

I looked at the soapy water, which reeked of gasoline. "It does look like he was cleaning up," I said to Steve.

"Lucky for you we didn't get her sooner. If we'd gotten here half an hour or so ago, I'd be calling the police."

"*Oui.* And now I can use your help to clean up the mess I made. It is not so easy to clean out several liters of petrol." He raised his arms in a dramatic gesture. "This is what the place has done to me."

The odor in the kitchen was strongest near a small plastic wastebasket that must have been moved from the office. "I think I'll start by emptying the wastebasket in the dumpster and rinsing it out," I said. A group of papers were soaked and twisted up like a torch. He was apparently going to light this wad, then toss it through the door. I separated one and started to skim read. "What are these papers?" I asked. They appeared to be a financial contract between him and Drew.

"Give that to me!" Lucas shouted, grabbing at the papers. "That is private."

Steve was already sorting through the contents of the trashcan. "Bank statements. Receipts."

"You were going to put these up in flames as well."

"I already explained," Lucas said indignantly. "I tried to leave my past behind by setting it on fire, but I changed my mind."

"And you wanted to destroy evidence that could prove you killed Drew," Steve said, "and maybe Fitz."

Did Steve think announcing his theory would make Lucas surrender on the spot?

"I did not kill anyone. I had nothing whatsoever to do with their deaths."   "Put that back in the wastebasket," Steve told me. "We'll turn it over to the police."

"Do they arrest people in America for *thinking* about crimes that they do not actually commit?" Lucas asked, his voice haughty.

"No, but they do for embezzlement," I said. "Drew was telling the truth about an employee stealing from his California restaurant, wasn't he?" I was talking through my hat, reasoning that I had nothing to lose.

"Is that why you killed Drew?" Steve demanded. "Was he going to turn you in for the twenty grand you stole from him?"

I dialed Detective O'Reilly on my cellphone, a number which, I'm sorry to say, I had committed to memory. Lucas made no move to stop me or to leave.

"I did not kill either man. I was long gone before Fitz came down with the poisoning. I would never have jeopardized my future by poisoning someone. And I was here in Crestview when Drew overdosed."

"Mark said Drew said your name before he died," Steve said. "Maybe he was trying to name his killer."

When O'Reilly picked up, I told him the state that Parsley and Sage was in and that we were currently with Lucas and had incriminating evidence linking him to money that was missing from Drew's restaurant.

"Do you have an alibi?" Steve asked Lucas. "Were you with anyone who can prove that you were in Crestview yesterday morning?"

"I was alone at my hotel room. The maid and the clerk at the desk spoke with me, however. The money records are all

Drew's doings. His records. I will tell that to the police, and they will set me free." He removed his apron and slammed it on the countertop. "My hands might smell of petrol, but they are clean. I will not speak with you ever again."

22

Lucas Leblanc continued to stay silent, sitting on a bar-stool, while we waited. His silent treatment was going to make his catering our wedding next week awkward. Steve and I pored through all of the records and contracts we could find. I was familiar enough with business practices to see that, although it was clear that somebody had been taking money from the till, nothing that Lucas was going to burn linked him directly to the crime.

Detective O'Reilly arrived. Lucas was maintaining his silent treatment, sitting alone at the end of the bar. O'Reilly seemed to surmise the situation as we greeted one another. He addressed us all formally—using our last names—and Lucas merely gave him a nod in return. "Thanks for the call, Ms. Gilbert," O'Reilly then said. "Or is that going to be Mrs. Sullivan soon?"

"She'll keep the name 'Gilbert,'" Steve said.

"We like our business name as it is," I said, "as opposed to Sullivan and Sullivan Designs."

"Good decision."

"I've done nothing wrong," Lucas said. "Gilbert and Sullivan arrived after a woeful moment that I was in the middle of reversing. Mademoiselle Gilbert jumped to the wrong conclusions."

"He was about to destroy evidence." Steve gestured at the papers that we'd spread on the counters as we attempted to salvage them. According to these records, there really was an employee who was stealing from Drew."

"As I already explained, those files are from Drew's office. They were sent to him. Look at the top of the paper. You see his name. He was trying to cheat the insurance company. And to frame *me* for embezzlement."

"No way," Steve said.

"These are the real records. It is true that the records he supplied to the insurance company show mysterious electronic deposits into an account that he set up in my name. They are the same amounts as the supposed thefts. He told *me* the money was profit sharing as I became a co-owner."

"I don't believe you!" Steve retorted.

"And Mr. Benson is not here to defend himself. I alone am left holding the bag. That is why I changed my mind about setting fire to this place. The insurance company would only see the money in my account. They would not believe I was set up. So, now, you want to arrest me for what I almost did, that is your choice. You want to arrest me for stealing money or insurance fraud, you have the wrong man. I must now try to mend my ways and get this establishment up and running. I am a great chef. We will make it a great restaurant."

"Not when you're behind bars," Steve said.

"I'm in the process of getting a warrant," O'Reilly interjected. "We'll seize all of the documents and computers, and go from there."

"Good," Lucas said. "They will point you toward the woman who killed him."

"The woman?" I repeated.

Lucas merely gave me a glare. Focusing his attention instead on Detective O'Reilly, he said, "I realized I had almost made a terrible mistake by burning the records that Monsieur Benson wished to use to incriminate me in his own fraud." He unbuttoned his vest and removed a tri-folded set of legal-sized documents. "You will see it was a woman who was being blackmailed by Drew Benson. Instead of that dark word—blackmail—they wrote up a contract, in which she is called his investor. I'm certain that Drew had no intention to pay it back, however."

"So this woman is now a part owner of Parsley and Sage?" O'Reilly asked. "Yet we have no proof that she was forced to give him investment money?"

He handed it to me, without meeting my eyes. "You see who was funding this restaurant for the past two months?"

"Barbara Elizabeth Quinn," I read aloud.

"Aunt Bea," Steve and I said in unison.

23

"Would you mind coming out to the stationhouse and giving me a statement?" Detective O'Reilly asked Lucas.

"If you would be so kind as to drive me there and back, I'd like to get some fresh air," Lucas said, rising from his seat—and frumpiness—at the bar. "You are welcome to take these papers with you," he added. "You will see how Monsieur Benson was suddenly getting large amounts of money from this woman everyone calls 'Aunt Bea', although he told me last week that she hated him almost as much as he hated her."

Detective O'Reilly opened the door for Lucas. He looked back at Steve and me. "Are you two going to stay here and continue to breathe in these fumes?"

"We're leaving in a minute," Steve said, "once we can see if there's a way to reduce them."

"Kitty litter and charcoal," I said. "Otherwise, we'll just have to air it out as best we can."

"Good luck," the detective said as he followed Lucas.

I looked at Steve. "It sounds as if Lucas was right that Drew was threatening Aunt Bea. Unless you can think of another explanation why Aunt Bea would suddenly decide to give him tens of thousands of dollars."

"Not off the top of my head," Steve said with a sigh. "She never said anything to you about giving him money?"

I shook my head. "Pretty much the opposite. She gave me the impression that she assumed this venture of his was going to fail. So I can't imagine he gave her a legitimate incentive to invest in it."

"We already know Fitz had been blackmailing my family members," Steve said. "Maybe he had something on Bea. And shared it with Drew."

"Fitz would never have shared anything with Drew," I countered. "They were enemies."

"My point is that killing her blackmailers would be one hell of a good motive."

Poison, as I'd been recently reminded by Lucas, was a woman's murder method of choice. And injecting an overdose of cocaine would also count as a similar method. No need to physically overpower the victim or to endure blood and guts. Still. I hated to think of Aunt Bea as a murderer. Or anybody connected to Steve's family.

"What are you thinking?" Steve asked, studying my features.

"It makes most sense that the same person who killed Fitz also killed Drew."

"Yeah. I agree."

"So the list of plausible suspects has narrowed from everyone at our shower—including the staff of servers—to a party guest who hated Fitz and also knew Drew was heading to Mark and Michelle's home, following Fitz's funeral."

"Then it's Mark," Steve said firmly. "Or Aunt Bea. My parents and sisters are innocent."

I knew how dearly he wanted to believe that, but his parents and sisters were in the immediate area, and Drew's murder might not have been premeditated. One of them could have spotted Drew in the act of shooting cocaine into his system and given him a second dose.

"Maybe it's Lucas," I told Steve. "Even though he wasn't at the memorial service, Drew could have met up with him at whatever Denver restaurant he'd gone to. Maybe Lucas even drugged Drew in advance, drove Drew's car, then took a taxi back to his own car."

Steve gave no response and continued to study my features. "You don't…actually believe one of my sisters or parents is a double-murderer, do you?" Steve said.

"No, I'm just…like I said, it could be Bea, or Lucas, or Mark." *Or Michelle. Or Eleanor, George, or Amelia.* "All three had a motive for at least one of the murders. It's just that… the police are going to have to take a serious look at *all* of your family members, since they were all in the vicinity of the crime scene."

"I know my family members, Erin! If they were capable of killing another human being, I'd know! That would be like saying that, just because Hildi kills mice and birds, she might kill another cat. And she wouldn't."

I stared at Steve for a moment, surprised he would make such an illogical statement. "It would actually be more like saying: cats kill other cats all the time, but I know *my* cat wouldn't kill a cat."

"I need to go get some air," he grumbled. "The gasoline fumes are messing with my brain."

I tried to give him a kiss, but he only allowed me to kiss his cheek. He hadn't shaved and his cheek was scruffy. I felt a pang as I watched him walk away. If our roles were reversed,

I'm sure I'd have felt every bit as isolated as he did. I didn't have his past history with his family members. I could imagine a scenario for each of them that could lead to their feeling so boxed in that they acted out of ruthless desperation.

Maybe that was a difference between him and me. I had become so jaded over the past couple of years that I now believed almost anybody could find themselves capable of doing terrible things.

My thought pattern led me to recall something that Aunt Bea had said to me, just before all of this began. *As time goes on, you get to recognize how easy it is to be on the wrong side.* Maybe Steve was right when he said that Fitz and Drew could have been working together, possibly to wrench Bea's money away from her. If she'd been contemplating killing them, it could go a long way in explaining her frame of mind back then.

The next day we learned that Drew had named Steve to be his executor. He arranged for a cremation, per Drew's will, and we scheduled the wake for him to be on Wednesday evening. My bridesmaids would be in town by then, and we agreed that Drew would have liked showing off Parsley and Sage to them.

Audrey seemed to be trying to kill me with kindness. She'd helped me plan a tour of the town's highlights for when my bridesmaids arrived mid-week. Having a hard time concentrating on the wedding plans, I did a brain dump on her, rehashing the minute details of my week in no particular order—the interview with the Denver police detectives, Eleanor's confession of infidelity, Lucas and the almost fire, and finally my conclusion that, other than Lucas—who was a longshot—all of the suspects were related to Steve, either directly or through marriage.

"Are you going to be able to…adapt if it's one of Steve's blood relatives?" Audrey asked me, quietly, as we lingered over our bowls of yogurt and granola.

"I think so. I hope so."

"Have you considered asking Steve if *he* can cope if one of the members of his family is guilty?"

I shuddered at that idea. "Do you think I should?"

She reached over the countertop and patted my hand. "Sweetie, my track record with marriage isn't very good. So maybe you should do the exact opposite of what *I* would do. But, yes, I'd use as gentle a voice as I could muster, and I'd ask that direct question. I think he might need to prepare himself for that possibility. If the worst happens, he'll have a heavy load on his shoulders."

I couldn't reply at first.

"Marriage is hard. It's difficult to stay with someone when it starts feeling so much easier not to. And even in the best unions, in-laws can pose problems. In this case, they pose lethal chasms for you. So I think it's critical for both of you to know for certain that you are Steve's most important relationship. More important than his parents or sisters."

"The thought of one of Steve's blood relatives being a murderer makes me want to drink the contents of Aunt Bea's wine cellar dry. Or to hope that the murders are never solved."

"Neither of those ideas sound practical, but if you decide to go with the first option, call me."

At two o'clock, my hunger pangs reached enough of a crescendo to remind me that I hadn't eaten lunch yet, it was almost. I made myself a turkey-avocado sandwich and started poring over the notes that Audrey had compiled for my schedule for next two days, up through the rehearsal dinner on Thursday. She'd entitled it: Frivolous Fun with Friends. Frivolity felt like the farthest thing from my mind. My phone rang. I looked at its screen. Michelle Dunning. Not wanting to hear any more troublesome news, I hesitated for a moment, then answered.

"Erin, I need your help," Michelle said, her voice strained. She seemed to be panting.

"What's wrong?" I asked.

"It's Mark. He's been drinking non-stop since last night. I got Zoey out of there and brought her to my parents' place. Plus I hid his car keys, so he can't drive. But my parents aren't here. Amelia said they had a scheduled art-museum thing with some friends. And Mom must have left her phone in the car again."

"What is Mark doing? Where—?"

"I don't want Zoey to see her dad like this. He's going to hurt someone. Or himself."

"I don't understand what—"

"He was banging on the door. Of my parent's house. Just now. Amelia's all freaked out. She thinks he's gone to get his gun."

"Well, good God, Michelle! Call the police! Now! Or else I will!"

"I will...I'll call nine-one-one. I just.... First I want you to contact Steve. I tried his cell and he didn't answer. I left a message, but—" She stopped and took a ragged breath. "I need someone to watch Zoey and help Amelia while I talk to the police. Amelia's...going over the edge."

"I understand, but your first priority is preventing your drunken husband from handling a loaded gun. Or, if it's already too late, getting him disarmed as fast as possible. Don't you see that?"

"I…suppose you're right."

"There's no doubt I'm right, Michelle. I'm going to call them myself."

"Okay, okay. I'm calling." She hung up.

I muttered an obscenity while, heart pounding, I called Steve's cell. I was bluffing about calling the police in thirty seconds, but I'd go ahead if Steve thought I should.

"Hi, hon. I was just about—"

"Have you listened to your phone messages?" I interrupted.

"Yeah. I got one from Michelle. Why?"

"Michelle called me, too. There's an emergency, and she needs…our help."

"She called it an emergency? All she said in her message was that she needs a babysitter urgently, and Amelia isn't up to it. What did she tell you?"

"That Mark's horribly intoxicated and she hid his keys and took Zoey to your parents' house, but they aren't there and Amelia's flipped out, and Mark's possibly getting his gun."

"God damn it!"

"She's calling nine-one-one. Are you at the office?"

"Yeah. I'll try calling the house."

"I'll meet you at the office in five minutes, tops." I hung up, wondering if Steve meant his parents' house or Michelle's. I dialed 911 and was told that the police were already on their way.

I swept up my purse and keys and raced out the door, not even pausing long enough to locate Audrey and tell her what was happening. In what felt like no more than three or four minutes, I pulled into my reserved space at our office. Steve was talking on his cell and standing by the door.

"She's right here," he said, thrusting his phone into my hands as he yanked his car keys out of his pocket. "Talk to Amelia," he instructed me. "I'm driving."

We got into his minivan. "Amelia, it's Erin," I said.

Silence.

"Are you there? Amelia?"

"The police are here. The lights are flashing. I didn't mean to do anything wrong."

"Are your parents home?" I paused, then asked, "Is Michelle there? And Zoey?"

"I just wanted my own place. I wanted to get an apartment. I want my own life!" She was shouting. I had to hold the phone away from my ear. Steve, I knew, overheard. "Mom and Dad said they'd help me find a place of my own. After your wedding."

"She gets like this when she's stressed," Steve said quietly. "Just keep her talking."

"Tell you what, Amelia. I will help you decorate your apartment," I said. "There are a lot of nice one-bedroom places in the area."

My cellphone started ringing. I got it out and put it on my lap while I talked to Amelia on Steve's phone. "What's your favorite color?"

"Yellow," Amelia answered.

I glanced at my screen. "Michelle," I mouthed to Steve.

"I love yellow," Amelia replied. "I love a nice buttery yellow on walls. With white trim." He gestured for me to give him my phone. I did so, and asked Amelia, "Would you like me to paint your bedroom yellow with white trim?"

"Michelle?" Steve said into my phone. He listened for a moment, then mouthed, "Earphone," to me. Meanwhile, Amelia was agreeing that yellow would look really pretty. It took me a moment to realize that Steve's concern was that he didn't want Amelia to hear anything he was saying to their sister. My earphone was in my purse, and I hooked it up within a couple of seconds, still giving an "uh huh" at appropriate times while Amelia described her ideal bedroom.

"Amelia's got Zoey and barricaded her bedroom door," Steve told me. "Talk her into opening the door so Michelle can get Zoey, and the police won't need to break down her door."

"Where's Mark?" I asked him, muting my mouthpiece.

"They don't know," he answered, rolling his eyes. Steve had pulled into the carpool lane and was holding at a reasonable speed—ten percent above the speed limit.

"You can put really nice wallpaper in your room," I said, no longer aware of what Amelia had been saying for the last several seconds.

"I want my own place."

"Is Zoey in your room with you?" I asked.

"She's hiding."

My every muscle tensed. I had a terrible image of Zoey cowering in fear under the bed, frightened of her aunt and scared for her mother. "Where is she hiding?"

"In the closet."

"In the closet?" I repeated for Steve's sake. Had Zoey gone into the closet by choice, or did Amelia lock her in there? "It's dark in there, isn't it? Does she want to come out and talk to me?"

"She doesn't talk much. She's two years old."

Locking a two year old in a closet was even worse than letting her hear her mom talk to the police about her father's violence. Fighting down my sense of panic, I said, "I'll bet she wants her mommy, though. Can Zoey say 'Mommy?'"

No answer.

I pounded my thigh in frustration. Steve was gesturing at me to move the conversation toward opening the door. "Amelia, can you please hand your phone to Michelle? I need to ask her something important."

"She's not here. She's talking to the police."

"Could you get her for me?"

"No. I'm scared of the police. I don't want to see them. I'm staying here until they leave. I want to get my own place, Erin. With buttery walls. I painted my room here too dark. It feels like a dark cave. Like a bear's cage."

I weighed trying to bargain with Amelia; to swap her bringing Zoey to Michelle in exchange for my promise to help her find an apartment. But I couldn't guarantee an apartment was an option. Steve was continuing to have his own conversation with Michelle. He was urging her to keep calm. I heard Zoey crying, "Mommy" in the background.

"Sounds like Zoey wants her mommy," I told Amelia. "Is she out of the closet?"

"Yes. She's trying to move the chair. In front of my door."

"Go open it, Amelia. You don't want to keep Michelle away from her daughter. The police can get all of you to safety if you'll just open the door."

"*I* could take care of Zoey."

"Take the chair away from the door, Amelia. Now. Let Zoey be with her mother. Steve and I will be there soon. We'll talk to the police with you."

I waited a few seconds, muted my mouthpiece again, and said to Steve, "What is going on down there? Are the police searching for Mark in the neighborhood? Did he take off on foot? Has anyone located your parents?"

"Zoey! Baby girl!" I heard Michelle cry through my phone, still in Steve's possession. "Amelia!" she yelled. "What the hell were you—"

There was a bang over the phone. It sounded more like a door slamming shut than a gunshot, but it still made my heart race. "Amelia? Are you there?" I said into Steve's phone.

"I don't want to hurt anybody. I didn't want Drew to die. Or Fitz. I just wanted them to leave us alone. I want to live on my own. I can't ever be alone. Not even in my head. The voices never leave me alone." She hung up.

24

My heart was in my throat for the next fifteen or so minutes. We arrived in the Sullivans' neighborhood in Denver. Their entire housing development was in a lockdown. A police car was parked perpendicular to the entrance to block access in or out. We explained our situation. The officer said that he could not let us in until Mark had been located.

While Steve and I were discussing what to do, George and Eleanor finally arrived in their car and drove up beside us. "What's happening?" Eleanor asked Steve through their car windows.

"Mark got soused and now the fear is that he'll grab his gun and start shooting," Steve explained. "The police have got Michelle, Amelia, and Zoey in a paddy wagon and will bring them out soon. Michelle's been keeping us up to date over the phone."

Eleanor paled visibly. "How's Amelia handling this?"

"Not well. Michelle says she's pretty much catatonic. She kept Zoey in her closet for a while and wouldn't let anyone in the room. They've got them all out of the house now."

"And what has *Mark* been doing while all of this was unfolding?" Eleanor asked.

"Nobody knows, but apparently a neighbor spotted him at least twenty minutes ago running across their backyard with a rifle in his arms. The police are doing a door-by-door search."

"Oh, dear God," Eleanor exclaimed.

George shut off the engine and came around to my side of the car. I rolled down my window, watching as a baby-faced officer approached George, who didn't acknowledge his presence. "Steve, Erin, I'm going to go on through to see Amelia."

"We can't let you do that, sir," the officer said.

"Then you'll have to arrest me," he said calmly. "All I want to do is tend to my daughter and my granddaughter. I know them well enough to know that they are both terrified."

"I can't let you do that, sir," the officer again stated. "We have to assume that there is an armed, dangerous man in the vicinity. We're asking for the public's cooperation and patience so that we can locate him."

"Has my son-in-law actually fired his weapon?" George asked. "Do we know if the gun is loaded?"

"No, sir."

"Are you certain that Mark even *knows* you want him to turn himself in?"

"Someone gets on the bullhorn every couple of minutes."

"In that case, I'm willing to take the risk that my son-in-law won't shoot me and go talk to my daughter before she suffers any *additional* emotional damage."

"I'm going, too." Eleanor held up her hand. "We'll sign whatever waiver you'd like."

"Let's just take the van," Steve said.

"You can't all go in," the officer said. He was looking over his shoulder, clearly hoping to get assistance from a more senior officer.

"For all you know, my brother-in-law could have passed out behind a neighbor's shrub all this time." Steve gestured to his parents to get in.

The officer squared his shoulders, glaring into Steve's eyes. "*Or* he could be waiting to ambush his *in-laws*. It wouldn't be the first time that's happened. I'm not going to be responsible for it happening again."

"Officer," Steve said, "I respect the work that you're doing and how dangerous it is. I realize I'm making it even harder. But my sister Amelia is too emotionally fragile to cope with this kind of upheaval. Every second we wait out here makes it more likely that she'll have a psychotic break. She nearly took her own life the last time. My parents *must* go through, and I'm going to accompany them."

My head and stomach were in a whirl. I held my tongue, but wanted Steve to just cede to the officer's authority. The officers were wearing bullet-proof vests. They were trained, but were just people, too, no doubt jittery and anxious at the possibility that a random guy with a gun would shoot them. Surely they would put Steve and his parents in handcuffs at any moment.

The officer's partner approached. His expression and stride were calm, and he bore an aura of quiet confidence. He was going to be sympathetic. I sent silent pleas for him to let us go get Zoey and Amelia. The policemen conferred, then the second officer told Steve, "I'll need to inspect the contents of your vehicle. Then I'll radio ahead that you're on your way."

"Against my strenuous objections," the first officer added in a semi-growl.

After another minute or two, the officers had inspected the vehicle to see that we weren't bringing in arms or ammunition. We slowly drove up onto the curb and around the patrol car. "Does this count as civil disobedience?" I wondered aloud.

No one answered. I resumed holding my breath, playing a mental game with myself that Mark's gun could go off only whenever I inhaled.

We drove down the deserted entrance road and turned into the Sullivans' cul-de-sac. As we'd been informed, there was a police van—paddy wagon—in their driveway, where Steve's sisters and Zoey were being kept out of harm's way.

An officer carrying a long, no-nonsense gun of some kind emerged from the van and held out his hand for Steve to stop. He then held up his index finger, and gestured with a jerk of his head that only one of us was to go past him and into the paddy wagon. Steve said, "Mom, you go first."

I quickly volunteered to be last. Steve and his parents had gotten into the paddy wagon without incident. As I got out of Steve's van, I looked from side to side before following our police guard's tacit instructions to stride past him quickly toward the wagon. I did a double take and gasped in surprise when I saw Mark staggering as he emerged from the side door of the neighbor's garage.

"There he is," I cried in disbelief. "Mark!" I shouted. "Put down your gun!"

Mark was startled. He took one staggering step, and tripped over his own feet. He dropped the gun while he fell forward, and a gunshot split the air.

I threw myself onto the ground. Three policemen emerged from the van and the house, all of them pointing their weapons at Mark, who, like me, was sprawled on the ground. They rapidly crossed the street toward Mark.

"Drop your weapon!" an officer demanded.

"Already did," Mark said.

"Back away from your weapon!"

Mark started doing an awkward looking crabwalk, then tried to rise and scoot away toward the garage door.

"Stop right there," the officer said. All three officers crossed the street toward him, all the while aiming at him. One officer picked up Mark's rifle, while another officer was putting handcuffs on Mark.

Steve climbed out of the police van and ran toward me. "Erin, are you all right?"

"I'm fine." My knees were a little sore, but I'd mostly hit the Sullivan's soft grass.

Steve helped me up and wrapped his arms around me. Immensely relieved, I took what felt like my first normal breath since Michelle's phone call.

"He wasn't shooting at me. Mark fired by mistake. When he tripped."

"What am I being arrested for?" Mark said, interrupting as one of the officers Mirandized him. "I own this gun. It's registered. I wasn't bothering anyone. Just drinking at home. Trying to sort things out with my wife. That's all."

I saw that the police helped Mark, his hands cuffed behind his back, get to his feet. "You discharged your weapon in a public place."

"These aren't *publics* here. This isn't a public place. It's my in-laws'. They're my family."

Mark was, indeed, extremely intoxicated. I glanced back and saw that Michelle had also emerged from the paddy wagon. Her face was white and her dark brown eyes looked almost black.

"Are you okay?" I asked Michelle, leaving Steve's side.

She shook her head. "I can't take this anymore, Erin. I can't. You don't know what it's been like for me. Growing up with Amelia, and being married to Mark. They're both such damaged people. I'm constantly walking on a high wire. Every day of my life."

"I'm sorry," I said, not knowing what else I could possibly offer.

George emerged from the van and helped Amelia out as well. Amelia was clutching a blue blanket that was draped over her shoulders like a cape. She was scared and wide-eyed. She looked like a little girl, ready to suck her thumb and curl into a ball. The Sullivan sisters were such a study of opposites—Michelle dark haired and sturdy; Amelia light haired with blue-gray eyes and tall and willowy, so much more frail. Eleanor also emerged and reached back to lift out Zoey, who truly seemed no worse for wear. The little girl was adorable—big, dimpled cheeks, big chocolate-brown eyes, and black hair. The adults were studiously blocking her view of her father across the street. He was flanked by two officers as a third led the way to a cruiser. Michelle's features softened as she lovingly took her child in her arms. Eleanor and George both put an arm around Amelia's shoulders as the three of them shuffled toward Steve and me.

"Amelia's decided to go to the resting room for a while," Eleanor said, "until she feels better."

"Resting room?" I asked.

"It's a halfway-house care facility," Steve whispered in my ear.

"I want to get my own place," Amelia intoned.

"After you leave the resting room, maybe I can help you find a place," I blurted out, knowing this wouldn't go over well with my in-laws.

"We'll see," Eleanor replied. That phrase was probably a no, but she kept her face neutral.

Amelia came over to me and gave me a hug, letting the blanket fall. George picked it up.

Meanwhile, Mark put up a mild struggle as the police tried to put him in the backseat of a police cruiser. His eyes were wild and he was unshaven and his clothes rumpled. Then he caught sight of Michelle.

"The police are arresting me," Mark shouted. "What the hell have you done?!"

"I followed Erin's advice and called the police before someone got shot!" Michelle yelled back. I winced at her mentioning my name.

The officers tried to shut the door to the police car, but Mark had wedged his foot in the door. "Self-defense!" he cried. "I've been getting threats. The entire city of Denver thinks that I've been beating my wife. It's a lie! I've never laid a hand on her! Let me talk to her!"

The two officers exchanged glances and stopped trying to shut Mark into the car. From conversations with Linda, I knew that, because they'd already read Mark his rights, every statement he made now to Michelle could be useful evidence.

"What, Mark?" Michelle asked, passing Zoey quickly into Eleanor's arms. She strode toward the police car. "What would you like to say to me?"

Mark, however, was apparently not as out of it as I'd thought. He stopped speaking, sank into the car seat and said, "I want a lawyer." The policeman shut the door.

An officer walked up to Michelle. "Ma'am, would you like to file charges against your husband?"

"No."

"Has he ever hit you?"

She narrowed her eyes at me. "No. It was an accident. I fell down the stairs."

"Are you certain about that, ma'am?" the officer asked.

"Of course I'm certain. My husband was laid off at work because of a stupid rumor that my brother started. That's why Mark got plastered. He also tends to get belligerent and paranoid when he's drinking. He probably thought he needed to protect himself from imagined boogeymen."

I glanced at Steve. This was the first I'd heard about Mark losing his job, and Michelle was blaming Steve for that. Steve grimaced a little; he was hearing this for the first time, too.

"Call me if you think of anything else you'd like to report. In addition to your *earlier* statements." The officer handed her a business card. "He'll likely be charged with public intoxication, along with unlawfully discharging a firearm. Once he sobers up, you can come to the stationhouse and see about posting his bail. Under the circumstances, we'll probably want to hold him overnight."

"Thanks," she said quietly.

We watched the police drive off with Mark in the back seat. I didn't quite know what to think. I felt put off by Michelle. She'd been so calm in her message to her brother that he hadn't reacted, yet was beside herself in her call to me. Maybe that was understandable family dynamics, but I felt manipulated. She seemed to want to have thing both ways— to have everyone on her side and not her husband's, but to take no action when he endangered people's lives.

Steve put his arm around Michelle's shoulders. I was a little surprised that he didn't resent her claim that Steve had started a rumor about her being abused.

"They don't prepare you for days like this in couples' classes at church," she said to him.

Zoey had started crying and was now hanging onto her mother's leg for dear life.

"It's okay, Peanut," Michelle said to Zoey, stroking her hair tenderly. "Daddy will be home tomorrow."

"You know what I always say," George said to Zoey. "When the going gets tough, the tough get ice cream."

"You never said that once, Dad," Michelle replied.

"Oh, yeah?" George bent down to Zoey's height and said, "What does Grampa say about ice cream, Zoey?"

"De tuh get I keem!" Zoey cried.

"Oh, my gosh!" Michelle smiled. "She says that to me at least once a day. I never understood what she was saying!"

"Yes," Eleanor said, with a smile in her voice, "Your father is turning your two year old into a sugar fiend."

"But an articulate one," George countered.

"Penny for your thoughts," Sullivan said after a long silence as we drove back to Crestview.

"I was thinking that this was one of the best times I've had with your family. During our trip to the ice cream shop, I mean, and then our dinner. Not the shootout."

"Funny. That's what I was thinking, too."

"I was glad to see you had such a nice conversation with your father tonight."

"So was I. Relieved, even. My parents have forgiven each other. That made it easy for me to follow their lead."

He paused, and I watched as his face grew sad. "I miss Drew, though. And Amelia. Even though she came with us. She just wasn't there. You should have known her when she was younger. She was my champion. Such a tomboy. A great athlete, popular, pretty. Then she had a psychotic break. Her sophomore year in high school. Started hearing voices."

Steve had told me this story before. "Was Amelia friends with Drew?" I asked.

"She was nearly four years older than us, so no, not really. We weren't even in high school yet. Drew started dating Michelle, though, a couple of years later. By then Amelia had pretty much been shut out by her peer group. She was in a private school that was better equipped to work within her parameters. She's just…had such a lonely life."

"Maybe you should talk to your folks about helping her find a place of her own, as she likes to say."

"Yeah. I mentioned that to my dad just now. He agrees. We're going to have to work toward convincing my mother, though." We stopped at a light. "I guess I should take you to Audrey's house now."

"She and Hildi will be fine on their own tonight. And it's been a difficult day. Let's go home."

25

The following morning was Monday. Five days until my wedding. Steve asked if we could stop by the office before dropping me off at Audrey's. He wanted to check if a missing delivery of glassware for Parsley and Sage could have been shipped there by mistake. While we pulled into his space, we saw a box by the back door. "Huh. That's probably it."

"Strange that they'd just leave out here, unprotected," I said, "without notifying you."

"It was supposed to go to the restaurant. The delivery service must have screwed up." We got out and headed toward the door. "It's sure heavy enough," he said as he lifted it.

"I don't even see a shipping label," I noted.

"Yeah. It doesn't really feel like sets of glasses. It weighs too much."

"Maybe a distributor tried to drop in and left us a sampling of bricks." I joked.

"That's probably it," he said, playing along.

Steve carried the box inside and put it on the oval-shaped cherry coffee table in the cozy corner of our office beside the exposed red-brick wall. We often sat here with new prospective customers to discuss our work and show them our portfolios. He and I stood looking at the mysterious box for a couple of seconds.

"I hope it's not a bomb," I said.

"Me, too. I don't hear any ticking sounds, or smell any noxious fumes." He removed an X-acto knife from his desk drawer, saying, "I'm going to take the risk and open it. You might want to duck and cover."

I chuckled a little. "Thanks, but I'll stand right here beside you. We'll both go up in flames. It will be terribly romantic."

"Maybe so, but that's going to wreck our wedding photos." He cut open the strapping tape and opened the box. We both peered down at the unexpected contents.

"Huh," Steve muttered. "Looks like bags of flour. And there's a note in the top." He pulled out a standard size sheet of copier paper. "'Mr. Andrew Benson,' he read, 'Here's the order you requested. Our finest quality flour.'"

He handed me the note. It was signed, *Mike Smith, CEO, India Flour Company*. Stapled to it was a second sheet with the handwritten words: *Ship to me, at this address*, followed by Steve's and my office address. "Does this look like Drew's handwriting?" I asked.

"Yes," he replied after glancing at it. "This is the strangest packaging for flour I've ever seen." He lifted one of the bags. It was in a 24-inch by 36-inch bag of extra-thick plastic with a label that read: All-purpose Flour and appeared to have been cut from an ordinary five-pound paper bag of flour, which was then glued onto the center of the bag. The plastic itself had been stenciled: 'White Flour, India Flour Company'."

Steve was also examining one of the bags. As we looked at each other, I could tell that his thoughts were mirroring mine.

"Is it my imagination, or does this look like one of those bags full of drugs from when a cop show on TV uncovers a smuggling operation?" I asked.

We brought the box and all of its contents to the police station. Not surprisingly, we wound up waiting for well over an hour in an interrogation room at the police station, with some nice female uniformed officer checking in on us every so often to ask if she could get us more coffee. By the time O'Reilly returned to the room, closely followed by Linda Delgardio, we were impatient and eager to leave, but well-caffeinated.

"The good news is only one bag contained anything but flour," Detective O'Reilly told Steve and me. "The bad news is that one bag contained cocaine." "Were you able to find out where it came from?" I asked. "Did you get any fingerprints, or anything?"

"Not yet," Linda Delgardio told me. She was playing second fiddle to O'Reilly today.

"Not counting your and Mr. Sullivan's prints," O'Reilly hastened to add. "And none of the delivery services in the area have any record of the package. Needless to say, we couldn't find any record of an India Flour Company. Is there any chance that this was a wedding present to you from Drew?"

"Zero," Steve replied.

"Could this have been intended for Drew's personal use?" I asked.

O'Reilly shook his head. "It's a hundred-grand's worth of coke. It was a bizarre risk to leave it unguarded by your door. You almost have to believe it was a setup. Unless Drew made all the arrangements himself and died before his plan came to fruition."

That was very possible, I thought. I could picture Drew setting up this shipment with the intention of having it blend in with everything else for the new restaurant. He had likely assumed that he'd simply pick it up and claim it was specialty flour for some of Lucas's gourmet recipes.

"Drew dealing drugs with that much money changing hands could certainly give someone a strong motive for murder," I said. A sorrowful look crossed Steve's features, and I cringed. It was inescapably obvious that Drew had been dealing drugs. I didn't need to rub it in.

With little to gain by keeping us there, O'Reilly allowed us to leave. Steve went home to "sort through some things." He was obviously deflated, and my statement hadn't helped. Rather than let my thoughts run me ragged, I decided to be proactive about looking into our "flour" shipment. I drove to Audrey's to ask my self-proclaimed sidekick if she'd come with me to drop in on Lucas Leblanc and see what he had to say. His being miffed at Steve and me had worn off the moment we hired him to cook for Wednesday's wake.

Delighted with my invitation, Audrey insisted upon driving and was all smiles as we made the short drive to the Parsley and Sage. "I have decided to find inspiration in Eleanor's affair with Fitz Parker," she suddenly declared, just as she was unbuckling her seatbelt.

"Wait. What? You're going to have affairs because of Eleanor?"

"No, silly! My point is that Eleanor was thirty years older than Fitz. That's the same age-gap as Lucas and I have. He always comes on to me. Eleanor's affair has made me realize that I can be flattered…and take advantage of his attraction."

"But, Audrey, think about how that particular story ends. Fitz blackmailed Eleanor and made her life miserable. Two men are dead, and it's possible they'd both be alive today if it weren't for her horrendous judgment to embark on that affair!"

"Only if you look at it from the negative side, and if that's where you choose to *end* Eleanor's story—the way things are right now."

"Well, that *is* the end for Fitz and Drew. They don't get to appear in Eleanor's epilogue."

Audrey sighed. "I'm in no way implying that I am willing to have an affair with Lucas. I'm simply saying that I should enjoy the notion of having that possibility. Being self-confident can give you the upper hand. Lucas represents our opponent, Erin. We're going to need an edge to prevail."

"Only if he's guilty of playing a role in the murders."

She shook her head. "He's the opponent because he won't want to give us the information we need in order to solve this crime. He's a hostile witness." She glanced at me and wiggled her eyebrows. "I'm going to soften him up until he sings like a canary."

"Yeah, that's just what we need," I grumbled as we got out of her car. "A soft canary." Audrey fell in step with me as I strode past her toward the door.

"You mock me now, Erin, but you forget that, as a dancer, it was my forte to capture and command the audience's attention. They would forget their concerns and hang on me every breath." She swept past me as I opened the door for her. "In short, the man is toast."

I now had an image of Audrey dancing the calypso around Lucas, who'd been flattened into a human piece of toast.

Lucas was in the kitchen when we entered. He'd been reasonably successful at restoring order and airing out the place after his near brush with arson. He greeted us warmly, dropped a handful of blueberries into his batter, and explained that he was happily working on a new dessert recipe. I couldn't help but stare at his flour. Currently, at least, it was in a large rubber bin. Surely he would have noticed if he was putting cocaine into the batter instead of flour.

Audrey wasn't exactly dancing toward him, but her pointy-toed stride did indeed resemble that of a ballerina crossing the stage to strike a pose. "Lucas, my darling man," she cooed, "whatever astonishing concoction are you in the midst of creating?"

"Ah, *ma cherie*, this is a Blue Brûlée à la Lucas. My second batch." He grabbed a spoon and dipped it into a creamy concoction nearby. "Here, mademoiselle, taste."

"Mmm. Heavenly," she said, staring with bedroom eyes into his. "You can spin the most mundane ingredients into a delectable ambrosia for the gods."

I had to resist rolling my eyes at her hyperbole, but Lucas put his hands over his heart and bowed, clearly smitten. "Speaking of mundane ingredients," I said, "did you order several bags of flour from the Indian Flour Company?"

"I have never heard of such a place." His expression and voice remained free of concern. If he was lying, he was doing an exceptionally good job. "Why do you ask?"

"We need your help, Lucas," Audrey quickly interjected. "This morning Erin found a bag of cocaine mixed among bags of flour at the door to her office. She has no idea who sent it, but it was addressed to Drew Benson, care of her business, Sullivan and Gilbert Designs."

"And…?" he said.

"And I'm freaked out and want to know who sent it to me and why," I explained.

"Ah, yes," Lucas replied with a nod. "The drug drop-off. That was a regular event in California. It is unusual that he used a friend's business address. Normally he would simply send it to the restaurant. But it always came in different, oh, let us say, disguises. It might be powered sugar one time, or carpet deodorant the next. I told the officers when they were asking me about Drew's death."

"I'm surprised they didn't arrest you for not reporting the crime in California, the first time a shipment arrived," I said.

He widened his eyes as if surprised by my statement. "I didn't know for certain that they were drugs. Drew told me that the powder was to assist building big muscles. I pretended that I believed him. Drew would sell the goods, then get another shipment. Two, three, or four times a year. I know nothing more. Whatever we did outside of the restaurant was never a topic for us to discuss."

"You knew he was dealing drugs…yet you entered into a fifty-fifty partnership with him for this restaurant?"

"He told me that he was done with selling his muscle powder," Lucas said with a shrug. "I knew nothing about those transactions. I was happy to keep it that way, and happy that he had ended it. Yet, now, here it has come around again. It seems he had gotten as far away as he could only to find that he had gone in a full circle."

"Did you tell the police all of this?" I asked.

He made a wavering gesture with one hand. "All that I *know* is that Drew had a habit he could not support, and he was getting farther and farther into debt. I told the police already. I think he was going out of his head. I think *he* killed Fitz Parker, then took his own life."

"Did Drew say anything to you about killing Fitz, or considering suicide?"

"No, but that is what the police will figure out. That is, I am certain, where the evidence will point."

In my dismay at Lucas's confounding story about Drew's shipments, I'd forgotten all about Audrey's presence. I met her gaze and saw that she looked unhappy. She would have enjoyed being the one to get this information—or, more accurately, this informed opinion—from Lucas. I stepped back and gave her an encouraging gesture to signal that she should take over the conversation.

"I don't blame you for a second," Audrey said in sugary tones. "We can all see how dangerous it is to concern ourselves with other people's…white powder of questionable origins. But why do you think Drew would have wanted to kill Fitz?"

"Perhaps they were competitors for customers." He gave Audrey a sideways leer as he smoothed his mustache. Her flirtation might have gone too far. "People have their strange habits. Nothing that one puts up one's nose compares to a good bottle of Beaujolais in front of a fireplace."

"I'll drink to that," Audrey said.

"Shall I open a bottle?" Lucas asked, looking first at Audrey, then at me.

"No, thanks," I answered quickly. "I'm strictly an after-five p.m. drinker."

"And I'll take a rain check," Audrey replied, "which hopefully won't need to be cashed in until after the wedding. We're hoping for clear skies."

As I stood up, I spotted an ashtray below the bar. It had a single cigarette butt in it, with that salmon-colored lipstick Aunt Bea often wore. The sight clicked in my head. I remembered now seeing that ashtray with its lone cigarette butt on Friday when Lucas had been mopping up gasoline. Lucas, I realized, had followed my gaze. "Was Bea Quinn here recently?" I asked.

"Yes, she was. I called her after last week's debacle with my foolish brush with arson. Considering that I want to make a go of it with the restaurant, I needed to talk about money with her."

"So...we just missed her then?"

"I'm afraid so."

"Was she in favor of opening Parsley and Sage in spite of everything?" I asked.

"She was. She's going to continue to be an investor, I am happy to say." His smile looked a bit plastic.

We said our goodbyes and left, but not without Audrey and Lucas exchanging some flirtatious banter.

As we got into Audrey's car, she immediately turned to head south, opposite our house. "We're going to drop in on Aunt Bea," she said, "auspiciously so that I can see her wine cellar for myself."

"Good idea."

"I have a good sense of smell, and I don't believe that we'd just missed Aunt Bea. There wasn't a whiff of smoke lingering."

"I'm pretty sure that cigarette butt has been there since Friday. Maybe Aunt Bea had poured the gasoline, not him."

"I suppose that's possible," Audrey said with a nod. She flashed a smile at me. "See? We make such a good team. If the design business starts to dry up for you, we could call ourselves 'Gilbert and Munroe Detective Agency'."

"If that ever happens, I would relocate our design business with Steve, not change professions. But I appreciate the top billing."

She shrugged. "It just sounds better than 'Munroe and Gilbert' somehow. But you're welcome."

Aunt Bea answered her door with a big smile. "Well if it isn't Audrey and my favorite honorary niece," Bea said as she ushered us inside. "What a pleasant surprise!"

"We happened to be out and about, and I was just saying to Erin that I haven't gotten the chance to see the fruit of her labor yet."

"Nor to taste the fermented fruit to which it was devoted," Bea rejoined. "Shall we select something?"

"I already had to decline a glass of red wine recently," Audrey said. "I can't hardly say no twice in a row. It seems the powers that be are determined to have me be blotto today."

"In that case, we'll just have a little Pinot Grigio," Bea said. She looked at me. "Should I make it three glasses?"

"No, thanks." I smiled at her, not wanting to sound ungracious. "I have lots of work to do this afternoon and need to stay sharp."

"How about a spritzer, then?"

"I'll just have a glass of ice water."

Aunt Bea used beautiful crystal stemware from her kitchen and poured the wine from an open bottle in the refrigerator, then took us on the tour of the wine cellar. I was thrilled just to get away from the sitar background music. Meanwhile, Audrey was all oohs and ahs, and both women were more than generous in their praises of my design.

Moments after our sitting down at the table outside the wine cellar door, Audrey stated, "So, Aunt Bea, you were at the Parsley and Sage recently."

"True. Only to drop in. I needed some documents for my accountant to peruse. I'd felt compelled to try to give Drew a helping hand. I had loaned him a few thousand dollars that will probably wind up as a bad debt now."

"You two had such an acrimonious relationship," I said. "Why did you want to be so generous with him?"

"There happened to be some...extenuating circumstances. I've known him for a long time, after all, and I'd like to think that my heart was big enough to forgive his youthful indiscretions."

"Mine have only ripened into fully developed bad habits," Audrey joked, lifting her glass.

"Whereas mine are now hobbies," Bea countered. They clinked their glasses.

I waited a beat, then said, "When Steve and I went to the restaurant a few days ago, we found Lucas cleaning up gasoline. Which he'd been spread across the floor in an attempt to burn the restaurant to the ground."

She widened her eyes in surprise. "You thought that *Lucas* spread the gasoline?"

"He *told* us that's what he'd done. He told the police that, too."

"Oh, dear. He covered up for me. I wonder why."

"You're saying that *you* poured gasoline all over the interior, intending to set a fire?" I was stunned, despite my earlier statement to Audrey. I realized now that I hadn't actually believed my theory. It made so little sense that Aunt Bea would attempt arson and that Lucas would try to take the blame.

"Until Lucas discovered what I was up to and stopped me. I was far from sober, and I didn't realize he was still in the restaurant office."

"But the office, too, had been dowsed in gasoline when Steve and I arrived there around one or two on Friday. I realized only when I happened to see your cigarette butt in the ashtray today that I'd actually noticed it there clear back then. On Friday. So at the very least, Lucas may have stopped you, but then wavered and poured gas all over the office." I thought back to his statements at the time. As he'd said then, he had probably panicked when he saw the incriminating records in Drew's office, then thought better of it.

"Why don't you start from the beginning, Aunt Bea," Audrey was saying.

Bea, looking more elderly and frail by the moment, sagged back into her seat. "Drew Benson has always known which buttons to push. It's his single-most defining characteristic. He knows some things about me. Private things. Such as my relationship with my ex-husband that I don't want my business associates in general and Mark Dunning, in particular, to know about. He presented a proposition to me that I was willing to accept. A mutually beneficial deal. He felt I had breached my side of the agreement when I told Erin about his drug habit at the party."

"Oh, dear," Audrey said. "I'm so sorry. That must have been dreadful for you."

"It was," Bea continued. "He tightened the pressure, and I conceded and give him the money that I probably would have given to him anyway. But on Friday, I'd...been feeling sorry for myself and had a bottle of wine for lunch. I knew I'd had too much to drink. That's the only time I smoke. But I was sitting right here in this very seat, smoking a cigarette, and found myself thinking: I could just let myself into the restaurant, drop a cigarette, and light the place up.

"Next thing you know, I fetched my gasoline can, and acted on the urge. When I lit up my cigarette, the fumes were nauseating. I snuffed it out, sat down on a barstool, and cried my eyes out like the drunken sot that I was. Lucas came out of his office then."

"Hadn't he smelled the fumes already? Or heard you?"

She shrugged. "He said he'd been taking a nap. He was angry with me, of course. I asked if he'd help me clean everything up. He insisted on driving me home, and took a taxi back to the restaurant. I'm sure they have records to verify that, so his taking the blame would never hold up in court."

"I suspect he dowsed the office himself," I said. "Since nobody actually lit the fire, he probably figured there was no reason to drag your name into it. Unless he was lying. Are you *sure* you didn't pour gasoline in the office?"

"Quite sure. I remember every moment. Including how I...made something of a fool of myself. I'm afraid I...proposed to him. Offered to make him to be my husband for the short time I have left in exchange for inheriting my money. He said no."

She turned beet red. Neither Audrey nor I said a word for a lengthy pause. I continued to ruminate on the fact that the office had definitely been dowsed in gas. Lucas had done that himself, either because he had gotten the idea from Bea and decided to finish what she'd started but we'd interrupted him, or because he, too, had second thoughts.

"So, there you have it," Bea said. "The moral of the story is, if you decide to indulge yourself and drink alone, be certain you *stay* alone. Put a childproof cover on your doorknob, or whatever it takes. Leaving the house when we were horribly intoxicated was both Mark's and my undoing."

26

A couple of hours later, Steve called me from our office. He sounded upbeat as we chatted for a minute. Then he said, "Amelia called and said she was doing a lot better. She's taking the bus up to Crestview to see us."

"Oh, good. Does she want us to pick her up from the downtown station?"

"No, she said a friend was bringing her to the house."

"Who's the friend?"

"She wouldn't tell me. She's bringing dinner, and she's staying overnight in our guest room."

"Really. That's good news, right? That she's being so adventurous?"

"I don't know. Sometimes it just means she's feeling manic, and that's followed by a depression. She's slightly bipolar, too."

My mood sank a bit. "Let's assume the best, then. Since she's sleeping over, I think I will, too."

"Now *that* is what I call good news," he said in sexy tones.

"This will make two nights in a row. I hope Hildi doesn't think I'm deserting her."

"Bring her with you. I can take care of her for the rest of the week. Now that my allergies have gone away, I'd be happy for the company…if you're still intent on staying at Audrey's until after the wedding."

Was I? I'd moved temporarily back into Audrey's in part because Drew was in our guest room. My notion that it would make our transition into marriage more significant if Steve and I slept separately now seemed so inconsequential. "I don't want to have to move Hildi back and forth again. She gets so stressed out. She'll be at Audrey's during our honeymoon."

"Okay. I'll see you soon," Steve said.

I told Audrey I was leaving for the evening, happy to have the excuse to be in my own home tonight. As much as I loved being at Audrey's in my old room, Steve's home was now truly my home. Even Hildi had made the transition easily enough; it was just transporting her from house to house that she hated.

All told, our house was in fairly good shape when I arrived, but I had some time to kill and started cleaning the kitchen. Steve arrived about fifteen minutes later. We'd only barely had time to greet each other when the doorbell rang. I smiled as I swept open the door, but my smile faded when I saw who Amelia's friend was: Lucas Leblanc. How did they even know each other?

"Surprise," Amelia said. "This is my pre-wedding gift to you both. Lucas and I are going to teach you how to ballroom dance to the song of your choice for your wedding."

"We will choreograph the dance, and teach it to you," Lucas said. "And the best part is, I have cooked tonight's meal!"

"How do you two know each other?" Steve asked, echoing my unasked question.

"We spoke briefly at your party," Amelia said.

"She was dancing in the corner," Lucas added, "and I told her that she should be my partner someday."

"So then I called *him* to ask if he'd be willing to help me with this little inspiration of mine...and voila!" Amelia explained, beaming. "Here we are!"

"Wonderful," I said. Although it would have been more wonderful if she'd come alone.

"It's always good to see you," Steve said, giving Amelia a hug and a kiss on the cheek. He shot me a little glance, however, that meant he was not thrilled with the evening's agenda.

"I know *I* would love a little help with our first dance at our wedding. This was such a good idea, Amelia."

"Actually it was Audrey's idea," she said. "She told me at the party that she'd wanted to teach you two a ballroom dance, but that she didn't have the time. So she suggested that I take it on."

"That sounds like Audrey, all right," Steve grumbled.

"Your brother is already a fairly decent dancer," I told Amelia.

"Oh, I know. I've been giving him tips for years now."

That remark at least made Steve crack a smile. He then suggested that we eat first, while the food was still warm.

Lucas's food was fabulous—beef wellington with spaghetti squash and roasted broccoli. We talked with Amelia about her living situation at the halfway house as we ate. She reiterated that she would be happier in her own apartment, and the two of us dived into Internet rental listings after we'd finished our scrumptious meals. Meanwhile, Steve was making chitchat with Lucas. I had yet to discuss my concerns about Lucas's nonchalance over Drew's drug shipments. I still held out a faint hope that Lucas had set up Drew to take the fall, and that he had killed both men, but would suddenly see the light and turn himself in to the police.

The men's pleasant background chatter began to grow contentious just as Amelia was excited about an ad she'd spotted for a room in a house not far from her parents' neighborhood. It *did* look ideal, especially because she knew the family renting out the room; they attended the same church.

"Let's not discuss Drew," I heard Steve state.

"I am only saying that I knew his habits well," Lucas persisted. "We worked side by side, six days a week."

Deep worry lines creased Amelia's brow as she looked up at her brother.

"Why don't you go ahead and call about the room?" I suggested to her. "You could use either of our bedrooms, where it will be quiet enough for you to hear over the phone."

"Steve?" Amelia asked. "Is everything all right?"

"No problem," he replied.

"I made the social faux pas of speaking ill of the dead," Lucas said. "My mistake."

The moment Amelia had shut the bedroom door behind her, Lucas added, "Even so, I am correct about Drew Benson. As I told Erin and Audrey earlier, I am quite certain that Drew killed Fitz and then took his own life in his despair at what he had done."

"And I'm *quite certain* that you're full of crap," Steve said, keeping his voice low. "Drew was not a murderer. If he did have in mind to take his own life, which he did not, he certainly wouldn't have killed himself on Michelle's front porch. Furthermore, he'd have left his fingerprints on the syringe. The killer had to have wiped all the prints off the syringe."

"Not necessarily," Lucas replied. "Drew had a handkerchief that he used to hide the syringe when he was injecting himself. If someone was to glance at him, it would look like he was simply dabbing a speck of dirt with his handkerchief."

Steve averted his eyes. A painful, heavy silence filled the room.

Lucas caught my stony gaze. As if I'd zapped him with an electric beam, he jolted to his feet. "But, tonight you are learning your special dance to share with your new bride. This is a dark discussion for another time, *oui*?"

"There's never going to be a time when I want to discuss my friend Drew with you," Steve said.

"I am so sorry. One of the first things I teach about dance is not to step on your partner's toes. I have already failed the very first step." Lucas walked over to me and touched my arm. "Please tell Amelia that something came up, and I had to run out."

"That isn't necessary," Steve said.

"Stay," I said. "For Amelia's sake. Please, Lucas."

Amelia emerged from the back bedroom just then. "They want to talk to me about renting the room," she announced cheerfully. She shifted her attention to Lucas. "Are we ready to begin?" she asked.

"I can only stay for half an hour," Lucas replied, "but you will be able to take things from there."

"Good," Steve said before Amelia could respond. "We're dancing to 'I'll Be,' which is a waltz. Let's clear out the living room furniture and build ourselves a dance floor."

I breathed a sigh of relief.

Lucas stayed for a full hour, and Steve made a great show of enjoying the process of learning our choreography steps and taking lessons on "constructing a good frame for your partner." He was, however, avoiding my eyes, as well as Lucas's. His every muscle was tight, and his dance steps were mechanical. I only hoped that Amelia was not picking up on his cues that he was uncomfortable and annoyed.

After an additional half hour of our practicing without Lucas, Amelia pronounced us "good to go," and said that she was going to take a shower and get ready for bed.

"I think I'll change my clothes," Steve said. "Dancing is hard work."

A couple of minutes later, I followed Steve into our bedroom. He was sitting on the bed, glowering at the wall. I sat down beside him and gave him a nudge with my elbow, hoping that he'd take it as a playful tease.

"Why did you and Audrey talk to Lucas about Drew's death?" Steve asked.

"We were just...asking him some questions. Trying to get a feel for whether or not he knew more than he was telling."

"Don't ask anybody any questions about the murders, Erin. Drew's death is as much as I can bear. I don't want to lose you, too."

"I understand. I don't want to put myself in the killer's crosshairs either. I'll mind my own business as best I can from here on out."

"Make sure you tell Audrey that."

"She does get a little carried away sometimes. That's part of what makes her so lovable, though."

"I sure hope it's not always going to be like this. Just because you used to rent a room from her doesn't make her my pseudo mother-in-law."

Stunned, I stared at him. "Whoa. Do you want to think about rephrasing that?"

"She convinced Amelia to teach us how to dance. And she partnered Amelia with Lucas, of all people, who's a lecher at best and a murderer at worst. She's got you back to acting like a female Sherlock Holmes. She's manipulating everything from our wedding invitations to our disk jockey."

"Because she voluntarily stepped in as our wedding planner under the worst possible conditions!" I cried. "She's also walking me down the aisle, because she's so important to me. She's been the closest thing to a parent I've had since my mother passed away. She's been nothing but loving and kindhearted to both of us!"

"Maybe so, but always on her own terms."

"She's self-assured. That's all. I admire her."

"So do I. But if you keep indulging her, you're going to get your head blown off."

"As I already said, I intend to tone that down."

"I'd feel better if I could put an ankle bracelet on you that could force you to stay put."

"How can you even sarcastically suggest something like that! That's the high-tech version of saying that you want to keep me barefoot and pregnant!"

"All I meant was—"

"I know precisely what you meant! We're each other's *partners*, not our lords and masters, regardless of how strongly we might think we know best. And you should be smart enough to stop talking right now before you make things any worse!"

Amelia tapped on the door. "Could you please give me a ride to Denver?" she said sadly.

Steve raked both his hands through his hair and cursed under his breath. She'd overheard our argument. "I'm sorry, Amelia," he said as he opened the door. "I'm just out of sorts. Losing Drew has been hard on me."

"I'm the one who's sorry," she said in a small voice. "I should never have come here."

"You're more than welcome in our home anytime, Amelia," I said, rising to plead my case. "We're both stressed with the wedding and the murders. We're just blowing off steam at each other."

"Because I barged in on you and brought Lucas with me. Now I just want to go home."

"I'll take you," I said.

"No, this is my fault." Steve sighed. "If this is really what you want, I'll drive you. But, Amelia, I didn't realize you could overhear; I thought you were in the shower. Please stay, and I'll drive you down tomorrow morning. I'll take you over to the house with the room that you like. We'll talk to them together."

Amelia shook her head, her eyes taking on the glazed look that she'd borne when the police were at the house. "I do terrible things. Even when I don't hear the voices. People are always dying."

27

"She decided to stay after all," Steve said when he returned to our bedroom half an hour later. I tried to tell myself that that he was actually angry at Drew, not at Audrey or me; I knew he adored Audrey and would normally never make nasty remarks about her. Even so, I was still too upset for Amelia's sake to coddle him.

"How's she doing?" I asked.

"Not well." When I gave no reply, he added, "Maybe you should talk to her in the morning."

"Actually, I think I'll try to talk to her right now." I promptly left the room and went down the hall to our guest room. I knocked lightly on the door. She didn't answer.

"Amelia, can I come in?" I asked.

"Yes," she answered dully.

When I entered, she was sitting in the rocking chair, hugging her knees to her chest. I closed the door behind me and sat down on the side of the bed. "Would you like to come help me get a teapot and a couple of cups? We can put Sleepy Time tea to the test."

She shook her head. "I'm tired of life. I can't keep fighting the voices in my head. And everybody always telling me I'm wrong."

"You're not wrong. Life is hard. For everybody."

"It's harder for me than most people. I never know for sure when I'm telling the truth—when I just imagined doing something, and when I actually did it."

"What I know to be true about you *today*, Amelia, is that you made the considerable effort to get from Denver to our house so that you could do us a big favor. I also know that, because of you, Lucas brought us a delicious meal. That you and he taught us a lovely dance that your brother and I will love having learned, and that, thanks to you, we will use that gift of yours on the most important and happiest day of our lives. Most of all, I know that Steve and I care about you and appreciate you for every single one of those things."

"Really?" she asked quietly.

"Really."

"I get so mad when I think about it. The drugs are what make me talk like this. They slow me down. I'm not stupid."

"What happens when you aren't taking your meds?"

"The voices tell me what to do. There's this one voice that wonders why I keep trying. That's the voice that makes it so hard for me to see my way out of this. I think I might have killed both men."

What she was saying couldn't be true. I couldn't let myself even think that it might be. "You didn't, Amelia. I'm sure that, if you did, you would remember. Those memories would have been as clear and real as when you taught us to dance."

"I'm not sure that's true, though, Erin. Remembering is like…looking through blurred glass. Sometimes memories look and feel a little different than my imagination, but both are still there. Drew and Fitz were killed. What if I did it, Erin? It's not impossible."

"Fitz's murder was premeditated. The cyanide was brought to Audrey's house. You couldn't have even known Fitz was invited. It's a thousand times more likely that you're innocent."

She nodded. "Let's go get tea." She stood up and led the way to the kitchen. Actually, as I quickly rehashed our conversation, my definitive statements proving Amelia's innocence weren't completely accurate. Fitz had been in touch with all the members of Steve's family. He might have told Amelia he would be at the shower. Even if she had no idea he was coming, she could have brought poison to the party intending to kill Drew, only to use it on Fitz when he insisted on taking her necklace.

I sent up a silent prayer that, however this terrible business with Fitz and Drew's murders wound up, Amelia would prove to be innocent.

The next morning, I returned to Audrey's house while Steve drove his sister home. Hildi gave me her tail-flick brush-off on her way out her cat door, punishing me for leaving her for two nights in a row. Feeling blue, I nursed a cup of coffee at the kitchen counter, when Audrey entered and peered at me. "What's wrong, Erin? Your bridesmaids are still arriving this afternoon, aren't they?"

"Yes." My two friends from Parsons were flying in from LaGuardia, and my maid of honor, a high school friend, was flying in from Boston. "But Steve and I had a fight last night, which his sister Amelia overheard. She wanted to leave because he was being so ungracious about her and Lucas teaching us a choreographed dance for our wedding."

"Oh, dear. That was my fault."

"It was a good idea, Audrey. It wasn't your fault. Steve was angry about Drew's murder and my being vulnerable to getting killed myself for asking too many questions about it. *I* was angry because I don't get to have the wedding of my dreams, but rather a patched-back-together one, and because I wished he'd chosen a better best man to begin with."

"Did you tell him that?"

"Oh, no. That would be too easy. Much better to carry the weight of my anger around with me…to slip it on like an ugly, scratchy, wet sweater and feel sorry for myself."

"Well. We all do that from time to time. Welcome to life on planet Earth."

"Thanks. It's a nice planet, overall." I sighed. I was also annoyed that Steve never apologized. So much so that I allowed myself to act like a brat, unable to act upon my knowledge that it never matters who apologizes first, just so long as one person bridges that divide and lets mutual injuries be mended.

"He drove Amelia back to Denver," I continued to complain to Audrey. "My parting words to him were: 'I'll see you on Saturday.' As if he needed the reminder to attend our wedding. That's about as lame as it gets."

Audrey snorted. "I've been married three times. Trust me on this. That's not even half of a pea in the soup of lame comments you're going to say to your spouse at one point or another. And that, later, you'll want to eat every bite of that pea soup."

I grimaced at her analogy. "That is *so* not reassuring, Audrey."

"Okay. Well, I'll try again. 'According to the Bible, love is not easily angered and does not keep track of its wrongs.' But, Erin, your friends *do* keep track. I can assure you, at this juncture, you're fifty points ahead of Steve on Audrey's Scale of Goodness. I know Steve well enough to be confident that he would agree with me. In other words, no worries, my dear."

I had to smile. "That's because you're only hearing my side of the story."

"Nah." She shrugged. "It's because I am all-knowing."

Later that evening, Mark Dunning rang the doorbell. I answered and was immediately ill at ease. So much so that I stared at him and didn't even say hello. He was unshaven and his shirt and slacks looked rumpled. He was less attractive than ever, and as always, I was struck by what an odd pairing he and Michelle were.

"Erin, can we talk for a minute?"

I stood in the doorway, not wanting to let him in, yet torn. Part of me suspected he could be getting a bad rap that he didn't deserve. It seemed too stupid for him to have killed Drew on his own front porch. Also, if they'd had an argument and Mark had lost his temper, how would he have gained access to Drew's needle to give him an overdose?

"This isn't a good time," I told him. "We're just about to sit down to eat." That wasn't strictly accurate, but we had been *discussing* the fact that one of us should be making dinner.

"Can we talk on your porch, at least?" Mark asked, his voice irritable.

"I…sure." I stepped out beside him, letting just the outer door close behind me. I could get away from him in an instant. If he tried to jab me with a syringe, that is.

"You've got this whole thing exactly wrong, Erin. I am not battering my wife. Or my daughter. Or anyone."

"Good."

"I didn't kill anybody. I didn't give Fitz cyanide, or Drew an overdose."

"That's good to hear. Thanks for stopping by and telling me that."

"I want to show you something before it fades." He started to roll up his sleeves. I glanced behind me to see if, by now, Audrey was watching us through the glass door. Indeed, she was.

"Take a gander at this." Mark's forearms were riddled with bruises.

"What happened to your arm?"

"*Michelle* pushed *me* down the stairs."

"You can't be serious," I retorted.

"Oh, I'm serious, all right. That's the irony of the situation. *She's* the one who hits *me*, yet I never laid a hand on her. But I'm the one who'll wind up going to jail on bogus-spouse abuse charges."

"I saw similar bruises on her arms."

"She banged her arms repeatedly so that they'd bruise. She's framing me."

Or maybe he'd bruised his arms to frame *her*. "Mark, if you're innocent, you won't go to jail. And if you can prove your side of the story, you can bring charges against her."

"That's easy to say from where you're standing, so nicely distanced. There's never been a rat's chance in hell that anybody would ever believe me. It was her all along. She's the one who would hit me. She wanted to make me hit her back. She taunted me. We all know Amelia's sick, but it's really Michelle who is the bigger mental case. If I were you, I'd steer clear of the Sullivan family. Steve's bound to have mental problems himself."

"Mark," I said, trying to keep my temper under control. "You're not helping yourself."

He spread his arms, which only made his pot belly more noticeable. "Why *would* I? Why would talking to you be any different from any other conversation I've ever had? That's the story of my life. I rub people the wrong way. I fought my way up with no high school degree. I grew up in a trailer park. My background makes me good at my job. I understand alcohol from the bottom of the keg to the finest of scotches. Michelle is jealous and insecure. She turns into a witch when we're alone. I'm only staying with her for Zoey's sake. And the baby's."

"Where is Zoey right now?"

He averted his gaze, the muscles in his jaw working. His reaction gave me my answer; she was home with Zoey. I turned away and grabbed the doorknob. "If Michelle is an abuser, your first priority should be protecting Zoey. Always. Nothing I can do or say will help. Furthermore, I love Steve. However dysfunctional his family may be, I am marrying into it anyway."

Mark snorted. "Funny. That's exactly what I said to myself right before marrying Michelle. And look at us less than three years later."

28

Late the next morning, my phone rang. I jumped with joy when I saw that it was my maid of honor, Carly Friedman. She and my two bridesmaids were flying in today and renting a car from the airport. Mentally crossing my fingers with the hope that she was calling to say that she and our friends Rhonda and Rachel were here, safe and sound, I pressed my "talk" button. "Carly?" I said.

"Guess what? The town of Crestview is considerably less cool than it was a minute ago, now that we're schlepping through."

"You're here!" I exclaimed. "Did your flight go well?"

"Meh. It took off and landed in the right airport. That's all I ask. Rachel is driving as we speak."

"Oh-my-god-Erin-you're-getting-married!" I could hear Rachel cry.

"Happy day, Erin!" Rhonda said a moment later.

Overjoyed, my eyes misted. "I am so glad you guys are here!"

"We are, too. Although your texts and messages feel like they're from a made-for-TV movie. What the *what* is going on!? The wedding planner, and now the best man? Is your wedding being managed by drug lords, or something?"

"Not intentionally. But…that's close to the truth. Sadly."

"So Steve didn't realize his best man was seriously into drugs? Isn't that a bit…unobservant of him?"

I grimaced and didn't answer.

"It's about time Steve joined the club," Rhonda said, apparently bogarting Carly's phone. "You've known that I'm an international weapons broker, Rachel's a hooker, and that Carly's a cattle poacher for years now, right?"

"Hey! It's my turn to be the hooker," I heard Carly object. "I'm letting *you* mind the livestock. Remember?"

I laughed. "Where are you exactly?"

"We've parked our rental car and are walking up to your house. And, oh, by the way, O.M.G. Nice digs!"

I dashed to the door and threw it open. There were Carly, Rhonda, and Rachel, heading up the front walkway. I literally hopped up and down in my excitement. We indulged in a group hug, then individual hugs, all of us chattering away as I invited them inside. We were acting like the teenagers we'd been when we'd first met, and none of us cared in the least if we were being a little overly loud and zealous in our greetings. Eventually the conversation rolled around to the house again, and I took them on a tour, reminding them that Audrey's house didn't belong to me.

"So, first things first, how is everything going with the wedding dress?" Rachel asked.

"I'm trying on the dress tomorrow to make sure it's been fitted correctly."

"Yay," Carly said to Rhonda with a big smile, "she saved that for us."

"Well, that and the fact that it won't be ready until tomorrow."

"This is something that I never understand," Carly said. "You buy your wedding dress months before the event, you get measured, etcetera, and yet it's invariably not ready until immediately before the wedding. What is happening to the dress in the meantime? Is every store employee taking it home for a couple of days?"

"*My* theory is that the dresses are where they're supposed to be much earlier than they claim," Rachel said. "They only want to make alterations once, though, and they're afraid that wedding nerves lead to extreme fluctuations in the bride's weight."

"Let's call the bridal shop and test your theory," Carly said.

I told them the name of the place. Rhonda dialed the number and spoke with the clerk. She nodded, and lowered the phone to say, "Yep. It's there." Rachel was soon doing a victory dance, set to the lyrics: "I knew it! I knew it! I'm so smart...."

"Okay, so let's go to the dress shop right now, then hit the bars," Carly suggested.

The four of us were soon in my minivan, heading to the bridal store in the northwest suburbs of Denver. Carly joked that wished they could bring their bridesmaid dresses with them to the store, so that we could get the full effect. We had collectively opted to allow each of them to select and wear their own black cocktail dresses, and simply consult with one another via photos.

Upon our arrival, the four of us crowded into one of their oversized dressing room. I was nervous. My designated saleswoman went to fetch my dress. It had been insanely pricey, but Steve had insisted that I should not even look at price tags when I shopped. The strapless, shimmery gown had looked and felt as like a white orchid that had enclosed me in its embrace. Even so, a week or so after making the purchase, I had second thoughts, but they left me whenever I looked at the photograph of my selection. Every so often in the last several weeks, I repeated that sequence.

My heart was racing as the saleswoman approached with my dress. I realized then how wonderful it was to be anxious about something good, instead of feeling that my life was in jeopardy. All three of my friends were squealing with their approval.

"Wow, Erin!" Carly cried. "This is like a Hollywood star's dress!"

"Feel how heavy the dress is," Rachel said.

"That's because the fabric is made from stardust," Carly said.

"Would stardust be heavy?" Rhonda asked.

"Sure it is. It's tiny sparkling...meteors. Or, well.... Let's just go with that image," Rachel said. "Put it on, Erin!"

A minute or so later, I was in the shimmery gown. Someone had zipped me up. At first I didn't notice that the room had suddenly hushed; I was too focused on staring into the two-seventy mirror, feeling that once again the dress had transformed me into this glamorous sight that bore only a passing resemblance to my actual appearance.

"What do you think?" I asked, turning around once more. Rachel, Rhonda, and Carly were quietly crying, dabbing at their eyes with tissues. "You're just so beautiful, Erin. I mean, holy crap!"

The saleswoman joined in with her own gushing, although that struck me as a basic job requirement. Soon they were ushering me out to step onto the raised platform to check the length with my shoes.

As we emerged from the dressing room, I thought for a moment that my eyes were deceiving me. But, no, unfortunately, Michelle was truly waiting for me right there in the bridal shop.

"Surprise," she said. "I called your house, and Audrey told me where you were going. I was in the general area anyway, and couldn't stay away. You look…absolutely stunning in that dress."

"Thank you." This was truly nice of her. It's just that I wanted to be strictly the bride right now, marrying the man of her dream in three days.

"You're more than welcome. I'm so proud of my little brother's excellent taste."

I introduced her to everyone, and she said, "I feel like I already know you. Erin's told me how wonderful you are."

"They are. And I've been woefully neglectful of all of them lately."

"That's true," Rhonda said.

"Yeah, you'd think that you had a lot of things going on in your life, or something," Carly scoffed.

"True," I said. "And most of it was unexpected. I fully intend to make it up to you guys." I had left out Michelle. "And to my sister-in-law."

"Oh, you've already been way too attentive to me," Michelle said. "*I'm* the one who kept dragging you away from your own wedding plans. Not to mention forcing Fitz on you. I'll never forgive myself for that."

"He'd have done a fine job anyway, if he'd gotten the chance," I said. Which was true. If he were to try to hit on my friends, they would have kept him in his place. Rhonda and Rachel were happily married. Carly was between boyfriends, but was nobody's fool when it came to habitual flirts.

Not surprisingly, the reminder of Fitz and Drew lowered my spirits. A moment later, though, I was swept back into the buzz of the dress and being the center of attention. Michelle had effortlessly blended in with my friends. The saleswoman brought us champagne, and we let ourselves get swept into the bubbling joy of it all.

Still feeling high, we accepted Michelle's offer to buy us a bottle of wine at the pub across the street. It was only a little after four, and we had no trouble finding an empty booth. "I don't know about you all," Rachel said, "but I'm voting to go with white. I don't want to spill red wine all over myself...and Erin."

We both laughed and Carly said, "That bar near Parsons. When Rhonda came up from SUNY Albany. Remember?"

We took turns filling in Michelle on our outlandish adventures. I had tried to hide an underage drinking incident from my mother my freshman year at Parsons, which included climbing up a fire escape to change my clothes, soaked with red wine, thanks to Rachel's errant elbow on a wine glass. In the process, I had barely convinced the police officer who saw us that we weren't committing a crime. I broke a heel off my shoe during my second climb back up. I concocted a ridiculous story for my mother to explain how I'd left wearing a white tee-shirt and returned in a light blue one. All which ultimately wound up with my mother hauling out a bottle of red wine from her suitcase and insisting that we all have a glass.

"That evening had gotten off to a bad start," Carly said. "Remember that crazy old woman at the bus stop? Erin tried to share her umbrella with her," she explained to Michelle, "and she started screaming at her in Russian or Bulgarian."

"She must have been thought Erin's umbrella would bring her bad luck," Rhonda said.

"Or else she was trying to wash her hair in the rain," Rachel joked.

"I'll bet the woman cast a hex on you that day, Erin," Michelle stated.

"A hex?" I asked.

"Sure. That would explain a lot." Michelle scanned my friends' faces, as if to get their support. "Erin's known something like six or seven people who were murdered," Michelle said. "It's like she's cursed."

"That's not the kind of thing someone should be saying, Michelle," Carly snapped. "Don't play head games with Erin now. She's about to be married."

"No, no, you misunderstand my motives," Michelle said, with a slight slur in her voice. "I'm looking at this from the opposite side of the spectrum. Let's try on the thought that this woman placed a hex, or a curse even, on Erin. That way, we can lift the curse right now. Erin can wear her dress joyfully—" she gestured in the direction of my minivan, where my gown was safely locked inside—"knowing all that bad karma is gone forever."

"You know how to remove curses?" Rhonda asked, intentionally exaggerating her Bronx accent.

"Of course. I use it for my daughter whenever she's scared about monsters underneath her bed." She chuckled. "It's a multipurpose bad-vibes remover."

"Who taught it to you?" Carly asked.

"My Aunt Bea. She was babysitting one day when I was a little girl, and Stevie pulled my hair. My sister, Amelia, meanwhile, had played the piano at this big recital, and everybody was raving about her performance. I got furious. Somehow or other, I convinced both of them that I'd put a hex on them. And so they were in terrible moods when Aunt Bea came over to babysit that night. She told us she'd execute her industrial-grade hex remover. And it worked."

"What happened?" Rachel asked.

"Aunt Bea said what we needed to do was think really honestly about *why* we did what we'd did and exactly what happened. That we had to reach deep down inside of ourselves, then tell ourselves *another* story. One that ends happily. So the new story *I* told was that Stevie was helping me to get a rubber band out of my hair, and that I'd thanked him. And that I'd helped Amelia to play by flipping the pages of the music for her, and then I told her how beautifully she'd played."

Michelle gave us a beatific smile. "Let's do that right now. Close your eyes, and tell Crazy Lady you're sorry for trying to share an umbrella, and that you wish her well. And imagine that Crazy Lady had realized that you meant well, then shared the umbrella, and gave Erin a hug when the bus arrived."

They all closed their eyes, then I closed mine, but Rhonda said, "You realize that, if this was the Bronx, when we opened our eyes, Michelle would have vanished with all our wallets, right?"

Everyone laughed, including Michelle.

"And I'd have knocked over Erin's glass of wine on her lap," Rachel said.

Eventually we all played along, and Michelle told us the last step was to hold hands. "Now we just look at each other right in the eyes and say: 'I forgive you and love you' in unison.' She led us in that little statement. "There. That's it. Hex removed, once and for all."

"Hooray," I said. "No more murder victims in my life."

"Do you know any rituals for getting criminals to confess and turn themselves in to the police?" Rhonda asked.

"Not even Wonder Woman has those kinds of skills," Michelle said. She peered at me with an uncomfortable intensity that made me think she meant that *I* was Wonder Woman.

29

The next morning got off to a rough start when Detective O'Reilly arrived at Audrey's door. I pretended not to be assuming the worst as I asked him to come in. He nodded and said, "Morning, Ms. Gilbert. I'm here because we have been unable to locate Lucas LeBlanc in the last thirty-six hours. I wondered if you have a couple of minutes to answer some questions."

"Has he gone back to California?"

"He appears to have left the country. We have information that links him to some drug deals. We were hoping he didn't realize we were on to him, but someone might have tipped him off."

I was doing my level best to keep my expression neutral, but I could feel my cheeks warming. Audrey and I had perhaps hastened his departure by letting him know that we'd taken the fake flour to the police. He'd claimed it was Drew who arranged the shipment. Maybe Lucas was the culprit all along.

"When was the last time you spoke to Mr. LeBlanc?"

"The night before last. He came over to assist with some dance lessons."

"Was anyone with him?"

"Yes, Steve's sister, Amelia."

"She left the halfway house to come to Crestview?"

I nodded.

"That was an unfortunate decision on somebody's part." He glared into my eyes, but stopped short of accusing me to be the deciding factor. "Were just the four of you present?"

"At Steve's and my house. Yes."

"Did Mr. Leblanc say anything to you about leaving town? Or anything that might have implied that he was thinking about taking off?"

"No. The opposite. He wanted to have us complete the restaurant project as quickly as possible so the place could open. My impression was that he planned to run the restaurant himself and become both the head chef and the owner. Did he remove items from the restaurant as well?"

O'Reilly gave me a shrug. "Just some personal items from the office."

"Are you considering the possibility that he was the murderer, and he's fleeing town to escape a lifelong prison sentence?"

"We consider this behavior highly suspicious. But his alibi that he was in Crestview during Mr. Benson's murder appears to be rock solid."

"I'm sorry to hear that he's disappeared on you. Obviously if I hear anything about him, you'll be my first person to call."

He straightened his shoulders. "I know Detective Delgardio is going to be at your wedding, and—"

"Linda's a detective now?" I asked.

"It's not official yet, but, yes, she's being promoted. As I was saying, she's agreed to invite me as her escort instead of her husband."

"So…was this her choice *not* to bring her husband, or did you force her into the decision?"

"I hardly had to twist her arm, Erin. She doesn't want to see more bloodshed, any more than I do. We'd post security guards, if we thought it'd do any good."

"Are you telling me this so that I will squeeze in another chair at her table so that her spouse can come, too?"

"No, just out of courtesy to let you know our plans. She agreed that it would be best to be sharp and keeping her mind on her job, rather than just acting like a guest."

"But she *is* a guest! I nearly put her in my bridal party! Please can't you get another female officer to attend as your plus-one? We'll find two seats for you. I promise."

He shook his head. "Del and I can handle it." He started to head out the door. "Be hearing from you soon, I'm sure."

"Please tell Linda that her husband should come, too. We'll fit you in at another table."

"I will. Thanks. Just not at the kiddies table. They never seem to like me."

"How odd. You're such a Spongebob Squarepants kind of guy."

He chuckled as he let himself out. Not even a minute later, my phone rang, with Steve at the other end.

"There's been a work stoppage at Parsley and Sage," Steve said to me in lieu of a greeting. "It appears Lucas, our de facto client, has skipped town."

"So I heard. Detective O'Reilly came over and just now left. Are you ever going to finish, do you think, or is this probably it for the restaurant?"

"Probably the last straw. With Lucas leaving town, the majority owner is going to be Aunt Bea, and she has no interest in owning a restaurant. Even if they find a second buyer or two, they'll probably want to redesign the interior their own way."

"The place never opened, though, so it's all brand new. And positively stunning."

"Yeah, I guess we'll see. In any case, it's over for the foreseeable future."

"That's a shame. You did a fabulous job."

"Thanks. But there *is* an upside. I'm officially done with work until we return from our honeymoon…assuming we can still leave the country. I can help with the wedding planning."

I grinned at the thought of him and his alphabetized seating charts. Audrey wouldn't put up with that for half of a second. "Did you tell Audrey that yet?"

"No, but I will."

"You can tell her your first task will be finding a seat at the reception for Detective O'Reilly. He wants to keep an eye on things. Meanwhile, I'll suggest that she contact Chef Hummel and see if he can be our caterer after all on such short notice."

"Yeah. Losing a caterer this late is a challenge. Good thing we've got Audrey at the helm." He paused. "I also called my dad and invited him up for lunch. It'd be nice if you could join us."

"You don't want to make it a father-son lunch?"

"No, I'd always rather have you by my side."

I grinned. "I can hardly say no when you put it like that. But I'm going to have to keep my presence at the lunch pretty short. I don't want to take too much time away from Carly, Rachel, and Rhonda."

To our immense relief, Chef Hommel was able to step in for Lucas. With Audrey eagerly filling in for me as tour guide at the picturesque Crestview Mall, I arranged to meet up again in forty-five minutes. I rushed off to join Steve and George at one of my favorite restaurants in Crestview, a small Italian place in a strip mall with little ambiance but extraordinary food. We polished off our entrees and were sharing a cheese-and-fruit plate when George finally broached the topic that was heavily on all of our minds. "This is all such terrible business with Fitz, and now Drew."

"It sure is," I said.

"There's so much violence over drugs. I keep trying to wrap my head around it, the ugly loss of two young men we knew personally. Such a waste."

"Detective O'Reilly came to the house and was telling me that Lucas was apparently a drug dealer," I said. "Maybe he was the mastermind, not Drew. Drew could have simply been an addict that Lucas was supplying."

Steve groaned and said to his father, "I have to convince Erin to stop trying to solve homicides like she's some kind of master detective. She's going to get herself killed."

I glared at Steve, but held my tongue.

George patted his lips with his napkin, then set it down. He peered into Steve's eyes. "Would you tolerate some advice?"

"Fatherly advice?" Steve asked, with that slightly crooked smile he got when he was nervous. "Of course."

"I wouldn't call it 'fatherly.' Raising you and your sisters always felt like your mom's territory. I thought I was doing my part as the breadwinner. But I *do* know something about being a husband. We can't build a safe haven for our loved ones, Steve. Walls that keep out danger also keep out…excitement, variety, life. If Erin was an avid hang glider, you wouldn't want to deprive her of that passion, just because it was risky, would you?"

"No, but that's a sport. And nobody is getting murdered."

"Erin has a great head on her shoulders, and is willing to help people who find themselves in jeopardy. When a couple decides to marry, they take each other as they are and hope to grow both together and separately as a product of their union. It's not a deli order; we don't get to say 'hold the mayo.' No hang gliding or being a master detective, now that we're together."

Steve let that sink in for a moment. "You're right. Well said, Dad." As he spoke, Steve reached over and took my hand. "I've been thinking. I know this is a bit out of the ordinary, and I've got my two good friends as groomsmen, so you don't have to say yes if you really don't want to, but I'd like you to be my best man. It feels right somehow."

George smiled slowly, and said, "I'd be honored."

30

That night, Steve and I drove to the wedding rehearsal at the Episcopalian church in downtown Crestview. Audrey and my bridesmaids drove together. We'd all dressed up for the dinner at the nice restaurant afterward, as had the women in Steve's family. His dad, however, was in his tuxedo. His explanation was that he'd decided to consider this a "dress" rehearsal.

It was a thrill for me to see the love of my life happy, and I felt exhilarated to be doing a run-through of the main event. Not surprisingly my bridesmaids hit it off with Steve's two groomsmen; he'd met them in Crestview several years ago, and they still lived here in town and were great guys. Audrey and Eleanor were clearly enjoying their catbird seats, giggling like the best of friends. As George and Rachel took their places flanking Steve and me, George joked about being the oldest best man ever. The priest promptly replied, "Not by a long shot. I once officiated at a wedding with a best man who was eighty two."

"Was this at a retirement home?" George asked.

The priest hesitated for a moment, and Eleanor, sitting in the front pew, chimed in, "Don't ask a priest a question you don't want answered truthfully, dear."

"My point remains that you are *not* the oldest best man," the priest said with a wink.

"Maybe you could be the *best* oldest man, though," Eleanor suggested. George laughed and, with a twinkle in his eye, started to reply, but was distracted by one of the double doors at the far end of the aisle being pulled open. My heart stopped for a moment when I saw that a uniformed police officer had entered. What would have been a witty rejoinder from George was no doubt gone forever; George promptly headed up the aisle to greet him. Audrey hopped up as well, and the three of them had a quiet discussion.

The quiet conference ended, Audrey and George looking grim. George walked over to Michelle's first row seat and said, "The police want to speak with you."

She gasped and looked frightened. She was sitting next to Eleanor, who put her arm around her shoulder. Eleanor's features and bearing grew stony, her eyes, fierce. Audrey, meanwhile, reclaimed her seat on the other side of Eleanor and said, "He said he just has a few questions."

"Don't worry, sweetie," George assured Michelle, and perhaps his wife as well. "They just want to ask you some questions about Mark."

"Why?" Michelle asked. "Can't it wait?"

"I'm sure this is just standard procedure for interviewing a witness," Audrey replied.

An officer tracking down a "witness" felt like anything but "standard procedure" to me. The policeman approached. "I'm Officer Dunlap, with the Denver Police Department, Ms. Dunning. We've had some conflicting reports about the sequence of events that transpired at your residence."

"Conflicting reports?" Michelle repeated. "In other words, you were talking to my husband, who must have told you I was here."

"We're in the middle of a wedding rehearsal," Eleanor said. "Can't this wait until Sunday or Monday? After my son's wedding? Or tomorrow, at least?"

"I'm afraid not. We're trying to solve a homicide, ma'am."

"I can show you both to my office," the priest suggested, "if that would be acceptable."

The officer responded with a slight nod.

Eleanor sank back into the pew, with a look of despair on her face.

"Mom?" Michelle said. "Can you come with me?"

"Unless your mother is your attorney, this needs to be a private conversation," Officer Dunlap said.

That sounded ominous.

The priest ushered Michelle and the officer away, and returned by himself. He said with a smile, "These matters are ultimately in far greater and more-capable hands than our own."

Steve's and my gazes met. He looked anxious. He probably saw a measure of frustration and despair in my features. He turned and looked at his sister Amelia, who was silently rocking herself in her seat on a pew.

"Before we proceed," the priest said, touching my elbow gently, "I'd like to take a moment and lead us in a prayer."

The tenor of the rehearsal was permanently damaged, although we all put up a show of pretending not to notice. Judging by my internal clock, we took another thirty or forty minutes to wrap things up for Saturday's main event. Michelle had yet to return.

Eleanor rose and excused herself to go check on Michelle. A minute later, Amelia suddenly sprang to her feet and darted down the hallway after her mother. Audrey started to rise, as well, then hesitated and looked at me, asking tacitly if I wanted her to get involved. I shook my head, and she sat back into the pew, looking tense.

The priest gave Steve and me a somewhat forced-looking smile. For all of the weddings at which he'd officiated, I doubted he'd had the police interrupt a rehearsal to interview a family member. "I'm sure the ceremony tomorrow will be every bit the blessed event that you've been anticipating."

"Thank you, Father," we replied in unison.

"I sure hope you're right," George said to the priest. "The circumstances have been anything but 'blessed,' for the past week and a half."

Just then Michelle rounded the corner from the priest's office. She had obviously been crying. When our gazes met, she made a slight motion with her head as if to say that she needed to speak to me. I squeezed Steve's arm and excused myself to see if I could reassure Michelle—afraid that she was about to drop yet another bombshell and would ask me to cushion the upcoming blow for Steve. The way things were going, the officer might be calling for backup so that they could arrest the entire wedding party.

When I neared, Michelle turned and led us partway back to the office in an obvious attempt to give us a measure of privacy. "Is everything okay?" I asked. Obviously the answer was no, but my mind was in a whirl and that was the best I could do.

She shook her head. "The officer left a couple of minutes ago." Michelle's voice was shaky and emotional. She cleared her throat, as if to get better control. "I just needed a little… time to myself. And Mom's still trying to calm Amelia down." She searched my eyes and asked, "Do you know who the killer is?"

"I really don't, Michelle. Do you?"

Her eyes welled with tears. "Erin, they're blaming me. The police think *I* did it."

"Why?" I asked.

"They know that Fitz and Drew both had big arguments with me. Mark said in his statement that he lost his temper because Fitz and Drew had flirted with me publically."

I had witnessed for myself that Drew still had had a thing for Michelle; his feelings for her had led him to attempt to intervene, and cost him his life. It was possible that Fitz was into her, as well, although I'd gotten no indication of that from him. "Is that the truth? That he was angry with you out of jealousy?"

"Yes, but it wouldn't have mattered. Mark has spent every day of our marriage angry with me over something or other. That's just the way it is. He also said that I have been physically abusing him, which is a total lie."

"Do you think Mark is the killer?" I asked.

She nodded, dabbing at her eyes. "I'm afraid that's possible. I'm sunk either way. If the police decide I'm a killer, I go to jail. If Mark is found guilty, *he* goes to jail, and *I'm* left with two little kids and no means of financial support."

"He belongs in jail, though. If he's guilty. You have your family here. We'll all help."

Michelle sighed, as if unconvinced. "We could use your help with Amelia now. Before she loses it completely." She grabbed my elbow and started ushering me down the hall. "I need you to reassure her that you're going to give me a hand with the police. Then she'll regain her control."

"I'm of course going to be supportive, but…I don't have any sway with the police."

Michelle furrowed her brow. "Steve said you helped him when he was in trouble and the police thought he was guilty of killing his ex-girlfriend."

"He probably overstated the importance of my role. A Crestview officer has become a close friend of mine. But I don't know anyone in the Denver police force."

Michelle glared at me. "Just…make up something reassuring to tell Amelia then. I can't stand to see my sister in so much pain." She swept open the door, we stepped inside, and she promptly shut the door behind us.

Amelia was rocking herself again. I got down on one knee in front of her, so that she couldn't help but look at me. "Amelia?" I said, vowing not to lie to her unless I had no other choice.

She didn't look at me. Her face had become so pale, I was afraid she was about to faint.

"I have a good friend on the Crestview police force. Her name is Officer Linda Delgardio, and I would trust her with my life."

Amelia covered her eyes. "I'm going to let everybody down. Nobody understands. I was only trying to protect my sister." She dropped her hands but was now veering backward and forward in her hardback chair as if she was moving to wild music that she alone could hear. "I killed Fitz and Drew. Because they were hurting Michelle. They were threatening to kill her if she didn't do what they told her to. I saw a note that Fitz wrote to Michelle and Mom."

"Oh, my God!" Michelle cried. She stepped between me and her sister and grabbed Amelia's shoulders so firmly that she stopped Amelia's motion at once. "What are you saying, Amelia?!"

"I'm so sorry," Amelia whimpered. "I did it. I killed them."

31

"Stop it, Amelia!" Eleanor cried, all but shoving both me and Michelle aside as she knelt in front of Amelia's chair and tried to gain eye contact.

Michelle turned away from her sister and faced me. "Erin. Don't listen to her. She would never kill anyone."

"I killed them both," Amelia said, her voice so emotionless it was eerie. "I told Fitz at the party to leave my family alone, and he just laughed at me. So I put poison in his coffee. I saw Drew using drugs at Michelle's house. I was babysitting Zoey. I gave him a second dose, because I wanted him to stay away from Michelle and Steve. Mark didn't tell the police that I was there, because he didn't want to get me in trouble. He covered up for me."

"Don't listen to her, Erin," Eleanor said, also turning to face me as she rose. "Amelia's lying to protect us." Her expression was one of abject despair. She put her arms around Amelia. "You don't have to do this, honey. You can't. I won't let you."

"Us?" I repeated, feeling desperate. Steve's entire family was crazy. How were we ever going to get past any of this?

Amelia started sobbing that she was sorry. Then she said, "I need to turn myself in to the police and confess."

"Erin," Eleanor said looking at me in despair. She was now seated on the floor in front of Amelia. "What do we do?"

"Get Amelia a lawyer right away, and listen to his or her advice." I turned to Michelle. "She didn't say any of this to the police officer, did she?"

Michelle started shaking her head and muttered, "No, thank God," just as Amelia said, "I'll tell the lawyer what I did."

"No, Amelia," Eleanor cried in a now-guttural tone, swaying as she got to her feet. "You're innocent. Stop making false statements! Or else I'll have to tell the police that *I* did it."

"Mom! No!" Michelle cried. "This is crazy!"

"Amelia," Eleanor replied, "I *know* you're innocent, because *I* did it."

"No, you didn't. You were with Daddy." Amelia stomped her foot. "You were at the funeral services for Fitz."

"I wasn't with your father the whole time." She shifted her gaze to me. "I killed Drew because I believed he'd raped Amelia."

I gaped at her. *Could she be telling the truth?*

"Mom! He never raped me, and you know he didn't," Amelia said. "You're only saying that so you can make it sound like you had a legitimate motive for killing him!"

"I know that *now*. But I didn't at the time. Amelia is innocent. So is Michelle. This was my doing. Mine alone."

Not only was Amelia no longer rocking herself, but she was suddenly articulate and forthright. What was going on? Was she putting up a front? Was Eleanor? I felt sick to my stomach.

My thoughts raced. Eleanor absolutely *had* to be giving a false confession to try to spare her daughters. There was a fierceness in her gaze that unnerved me. *How can I possibly stop this avalanche?* Maybe, in her shoes, I would do precisely the same thing. "You can't do this, Eleanor," I protested, despite knowing I was wasting my breath. "Steve and your husband are just a short distance away. What's your false confession going to do them?"

"It's my moral obligation to confess," she said evenly.

"I'm getting Steve," Michelle said over her shoulder as she darted out of the room, closing the door behind her.

"How did you get the poison, Amelia?" I asked pointedly, thinking that proving how flimsy her story was could bring a quick end to both her and her mother's ruses.

"I ordered it from the Internet."

"What was the precise name of the poison you purchased? What did it say on the label? Was it liquid or powder?"

She narrowed her eyes and met my gaze. "It was cyanide. A white powder. That's all I remember. Computer records of my purchase will still be listed on my store account, and on my hard drive. The police will examine my computer and can prove that I did it."

Eleanor's eyes widened for an instant. "That only proves that cyanide was purchased using your computer."

Eleanor closed her eyes for a moment and clenched her fists, as if steeling herself. "Even if that's true, which it isn't, you weren't in your right mind. You aren't guilty of murder."

Michelle reentered. "I had to get Daddy to fetch Stevie," she said. I assumed that meant he was in the men's room.

"And I can't believe for a moment you'd have killed Drew," Eleanor said to Amelia. "You always liked each other."

"So did *you*," Amelia retorted. "You used to call him your second son."

"I did, didn't I?" she said wistfully. "I'd forgotten that." Eleanor raked her hand through her hair, in a motion that reminded me so much of her son that I felt a pang. "How he used to make your brother laugh."

"What's happening?" Michelle asked her mom. "Amelia isn't still trying to insist she did it, is she?"

"She's confused," Eleanor began. "She—"

"*I* killed them!" Michelle shouted. "I'm not letting either of you take the rap for me!"

Dear God! Twenty-four hours from now, I was going to be in this chapel, marrying Steve Sullivan! How the hell could this be happening! "You've all got to stop this!" I cried, losing my thin grip on my emotions. "It's a federal offense to confess to a crime that you didn't commit." I wasn't actually sure if that was true, but it certainly *should* be a criminal offense.

"In which case, I'll go to jail for my having committed a crime," Eleanor fired back. "And that's what I'll deserve. I'm getting the priest and confessing to him."

I blocked the doorway. "Please don't do this," I told Eleanor. "I know why you're making this false confession. But you can't blame yourself for murder just because you made a mistake in judgment. Even if it had terrible consequences."

The sound of footsteps resonated in the stone hallway. They were Steve's; I could recognize his gait. I rushed into the hallway. My eyes misted with relief at seeing him and knowing he could help.

"What's going on?" he asked me.

"Michelle is scared she'll be arrested for the murders, so Amelia claimed she did it, and now your mom's claiming *she* did it to protect Amelia."

Steve gaped at me and said, "You're serious, aren't you?"

I nodded.

Steve marched past me, clearly livid, and I closed the door and followed him. "Are you trying to scare Erin off from marrying me?" Steve demanded, scanning the faces of his family members.

"I'm telling the truth," Michelle said. "It's *Mom* who's lying to protect me."

"She's protecting *me*, Stevie," Amelia said. "I killed Fitz and Drew."

"No, I did," Eleanor and Michelle said in unison.

"Mom, you cannot plead guilty to a crime you didn't commit and go to jail in anyone's place. Drew had a lot of faults, but he was my closest friend and meant a lot to me. You're turning the investigation of his murder into a circus."

Eleanor was grinding her teeth but said nothing.

"Michelle, stop acting like the watchdog and protector of the family. You have your own life to lead, and your daughter and soon, an infant, to take care of. Just tell the police the truth.

"Amelia," he said, softening his voice. "What you tell the police will have a permanent impact on many people's lives. Are you absolutely certain that you killed both of these men? That it wasn't something you dreamed you did in retrospect?"

She nodded.

"You remember buying the poison," he prompted, his tone of voice skeptical.

"I used Mark's name. I said it was for killing pests on that property they own on the Western slopes. Where they're raising the grapes."

"You remember crushing the pills?"

"It was capsules. I opened them. I put it in his coffee. Then I saw Drew put a needle in his arm on Michelle's porch. I was there, babysitting. He rang the doorbell, but I didn't want to answer. Mark had run out on an errand. So it was just me and Zoey. I watched from the window. I went out and said he had to leave…that there was a little child in the house, so he couldn't be there. He said he was just trying to wake himself up and gave himself some vitamins. But then he went to sleep. I gave him another injection. And he died."

Now she sounded both articulate and believable. The effect was harrowing.

"Did you tell Dr. Whiting about this?" Steve asked, his voice and bearing now tense.

"No," Amelia said, shaking her head. "I didn't want Doctor Susan to know what I did. She likes me. I didn't want her to start hating me."

Steve looked at his mother, his stoic expression nearly crumbling. The sight broke my heart. "I'm calling a lawyer," he said, putting his hand on Amelia's shoulder. "We'll go talk to him together."

Eleanor was sobbing. "You can't force me to endure this," she said to Steve. "I don't believe Amelia, but the police *will*. She thinks she's telling the truth, but she isn't. I know my daughter, and she isn't capable of killing anybody."

"I agree, Mom, but we have to do the right thing here. A lawyer can get a psychiatric evaluation of her and sort the truth from the delusions."

"But what if the police arrest her, and she gets convicted?"

"We'll have to deal with what happens next. We have to have faith in the legal system that she won't be convicted."

Michelle muttered that she would go fetch the priest, and the rest of us waited in silence. A short time later, the two of them returned. "What is going on?" the priest asked us, his voice gentle.

Eleanor hesitated.

"Mom," Steve said. "You're talking to a man of the cloth. Tell the truth."

"I need you to talk to my daughters separately," Eleanor said, as if agonized. "Amelia's intent on making a false confession. If she does, Michelle seems prepared to follow suit. This is the worst day of my entire life."

32

Audrey and the wedding party went ahead to the rehearsal dinner, which was too late to cancel, with the instructions that they were to explain that we were unavoidably detained, and that Steve and I would get there as soon as we could. From that point forward, where I was concerned at least, it was a matter of prayerful, private waiting.

On a ten-point scale of spirituality, I'm probably a six. I am one-hundred percent certain that God exists, and that he has gifted us with this amazingly beautiful world, so rich with possibilities. In my opinion, however, far too often, religion and spiritual practices mutate into divisiveness, instead of a loving, supportive, and enlightened spiritual community. Personally, I'd take an atheist any day over a deeply devout worshiper who believes his hateful actions are heaven sent; Hitler, after all, considered himself a good Christian.

The pastor had asked Eleanor to leave, and so she, George, Steve, and I maintained a small vigil in the worship space, sitting in the last pew closest to the office hallway. As an hour dragged by with the priest still in private conference with Steve's sisters, I was praying all but continuously. Steve and

Eleanor were praying as well, although George struck me as having been so overwhelmed by these circumstances that he had a glazed look to his features, as if he'd tuned out.

Finally, Michelle and Amelia appeared, Michelle with her arm around Amelia's shoulders. They gave us identical wan smiles, the similarity in their attractive features more apparent to me now than ever.

George stood up, but said nothing. We anxiously watched them approach. "Amelia and I have agreed to wait until after the wedding, then to speak to lawyers," Michelle announced. "Amelia realizes that she did *not* kill anyone."

"No," Amelia said. "I just agreed not to tell the police anything I don't know for absolute certain is the truth. And I realize that my memory is fuzzy."

"Thank God," Steve said. He gave his sisters a three-way hug.

"We need to get to the restaurant," Michelle said. "We should already be there."

"Everything's all right," Eleanor told her. "Audrey and the wedding party have volunteered to take charge and fill in for us. We're only going to be a few minutes late."

I realized then how numb I felt. It was as if my brain had been frozen and only the surface was registering my surroundings. "The rehearsal dinner just recently started?" I asked.

"Fifteen minutes ago," Eleanor said.

Steve's and my gazes met. He looked as weary as I felt. He forced a smile and gave me a little nod. We were going to have our dinner. And put on our smiles.

Eleanor grabbed George's arm. "We're all made of stern stuff. Let's go and have a good time."

Steve put his arm around me, and we started to follow his parents.

"Oh, and I invited Aunt Bea last night," Eleanor added, "and dutifully apologized for losing her invitation."

Steve's arm muscles tensed.

Steve and I pulled into the restaurant parking lot right behind George and the Sullivan women. Steve was being stoic, and our conversation so far had been limited to reassuring each other that all would be well. This was clearly not the time to discuss the guilt or innocence of Amelia or Michelle. There was also no need to discuss how strongly we both hoped that they were innocent, and that somehow Lucas Leblanc had managed both murders despite his solid alibis. Steve took a deep breath after shutting off the engine.

"There's Audrey's Mercedes," I said, pointing with my chin.

"Good. I'm lucky she's there for us. Despite my being such a blockhead."

"You're not a blockhead."

"Sometimes I am."

"Well, hardly ever," I said, winking at him and knowing he got the Gilbert and Sullivan Pirates of Penzance reference. "Ready to do this thing?"

He watched his family emerge from his dad's car. "I'm a bit shaky, but yeah." He reached for my hand. "You'll be my rock, if I have to lean on you tonight?"

"Of course. Just like you're always *my* rock."

He gave my hand a squeeze, and we got out of the car. Steve held the door for his parents and sisters, and I hung back beside him. The maître d ushered us to our private room, where our tables for thirty guests were arranged in three long rectangles of ten. Most of our guests were already seated. Someone—probably Audrey—led them in a round of applause, which made me smile.

Steve smiled, too, and held up his hand. "Thanks for coming, everyone, and for your patience. The rehearsal took a little longer than it should have. Unfortunately, *I* kept messing up," he joked. "But the love of my life is still here by my side. Like always, she's been lighting the way for me."

And just like that, all felt right in the world. We took our seats in the center of the center table, and we were soon swept up in wonderful conversation and delicious Prosecco and appetizers.

While the servers were taking our orders from our special menu, I made a quick scan for empty seats. All of our guests were here; there wasn't a single empty chair. Aunt Bea was seated between Eleanor and Audrey, and she gave my shoulder a quick squeeze and told both me and Steve that she was so very happy to be here. Steve mustered a gracious reply. A short while later, she excused herself, presumably to use the restroom.

A minute or two later, Mark Dunning entered the room, weaving a little. The conversation at our table stopped. He headed toward Aunt Bea's currently vacant seat, and plopped down.

"Mark!" Michelle snarled. "What are you doing here?"

"I got an invitation and I accepted," he said with venom in his voice. His eyes were a little out of focus and he had to struggle to stay balanced in his seat.

"Mark," George said calmly, "things have only escalated in the last couple of hours. Please be a gentleman and leave."

Audrey grabbed Mark's arm and said, "I'm here without a date for this evening. Let's ask if we can get a table for two in the main room, shall we?"

I couldn't help but grimace. It was magnanimous of her to sacrifice her enjoyment of the evening, but I wanted her here with us.

"Thanks, Audrey," Mark said, slurring his words, "but I want to stay put."

Aunt Bea returned to the room just then. She grimaced at Mark for a moment, but then managed a smile. "Well," she said. "We'll need to squeeze in an extra seat."

"Stay away from my family," Eleanor implored to Mark. "You've done enough damage already."

"Mom, Dad, he's my husband," Michelle said with a defeated sigh. "He's still part of this family." She turned her attention to Mark. "You have to sober up, Mark. Once and for all. Your children deserve a better father than this."

"Yeah, they deserve a lot better than me—an out-of-work bum." He glared at Bea. "Thanks to you."

A server came with a chair and positioned it at the corner next to George. I could see that our guests at the two other tables flanking ours were trying not to stare at us; they averted their eyes when I looked their way.

"If you choose to stay at this wonderful family celebration," Bea said, "show some respect to our companions." She took the new seat. "It's not about you and your situation at work."

"Aunt Bea is spreading lies about me to my boss," Mark exclaimed loudly. "I was the number one salesman! And now he expects me to believe that business is down. Well, let me tell you something. When times are hard for everyone else, the booze business booms!"

"I can see that you're angry," Aunt Bea said to him. "As well as highly intoxicated. This behavior makes you look guilty."

"I don't *care* how it makes me look. I know the truth. I didn't kill anyone," Mark stated. "I also know who *did*. But nobody wants to listen to me."

"Who?" Aunt Bea asked.

"*You!*" He scanned our faces, looking each of us seated at the center table in the eye. "She's behind all the killings and all the infighting between us. Can't you see that? It's as obvious as the nose on my face!"

"That's a ridiculous, baseless lie!" Aunt Bea declared.

"She's the one who got me into this mess with her false accusations. She tricked me into getting loaded and behaving like an ass. Thanks to her, I got fired for nothing."

"Thanks to *you*," Michelle said to Mark with a haughty voice, "the entire neighborhood was in lockdown for three hours! You fired a shot into the air! You were drunk as a skunk with the police trying to talk to you! You call that *nothing*?"

He spread his arms. "It had nothing to do with my job! I wasn't on the clock!"

"You're not *fired*," Bea said. "You're on probation. For thirty days. At least get *one* of your facts straight."

"Um, maybe I should make a toast," Carly said. "This is our dearest friend, Erin, who is getting married tomorrow, to the wonderful love of her life. It's time we put our differences aside."

"Hear, hear," Aunt Bea said.

"Yeah, right," Mark grumbled.

"You're drunk, Mark." Michelle rose. "I'm going to drive us home. I ruined the rehearsal, and now we're *both* ruining the meal along with my darling brother's and Erin's celebration. Let's leave now while there's still plenty of time for everyone *else* to salvage their party."

Mark scanned our faces and, apparently, realized he needed to cede to his wife's wishes. He rose and followed Michelle through the doorway without another word.

A few moments later, I spotted Amelia sneaking out of the room. I excused myself and followed. She headed into the women's room. Her shoulders were shaking with sobs once again. I trotted in after her.

"Amelia? Can I get you anything? Club soda? Tonic water?"

She shook her head, took a couple of deep breaths and said, "Oh, Erin. You have no idea what you're getting into by marrying a Sullivan."

"I *do* know, Amelia. I love Steve. I also love you, and your family."

"Maybe you love injured souls, then, Erin."

I handed her a pair of tissues from the box on the counter behind me.

Amelia took a deep breath. Staring at the ceramic tile floor, she said, "I thought I was guilty. But now I don't think that's what happened. It was Michelle."

33

My nerves were turning the butterflies in my stomach into humming birds as Steve drove me back to Audrey's from the restaurant. Much as I wanted to pretend nothing unusual had gone wrong at our dinner, Amelia's statement had pushed my hand. I hadn't planned on driving with me instead of my squeezing into Audrey's car with our bridal-party houseguests, but I'd been too alarmed by Amelia's statement about Michelle to wait until tomorrow—the day before our wedding—to discuss the subject with him.

"Aunt Bea seems to be aging really quickly," I said, intentionally starting us on a relatively gentle subject. "I think all of the deaths and the stress surrounding our wedding has been getting to her."

Steve let my statements hang in the air for a while, before saying quietly, "I think so, too. She looks ill. But that strengthens Mark's theory."

"You think Aunt Bea actually murdered Fitz and Drew?" I asked, skeptical.

Steve gave no response, but his furrowed brow indicated that the answer was yes.

"I can at least *conceive* of her poisoning Fitz's coffee…setting aside the fact that she had no motive. But there's no way I can begin to picture her getting out of her car, walking up to Drew on Michelle's porch, searching Drew's pockets to find his liquefied drug stash, and then giving him a second injection…assuming he was out of it after giving himself a first injection. How would she know how to do that?"

Steve's jaw muscles tightened. After what felt like a lengthy pause, he said, "She could have managed. If anyone could ever figure out how to get her own way, Bea's the one."

"But…that's a long time to be standing on someone's porch in the middle of the day never once being seen by a neighbor or a passerby."

"Yeah. Maybe it was Mark, after all. Or the police could be wrong about Lucas's whereabouts that day. Maybe Lucas gave him some higher grade cocaine than typical, and he accidentally overdosed."

"I guess that's possible," I said honestly. "That would be a load off everyone's mind." I paused, wishing Steve would launch into a lengthy conversation so I wouldn't have to voice my next statement. He said nothing, though, and we were nearing Audrey's street. He had a right to know what was happening with his own sisters. "Amelia thinks Michelle is guilty of both murders."

"She told you that?" Steve asked, his voice heartbreakingly sad.

"When we were in the women's room together. Michelle had a motive for killing Fitz. He was blackmailing her. She could have been there when Drew arrived, and they could have argued. He'd proved to be a ladies man right when she was looking for a safe exit from her marriage. Drew was flirting with my friend at our shower and took her on at least one date. Michelle loses her temper easily, and, like you said, she can hold a grudge like nobody else."

"Michelle would never do that, Erin. She's hot-tempered and self-absorbed, but she's not a killer."

"She's family. It would be terrible to discover that your sister is capable of taking another person's life. But…I can't help but think that most killers have siblings. Lots of them probably didn't want to believe their siblings were capable of murder. Meanwhile, Steve…I need to ask you this question. And I want you to give me an honest answer. Okay? This is important."

"Of course, Erin," he said. "Let me pull over." A red light turned green, and he stopped the car alongside the curb and faced me.

"What's going to happen to us if the unthinkable turns out to be *true*? What if Michelle's guilty? Or if it's Amelia? Or one of your parents, as ridiculous a suggestion as that is."

Steve grimaced, but continued to hold my gaze. "It will break my heart. But at some point, I'm one-hundred percent certain that I'll remember that I'm married to the love of my life. Then I'll do what comes next. I'll face up to whatever it takes to accept that a family member of mine was guilty of killing my friend."

"Are you sure?" I asked. "Even if I wind up testifying against your family member, you won't hate me forever?"

He managed a small smile. "No, Gilbert. I'll *love* you forever, no matter what. But it's a moot question. Nobody in my family is guilty of murder."

I awoke early after a terrible string of violent nightmares. The dreams were set in Aunt Bea's wine cellar, although the space had warped into cavernous dimensions. Sometimes I was the killer. Once I was the victim, not dead but unable to communicate that I was alive. Michelle had choked me, but then she morphed into Amelia. Even then, I had the pervasive sense that I was responsible for the violence, and that Steve was there on the periphery, waiting for me to join him, unaware of my predicament. This was an inauspicious beginning to the eve of my wedding, if ever there was one.

A thought that lodged itself into my head like a burr was that I had missed a major clue having to do with the wine cellar. I still had a key to the basement door in Aunt Bea's house. She'd given me the key shortly after signing my contract. I'd never needed to get inside her house when she wasn't home, and we'd forgotten all about it. In four years of private clients, this was the first time I'd ever forgotten to return a key during my final walkthrough. Maybe that alone had caused me to fret about the wine cellar; my unconscious was merely trying to remind me of my oversight.

And yet, I couldn't let go of Steve's remark last night as he drove me to Audrey's. He believed that Aunt Bea was highly capable of manipulating a situation and could have gotten Drew to allow her to inject him with a drug. I could only think of one outlandish reason that Drew could have allowed Aunt Bea to inject him with a drug: if Aunt Bea was Drew's cocaine supplier.

In my sleep-deprived stupor, I became fixated on that possibility. Bea could have brought drugs into the country more easily than most people. She operated primarily in South America and India, two places with considerable drug trafficking. Maybe the reason Bea wouldn't allow anyone to touch her wine bottles was that they might not have held wine, but rather were filled with illegal drugs, perhaps in powder form.

If I could sneak into her wine cellar, I could examine her stock more closely. Even if the bottles were made with dark green glass, I'd be able to tell by shaking them if the contents were liquid or powder. I could abscond with one or two of her wine bottles and bring them to the police to examine. Then after my hope had fizzled, and we were forced to face the horrid reality that one of the Sullivans was a murderer, I'd replace Aunt Bea's bottles and apologize on bended knee. Worst case, I'd get caught in the act of snooping, and once again, I'd fess up and apologize.

I left a note in the kitchen for Audrey and my bridesmaids that I was "looking into some last-minute wedding preparations" and that I'd be back before noon. Halfway to Bea's house, I got hold of my senses. I couldn't simply park my van in her driveway and think that she'd fail to see it, or to hear me creeping around in her basement. Not to mention the slim possibility that she'd installed a security alarm in the last week or so.

I decided instead to knock on her front door and make an excuse for examining her wine bottles. I could tell her that I wanted her to educate myself on wine purchasing in advance of our honeymoon in Paris, then I'd insist on examining some bottles to look for residue. Or for leaky corks, even. If my excuses fell short, I'd tell her the truth about my nightmare and my theory that not all of her bottles contained wine.

I rang Bea's doorbell repeatedly and also knocked. No answer. I promptly reverted to my original plan. After rounding the house, I let myself into her basement, thinking all the while that I would apologize for my terrible behavior upon my return from Europe. The chances of my search turning up anything seemed ridiculously remote, yet little was at stake by my airheaded actions; people tended to expect brides to get a bit crazed.

I went straight for the most expensive bottles she possessed. With just a passing thought that this was perhaps the lowest behavior I'd ever sunk to—entering an elderly client's home uninvited and shaking her bottles of wine—I got to work.

Right away, I found something puzzling. Some of the bottles seemed heavier than others, and they truly didn't feel the same way when shaken. Some of the reds had almost no sensation of having liquid in them. There seemed to be no space for air—as if they'd been filled to the tippy top and then corked. I gathered six bottles to compare. I was inspecting them closely when the door creaked open.

I gasped and turned. Aunt Bea stood at the door, staring at me.

"What are you doing, Erin?"

"I rang the doorbell, but you didn't answer. So I let myself in with your key. I've been looking at your wine bottles."

She glared at me. "You know I don't like anyone to touch them."

"I know. I'm sorry. This was inexcusably presumptuous of me. I've been under so much stress, I can barely control my own behavior lately."

She glowered at the half dozen bottles that I'd set on the end cap of one of the wine shelves. I'd designed this flat space for just this purpose—to set out a few bottles that had been culled from the many racks.

"You scared me, Erin. When I heard someone rattling around down here, I thought it had to be Mark, trying to round out his litany of crimes by adding the theft of my wine collection."

"You really think he might be the killer?"

"I'm *certain* he's guilty. Aren't you? He had both the motive and the opportunity."

"Not the evidence, though. That's why he hasn't been formally charged with murder."

"He still hasn't? Even after his boorishness last night, and the police questioning Michelle?" Bea asked with obvious alarm.

"No. My friend, Linda, is an officer—soon to be named a detective—and she'd have told me right away."

Aunt Bea looked deeply worried. Her whole body was trembling, and she looked even more frail than she had last night. "The police will gather the evidence they need. I hope."

"Are you okay, Aunt Bea? You seem to have lost quite a bit of weight. And you look as exhausted as I am."

"I couldn't sleep last night," she said.

"Neither could I. Wedding night jitters, I suppose."

"So you jittered yourself into my wine cellar?"

"Yes. I...wanted to see if I could find any physical differences in wine bottles themselves that can indicate that a particular wine is a really outstanding vintage." Even as I said it, I realized how lame it sounded.

"There isn't," she replied, impassive, considering our bizarre circumstances. "Unless you count how steep their price tags are."

"I really think there's something wrong with this bottle. There's a circle on the bottom of the insides that looks almost like a cork."

"You shouldn't be turning the bottle over to look at its bottom," she scolded. "It's not good for the wine."

"It isn't? I thought wine was supposed to be stored slightly tilted toward the cork."

"No. That's old-school." She leaned her cane against a shelf and took the bottle from my hands. Her cane tipped over. I picked it up as she replaced the bottle on the shelf, neck out.

Without stopping to think, I said, "Your cane is lighter than I expected."

"Yes, it's hollow."

"Of course it is, come to think of it. It's gold plated. You wouldn't want a solid gold walking stick, after all."

"No. If it were solid gold, some thief would snatch it away the minute I left my house." She gestured at the length of shelving. "Did these other bottles pass muster with you?"

"Umm…a couple of them had that strange circle on the bottom, too."

"It's just the thickness of the indent in the glass that you're seeing. But enough of this nonsense. Why are you really here?"

"Well, it's pretty difficult to explain. More like really embarrassing. I'm still trying to eliminate Steve's immediate relatives from the suspects list. Last night I kept thinking about how only someone who was familiar enough with drugs as to give someone an injection could have killed him. So it seemed to me that, other than people in the field of medicine, drug dealers, users or—"

Aunt Bea suddenly pivoted and swung the bottle in her hands as it were a baseball bat. She cracked against the upright corner of her wine shelf as if she were christening a ship.

I gasped and stepped back as red wine pooled on the floor. I eyed the remaining neck of the bottle in her hand. A golden-colored rod was sticking out of it. That was the circle I'd seen, which had extended from the neck to the bottom of the bottle.

I stared, uncomprehending for a moment. Then it clicked. It was a rod of pure gold. Bea had indeed been smuggling, but not drugs. She was smuggling cylindrical bars of solid gold in her wine bottles.

34

Ignoring the glass shards and the puddle of spilled wine pooling around her shoes, Bea grabbed the gold rod with her left hand and yanked it free from the bottle neck. "Don't make me use this on your face, Erin," Bea said, brandishing the jagged edge at me.

I was so stunned by Aunt Bea's actions that I didn't know how to react. My heart was pounding with fright, yet I couldn't quite grasp the concept that my life was in danger. "You killed them? Both men?"

"Calling them 'men' makes it sound like a worse crime than it actually was," Bea said, her voice remarkably unemotional. "I killed a pair of drug dealers." She knocked her cane over again as she groped for it blindly. It rolled, the bottom of the cane facing me. I could see that the tip of the cane was solid cork.

It came together for me then. I had been right the first time. "You killed a pair of drug dealers who sold the drugs that *you'd* smuggled through customs inside of your cane. You could access the drugs by pulling out the cork bottom from your cane."

"Not exactly, Erin. My cane didn't hold enough drugs to support even one addict's needs. The contents of my cane were for my recreational use only. The finest quality cocaine in the world. Although I've never once shot the drug into my own veins. Just into Drew's."

"And the gold rod in your wine bottles? Is *that* hollow and filled with drugs, too?"

"No, that is solid gold." She glanced at the gold bar in her left hand. "This is a *golden rod*, as I like to call it. My favorite color."

"The rods were created so that you could smuggle gold into India? To feed that country's citizens' insatiable desire without having to pay their enormous fees?"

"Yes. I never should have brought the bottles here. I usually send them straight to India from Damascus. But I had problems with one of my major…beverage importers."

"Mark Sullivan?"

She narrowed her eyes. "Yes. He's been difficult."

"So you framed him for murder."

"I tried to, yes. Don't expect me to feel bad for that, Erin. He's a wife beater. Michelle didn't have the backbone to press charges. You don't want to set a man like that free, any more than I do."

Bea's cane was not far from my reach. I could probably lunge for it and use it as a defensive weapon before she could jab at me with the broken wine bottle. She followed my gaze. Stalling, I said, "It's so clever how the diameter of your cane is the same size as the typical neck of a wine bottle."

"Aren't you going to grab it? Knock the weapon from my hand?"

I sighed. I was staring straight into her eyes. She lacked all conviction. She also looked as if she lacked the strength to hurt me. "You don't have the stamina to overpower me and stab me. You're still breathing heavy from breaking the bottle."

"True. I have a flare for the dramatic, but, clearly, the cancer has gotten the best of me."

"Cancer?"

She nodded. "Of the liver."

Liver cancer was always fatal, and progressed rapidly. "How long have you known you were ill?"

"Less than two weeks. My oncologist doubts I have more than three months left. I'm sorry not to have been more forthcoming with you. Or with anyone. I didn't want to spoil everyone's mood before your wedding. Yet now I let the cat out of the bag. As well as the gold out of the bottle."

"I'm just so…." *What was I? Confused? Baffled? Mostly just sad.* Maybe Drew and Mark were blackmailing her. Even so, Drew was Steve's friend, and she'd killed him. Steve's intense dislike of her had been justified. Yet I felt sorry for her. "I wish I hadn't built this expensive wine cellar when you could have done some extravagant bucket-list item with the money."

"Don't worry yourself. I've made up for my miserable existence many times over in the last decade. I'm prepared to meet my Maker. I've traveled all over the world. I was already more than ready to stop. That's why I bought this place. And this room gives me so much pleasure."

But you killed two people! How can you be nonchalant about dying with that *on your conscience?*

In defiance of her low-energy mood and physical weakness, Aunt Bea continued to hold the neck of the bottle in front of her as if it was a knife that she intended to stab me with.

"You don't want to kill me," I told Bea, hoping that was the truth. "And you know you won't be able to overpower me.

Put the bottle down. Besides, the police are already on their way. I called them the moment I discovered something was fishy with several of your bottles."

"Don't lie, Erin." To my great relief, she dropped the broken bottle into the pool of shards and wine. She set down her bar of gold between two bottles on the shelf. "You can go ahead and call the police now, though. It's time to stop all this madness. I'm too old and tired. That's a line from 'The Little Engine That Could.' And fact of the matter is: I *can't*."

I felt more sad than relieved. I didn't understand what she was doing or why. I hadn't posed much of a threat; if she'd simply demanded that I leave her house, I would have obeyed. Then I would have suggested that the police get a search warrant and discover what was going on with Bea's wine shipments. Unable to understand her current behavior, I couldn't predict what she would do next.

"Watch your step," she said over her shoulder, as she shuffled out of the wine cellar, leaving her cane behind. My heart was still pounding as I followed her. Maybe she'd hidden a gun out here; perhaps she'd shoot me or turn it on herself. Instead, she merely plopped into the closest chair at her table, her back toward me.

I rounded the table cautiously, concerned about her health, even though that seemed pointless. Her face was pale and damp with perspiration, and she was still out of breath.

"You can turn my cane into the police as evidence. There's bound to be at least trace amounts of cocaine. That's how I smuggled drugs in and out of India. And they'll see for themselves how I smuggled gold from Dubai into India."

"So you killed Drew? And Fitz?"

"I had no choice, Erin. They were both onto me and were both blackmailing me. They wanted to take over my business and build it into a drug empire. The last straw was when Eleanor told me the day of your shower that Fitz was blackmailing *her*, as well as me. I have such a limited time left on this earth. I didn't want drug dealing and smuggling to be my only legacy. My best option was to get rid of those two despicable young men."

"But *now* your legacy is going to include killing two people. Did you think you were going to get away with it?"

"My intention was to frame Mark. But all I really wanted was to stay out of jail long enough to watch you and Stevie get married." She chuckled ruefully. "Missed it by a day and a half."

"I don't understand, Bea. Why did you smuggle drugs? And gold? Was it just for the money?"

She sighed and looked up at me. "No, it was mostly for vengeance. At least, originally that was my strongest motivation. I was tired of being treated like a nobody. That's how it had been, my whole life. Always in the shadow of my flamboyant, miserable husband. Then, one day, I woke up and saw things clearly. My abusive husband had left me. I had no children. I'd never had an outside job…he'd been against all of that. He never wanted me to have a life of my own. I looked at myself in the mirror that morning and saw this fifty-five year-old image staring back at me. All of that time, gone. So I decided I was going to live large from then on out. I'd take full advantage of being the person in the room who would draw the least attention. I'm no one anyone would ever suspect of being an international smuggler."

She paused and eyed me from head to toe. "You still haven't placed your call to the police, Erin. Go ahead. I'm sure your phone's right in your purse. I'm not going anywhere."

Still edgy, disbelieving that she would truly just sit there, I kept an eye on her and dialed 911. When the dispatcher answered, I gave her my name and Bea's address, and said that Bea Quinn had just confessed that she'd killed Fitz Parker and Drew Benson and wanted to turn herself in. The dispatcher asked if this was some sort of a prank. While I was assuring her that it was all on the up-and-up, Bea asked to speak with her directly. I handed her my phone.

"This is Barbara Elizabeth Quinn, and I did indeed kill the two men that my friend Erin told you about just now. I'd appreciate it if you'd send a patrol car immediately to my house." She paused as she listened to the dispatcher and said, "No. Thank you for offering, but I'm unwilling to stay on the line with you. I was right in the middle of a conversation. Just tell the officers to ring the doorbell, and I'll come right out with them." She hung up.

"As I was saying, Erin, I didn't see the harm in transporting gold. Buying low and selling high is the way capitalism works, and their fixed-limits on gold imports simply ensure that the rates remain sky high. I looked at my misdeeds strictly as a business opportunity." She sighed again and shook her head. "What I didn't realize at the start was that, once you blur one line by telling yourself you're simply making a harmless infraction, it's just too easy...and too tempting...to cross the next line. *Then* you tell yourself: I've already got a proven system in place. And that, well, drug addicts got *themselves* into their addiction. And so dealing drugs doesn't damage anyone who hasn't already been abusive to themselves."

"So you justified selling the drugs? Then you used drugs to kill? Twice?"

By supporting her weight on the table and the back of her chair, she got to her feet and staggered over to the highboy in the corner. She grabbed a pair of red-wine glasses from the cabinet, then the bottle of red wine and corkscrew. Shuffling back to the table, she said, "I knew this day was coming, so I picked out my very best bottle for the occasion. Share a glass of wine with me, Erin. I'm assuming with my confession to poisoning, you're hesitant and fearful. But I'll drink first, and you can pour."

"No, thanks."

She opened the bottle with finesse and poured two glasses before dropping into her seat once again. "I should have opened this bottle sooner, to let it breathe." She took a sip and closed her eyes. "Heavenly. This is the nectar of the gods, Erin. I'm an old woman. I'm going to be in jail for the rest of my life. It's an excellent wine. At least try a sip."

"No offense, Aunt Bea, but for all I know, you've already poisoned the bottle and are going to kill us both if I drink any."

"You saw that the seal was unbroken and the cork was intact," she scoffed. "I promise you, Erin, if this was suicide, I'd just gulp it down, then turn red and writhe on the floor. That's not my style. I'd just as soon go out the natural way...let the cancer take me at its own pace." She took another slow sip. "Furthermore, I have no intention of killing you. I want you and my ersatz nephew to have a long, happy marriage. I already told the police my story, so what would my purpose be?"

This might be the strangest and stupidest decision of my life, but I could find no fault in her logic. I pulled out the chair next to hers, sat down, and indulged in a sip of wine. The flavor was sublime.

"Wow."

"You see what I mean?" Bea asked. "A flavor like this should be illegal. How could I, or any rational person, ruin it with cyanide?"

I laughed at the irony in her last statement. We sat in silence for a moment, luxuriating in my second sip of wine, but I was still so puzzled by her confession. "How did you even know that Fitz was going to be at my party?"

"Audrey had shared the guest list with me earlier."

"How did you get the cyanide?"

"Oh, please, Erin. I have all sorts of ignoble connections."

"And you drove out to Mark and Michelle's house, found him on the porch, and convinced him to shoot up some coke with you?"

She grimaced.

"I'm truly just trying to understand."

"He didn't need any convincing. He was already so high, he couldn't function. I gave him a second dose."

"Just to stop him from besmirching your legend?"

"And to undo the damage I'd done by not blowing the whistle on him. This was my deal with the devil to stay out of jail, clear back when Drew and I crossed paths in our dealings in California. I killed Drew for the good of the people in my life I was leaving behind. He brought everyone crumbling down around him. That boy had every gift in the world—loving parents, friends, community, good looks, a sharp mind, a big inheritance. Yet he was all about wanting more. He wasn't strong enough to kick his habits. He was going to OD all on his own one day. I simply hurried the process."

"But...killing someone as your last act on this earth...." *Not mention that one of them was the best friend of the man that I loved.*

"My only regret is that I wanted to frame Mark, but failed. He weaseled out of it."

"He's innocent."

"No. No, he's not. He's committed crimes against his wife. He's pilfered money from customer accounts."

"But he didn't murder anybody."

"And *I* did." She lifted her glass. "Here's the toast I intended to make at your wedding. 'To two of the loveliest people I know. May you always find the little byways in your life's journey that give you unexpected adventures. May you remember every day how blessed you are to find each other. May your love be the beacon that guides you through the dark and troubled times. May your dark and troubled times give you the strength and maturity to never take yourself too seriously or take your love for granted. Cheers.'"

We clinked our glasses and had a sip. I was getting choked up and had to quickly take a second one to swallow the lump in my throat. The doorbell rang. "That would be the police, here to arrest me. Let's go let them in, shall we?"

35

The next morning felt surreal. It was impossible for me to process the fact that Aunt Bea had been arrested for two murders, and that twenty-four hours later, I was sitting in a beauty salon with my bridesmaids, getting my hair and nails done for my wedding.

All that morning and into the afternoon, Audrey and my bridesmaids kept filling my champagne glass, taking care of my every need. I allowed myself to be whisked off to the hotel suite a short distance from the church. Next thing I knew, I was in my dress, and Audrey was handing me my bouquet and making me turn around to face the full-length mirror. It was at that moment, as I was holding my bouquet of pure white calla lilies and seeing myself in my Vera Wang gown, that I suddenly became giddy.

My journey through hell was over. The killer had been arrested! Steve's family members had been exonerated. Here I was, looking at myself in my wedding dress, feeling beautiful and so phenomenally lucky to have my dreams come true. I started giggling, as did Rachel, Carly, and Rhonda.

Audrey snorted and said, "You young people just don't know how to hold your liquor."

"I'll drink to that," Rachel said, and the four of them clinked glasses. I was too busy staring at my own reflection, telling myself that this was real. I'd gotten my dream career, my dream house. I had tried-and-true friends who meant the world to me. I was marrying the love of my life within the hour. And I believed that in heaven my mothers—my adoptive mom and my biological mom as well—were lifting their own champagne glasses to me in our shared happiness.

Someone knocked on the door, and Audrey answered. Steve's mom stepped inside. She gushed about my dress and exchanged some chit-chat with my friends. Then our gazes locked, and her eyes teared up.

"Let's step inside the bedroom for a moment," I suggested.

She nodded, and we sequestered ourselves for a private conversation. The moment she'd shut the door behind us, she said, "Oh, Erin, I'm never going to be able to apologize fully enough. There aren't even words to describe how grateful I am to you for hanging in there with my family, and especially with me, in spite of how I treated you."

"You don't owe me an apology. You were doing your best with an impossible situation. And, as for gratitude, you and George raised my favorite person in the entire world. *I'm* the one who's grateful and indebted to *you*."

"My heavens. Your mother raised *you* to be incredibly gracious. But, Erin, I need you to hear me out." Eleanor perched on the edge of the bed; I had too much adrenaline to sit. "I heard about Aunt Bea, of course, and how you had to be interrogated by the police at length yesterday…right when you should have been spending the day happily with your bridesmaids. I owe you so much. I was scared out of my mind that

Michelle had killed Fitz, thanks in no small part to my horrendous bad judgment regarding Fitz. I honestly couldn't think straight. But she's innocent. You solved two murders. And you saved my daughter from imprisonment. She's finally decided to file for divorce. Mark's moving to Spain next month. He has a brother there who's taking him on as a business partner."

"Wow. That's surprising, to put it mildly. What are they doing about his parental rights?"

"He's giving them up. Michelle didn't to go into many details, but apparently, he lost his temper and shoved her on the sidewalk, in front of a witness last night. That's why he's agreed to leave the country. In exchange for her not filing charges, he's going to be out of my family's lives once and for all."

"Which means he's out of *my* family's lives, too," I said. "That's wonderful!"

"Yes." She smiled at me with obvious sincerity. "I'm so lucky to be getting you as my one and only daughter-in-law."

"That's so sweet of you. Thank you."

"I've never disliked you, Erin. Quite the opposite. You're a sweet, yet strong young woman...exactly the sort of person I envisioned Steve wanting to spend his life with. It's just that, truth be told, I hoped that he'd wind up with someone who wasn't in his field, let alone his business partner. He's had his heart broken so badly with that con artist who went into business with him."

"Yes. I knew her. And I understand how much of a déjà vu our union must have seemed to be."

"With the operative word being 'seemed.' You're nothing like her. I went from rags to riches in terms of my daughter-in-law. I'm so fortunate that you are still marrying into my family despite all of its quirks and drama. Not to mention our false confessions. We've behaved like characters in a terrible soap opera."

Blessed by our drastically improved relationship, I smiled at her. "One with an extraordinarily happy ending."

"Indeed."

Eleanor gave me a hug, and we reentered the living area. She exchanged goodbyes with all of us, then she gave me a proud, maternal-looking smile and said, "I'll see you in fifteen minutes."

Audrey ushered her out the door, then turned toward me and said, "Well, Erin. It's time to seal this thing for all eternity." She held my gaze, and I could see the mixture of pride and excitement in her eyes. "Are you ready for your grand entrance?"

"I do," I said. Then I laughed and said, "Just kidding. I *am*. Let's go."

Pachabel's Canon in D minor started playing, which I'd selected simply because it's so beautiful. But as Audrey and I walked down the aisle, I was grinning at the thought that I would have preferred to have been gyrating to "Tell Me What You Want" by the Spice Girls as I moved toward Steve. It was probably fortunate that tastefulness had prevailed, however. I knew that the loving expression on Steve's face was priceless, and that I would remember it for as long as I lived. And, dear lord, but the man knew how to wear a tuxedo!

The priest spoke the "dearly beloved" phrase that I'd heard countless times. For the first time, I grasped its full meaning. I couldn't possibly have loved the people gathered here to witness this sacred event in my life any more than I did. My heart was full of gratitude and love.

To my surprise, Audrey started getting more and more emotional during the ceremony and was weeping audibly during our exchange of vows. She was sitting in the front row, immediately beside the aisle. I saw Steve hesitate and glance down at her. That must have set off his reaction to how phenomenal this moment was. Up to that point, I had been keeping a lid on my own emotions, despite Audrey's sniffles. But when Steve's voice cracked, I started crying, too.

In an obvious ad-lib, Steve said, "You're the woman who makes me so happy I can cry. I'm so blessed to be able to spend the rest of my life with you."

During the reception, I was swept into a joyous buzz in which all I could feel was overpowering love and happiness. I kept pausing and telling myself to remember this moment—every smile on every face, every embrace, every amazing conversation with our one-hundred-plus well-wishers. I wanted to always be able to picture a panoramic view of the hall, with its sweeping view of stunning scenery: mountains, woods, and Crestview Creek. Of the strings of lights on the ceiling that recaptured the beauty of a starry sky. The crystal glasses, silk tablecloths, Ikebana centerpieces, and the ornate china. All of our guests looking so beautiful and so happy. I could not think of a single moment in which I felt as overwhelmed with joy as when Steve and I performed our first dance with Amelia's choreography.

As guests joined us on the dance floor, I was startled to see that Mark had not only come to our reception, but was escorting Michelle onto the dance floor. Steve and I stopped dancing and stared at them as they approached.

"At ease, brother dear," Michelle said to Steve, in what could only be considered a snide tone of voice. "I asked Mark to come. It's our last hurrah."

"Yeah," Mark said. "I agreed to stay on the wagon, in exchange for the free meal." Then he turned toward Michelle, took her hand led her into an energetic samba. Michelle's grin as she danced with him was almost a sneer that, for all the world, seemed suitable for a movie villainess.

I whirled around toward Steve. He was gaping at Michelle. We resumed dancing, but as he took me in his arms, he said, "Michelle's up to something. That was her evil-genius expression, which she's had ever since I can remember. She'd make that face and put Super Glue on my lip balm, or something of that ilk."

"Yikes! I'm glad she wasn't *my* sister."

"She kind of *is* now."

"Maybe she's just feeling triumphant for forcing Mark to leave the country."

"That's probably it exactly," he replied. His voice lacked confidence, though.

As the evening progressed, Mark was on his best behavior. He wasn't drinking, and every time I spotted him, he was by himself or with Michelle, keeping his mouth shut.

Steve and I made a point of visiting all of our guests tables, making sure to chat with each of our guests individually. When we joined Mark and Michelle, Michelle pulled an unwrapped DVD out of her clutch purse. "Mark and I got you a present from Paprika," she began, "which is already on the gifts table. But Erin, this is my personal gift to you." She handed it to me.

"It's various family photos and videos throughout the years, dating back to when Stevie was just a newborn."

"Thank you, Michelle. I'm touched," I told her honestly. "That was so thoughtful of you to do put this together for me."

"Oh, it was nothing, really." She turned toward Mark, who was staring at the disk as if alarmed. "I know this is a surprise, Mark, but I'm certain Erin will be really happy to see its contents. Don't you think?"

"I'm sure she will," he said evenly. He seemed to be struggling to keep a lid on his temper. Maybe the disk had embarrassing recordings of him, or it showed her and Drew together. Just then Rhonda and her husband were passing Steve's and my chairs on the way to the dance floor. Her husband set down his glass of Beaujolais between us. "Forgot I had this in my hand," he said to me with an affable grin. "Whoever supplied your wine and champagne is my new best friend."

Rhonda winced at his remark. Determined not to let my spirits sag with thoughts of Aunt Bea's imprisonment, I simply said, "I'll tell her you said so."

As I turned back to speak some parting words to Michelle, that haughty expression of hers was back on her face. I merely thanked her again, then ushered Steve toward some former-client friends of ours.

An hour or so after our cake-cutting ceremony, some of our guests were departing. I'd all but dismissed my concerns about Michelle's haughty expression. I spotted her alone, and took the opportunity to sit down next to her for a reasonably private conversation, hoping she could dispel my fears completely. After a brief exchange of chitchat, I said, "I admire you for making the decision to raise your young children alone."

She nodded. "Thank you. It's going to be hard, but I've got a supportive family."

"Yes, you do."

"Frankly," she said, after taking a long sip of her wine, "I *do* feel like the unintended victim in all of this."

She was slurring her words and her cheeks and nose were a little red. I bit back my urge to ask if she should be drinking while pregnant. "Oh?"

"My future's so tenuous. I'm going to have to go back to work. Which I always intended to do, but not while I'm pregnant with my second child."

"Are your finances really that precarious?"

She nodded. "But it's okay. Aunt Bea said she'd allow me to inherit her business."

"She *did*?" I asked, truly surprised.

Michelle chuckled. "Well, not *all* of them, of course. Minus the drug smuggling. And probably the gold marketeering."

"*Probably?*"

"I wish she could be here. Even after knowing what she did. She just wanted to protect me from Mark."

I studied her features, confused. "By...killing Drew? And Fitz?"

Steve, I realized, was now standing behind me. "How could Aunt Bea's actions protect you from *Mark*?" he asked.

"I meant to say Fitz. She knew he was blackmailing me. I told her a week earlier, when we were discussing the invitations."

"But, that's not what she told me yesterday. She said she'd found out the day of our wedding shower that Fitz was blackmailing your mom."

"Bea must have been confused." She started to set down her wine glass, but jerked her hand and splashed wine on her lap. "Clumsy me. I'll be right back."

She rose and headed for the women's room. Steve took the seat she'd just now vacated. He raked his hand through his hair. "She's lying, Erin. I can always tell when she's lying through her teeth."

"She meant it the first time, when she said that Bea was protecting her from *Mark*," I said. "And Bea told me a couple of times that she'd tried, but failed, to frame Mark for the murders. But how would killing Fitz and Drew protect Michelle from her abusive husband?"

"It makes no sense," Steve agreed.

"If she's lying about talking to Aunt Bea about Fitz's blackmail, she could be lying about everything else," I said. "Mark's abuse. Her whereabouts during the murders. What she knows about the murders."

Steve was staring straight ahead. He had spoken so quietly, his voice was a cracked whisper. "My family has bent over backwards to protect one another. All of those false confessions at the rehearsal."

"That was like the scene from 'Sparticus.'"

As I heard myself, I felt as if I'd just been sucker punched, and I groaned.

"What is it, darling?"

"Yesterday I asked Bea how she'd gotten the cyanide, and she told me she had nefarious connections. I should have stopped to wonder how Bea could have gotten cyanide that fast. The way Aunt Bea reacted yesterday. She—" The chill up my spine was so intense, I not only got goose bumps, but a case of the shivers. "She told me her only regret was not being able to frame Mark, that she felt bad for Michelle. Bea all but announced that she was *also* making a false confession, Steve."

"Are you saying that Bea was trying to protect Michelle from going to jail to pay for her crimes?"

I nodded. "Your mom told me today that she'd been worried sick all this time that Michelle was guilty. And how relieved she was at my solving the case. But, unless she had really good reason to suspect her, shouldn't she have believed in her own child's innocence? Meanwhile, Aunt Bea all but fed me clues, incriminating herself. She *wanted* to go to jail in Michelle's place."

"It's possible they were both wrong about Michelle…my mom and Aunt Bea," Steve said. "In any case, I'm certain that Michelle knows more than she's telling anyone."

"And *I'm* all but certain that Aunt Bea's innocent." I grabbed Steve's hand with both of mine. "Meanwhile, we're leaving in the morning for two weeks. I don't want Aunt Bea to be sitting in jail all that time. Especially not when *I* played such a big part in putting her there." I doubted that the police would incarcerate her—an elderly, dying woman—for smuggling cocaine. If she retracted her confession, the trace evidence in her cane would only indicate possession.

"I agree. But we don't have any actual evidence. All we can do is tell Linda Delgardio and Detective O'Reilly about our concerns over Aunt Bea's innocence and Michelle's…complicities." Steve looked on the verge of tears. "Maybe's she's covering for Mark. Maybe she just couldn't stand the thought of raising her kids with the onus of having a convicted murderer for a dad."

"So she's letting Aunt Bea go to jail for a double murder?" I asked, incredulous.

He rose. "We have to give the police a heads up. But this is *not* going to be on *your* head this time. *I'm* going to go get Detective O'Reilly and Linda. I'll tell them our suspicions. Promise me, Erin…stay with our other guests until I get back. If Michelle tries to talk to you, make an excuse, and join the largest group you can find."

"I promise. But…shouldn't I just come with you?"

He shook his head. "I need to be alone when I report this. Again, this one is on me, not you."

Steve crossed the room in search of Linda and O'Reilly. I watched as his father pointed to the door, and Steve went outside. That exit led to the parking lot, and my first thought was that Linda might have left. Then I spotted her husband's bald head among a group of guests near the dance floor. Linda was definitely still here and wouldn't hesitate to call in an on-duty officer if O'Reilly had already left.

A moment later, I saw O'Reilly enter the room, scanning his surroundings and then heading toward Michelle, who had just reentered the room. I breathed a sigh of relief.

Just then, a waiter tapped my shoulder. "One of your bridesmaids asked me to tell you that you are to come to the storage shed for a surprise."

"The storage shed?" I repeated.

"Yes. She said to tell you it was a surprise for the bride. If you go right out the front door," he said, pointing, "and you look to the left, you'll see a dirt path. It leads to a storage shed behind the restaurant. If you hit our auxiliary parking lot, you've gone too far."

"Okay." I glanced around and saw that Rachel and Rhonda were still on the dance floor with their husbands. "Was it Carly? With Auburn hair?"

"I think so," he said with a shrug.

"This is very strange, but thanks." I caught Michelle's eye as she crossed the room with Detective O'Reilly heading toward the front entrance. She looked scared and shook her head at me. O'Reilly must have told her that Steve and I doubted her innocence.

Eager to talk to Carly, I left the room with a minimum of exchanges with our guests. I felt horrible. I'd just convinced myself that my sister-in-law was a murderer. I'd destroyed the only family I had.

I soon saw the path, which I could tell was wending along a rugged path toward the back of the hotel. The full moon was casting eerie shadows. I watched my footing, thinking that my two-inch heels were not making this pleasant.

I had gone only about twenty or thirty yards when I sensed that someone was waiting up ahead next to the path, the person's silhouette mostly blocked by the spruce tree between us.

I stopped, my senses on red alert. "Carly?" I asked hesitantly, feeling on edge.

Someone stepped out from behind the tree. It was Mark. "'Fraid not." I stared, not wanting to believe my eyes. He was holding a gun in his hand, and he aimed the gun at me. "I bribed a waiter to lie to you. I'm afraid I can't let you watch the DVD that my wife just gave you. I should have known she'd be incapable of keeping her end of our agreement."

Oh, my God. The two of them had worked together. Probably with the ultimate goal of taking over Aunt Bea's lucrative business. "I have no idea what you're talking about."

"The bitch that I'm married to went behind my back and set up surveillance cameras throughout our house. *Including* our porch. She was trying to trick me into admitting on camera that I'd killed Fitz. She took all her equipment down before the police could find them, right while I stupidly drove Drew to Crestview, in order to make sure he was too far gone to be saved. I... lost my head when her black lover showed up at my house. She got a recording of me giving him a lethal overdose...which she gave to you. I need that DVD, Erin. Where is it?"

"In my purse. Under my chair at the reception hall. I'll go get it for you." I whirled around, intending to run and scream for help.

"Stop!" he said.

I heard a metallic click and froze.

"That was me removing the safety from the trigger. Don't scream, or I'll shoot you in the back. Then I'll shoot every person who comes up this path to rescue you."

I turned around again, my fear morphing into rage. "This is pointless, Mark. Two detectives are talking to your wife, right now. She'll tell them about the DVD. It's too late to escape. If you kill me, you'll be a triple murderer."

"Right. Which means I've got nothing to lose. I'm spending the rest of my life in jail, no matter what. This isn't how I wanted things to turn out, but Michelle forced my hand. So I'm taking you hostage, and we're driving to Mexico. As long as you cooperate with me, I'll let you go at the border."

He gestured for me to come toward him. "Lead the way, Erin. My car's parked at the other side of this path. Don't scream. Don't try to get away. As you pointed out yourself, I'm a desperate man."

"But if you shoot me you won't *have* a hostage."

"I'll grab the next girl I see. Maybe one of your little bridesmaids in their pretty black dresses."

I gritted my teeth, filled with hatred for Mark. This was like arguing with a toddler. I could use as logical an argument as I wanted, but he was operating on pure adrenaline and raw emotions. I started walking. "Why did Michelle give me the DVD?" I asked. *She could and should have given it to the police! Over a week ago!*

"She was blackmailing me. It was her protection. She forced me to promise to leave the country by the end of the month and let her divorce me. She's a computer whiz. She set up her computer so that unless she keyed in the correct password each month, the video would be automatically sent to the police. She claimed she was doing it for both our benefits. Giving me the chance to build a new life for myself. Giving her the chance to raise her kids without the stigma of knowing their dad was a murderer, rotting away in a penitentiary."

Steve was right. Mark acted alone. But, inexplicably, she'd set me up for a fall. I continued walking as slowly as possible. I had no intention of getting into his car with him. Or, at least, I wouldn't if I could possibly help it.

He snorted. "Stupid thing is, Zoey's not even my kid. When she was born, I just thought she had a naturally darker complexion than either of us. But, nope. Michelle tricked me into marrying her. I guess she couldn't dig up a black man willing to marry her that quick."

We were nearing the storage shed. I was running out of time. My gorgeous gown was a handicap. I couldn't possibly outrun Mark, and all of my white fabric made me an easy target.

A good-sized rock was by my feet. I waited until Mark was just a step behind me, then I dropped to my knees, grabbed the rock, and slammed it into his kneecap. He yelped in pain and fell, right beside me. I pounded the rock straight into the gun in his hand. He dropped the gun.

I heard voices in the background. "Help!" I yelled.

Mark lunged at my throat. "I warned you! I'm going to kill you with my bare hands!"

He had me flat on my back in an instant, with his big hands wrapped around my throat. He was incredibly strong. I was struggling to breathe.

My vision was fading into gray.

"Stop or I'll shoot!" someone yelled. It sounded like Steve. "Let her go!"

Mark's grip eased. An instant later, Steve loomed over Mark. He punched him in the face, knocking him to the ground.

"Freeze! Police!" Linda Delgardio shouted, running up the path toward us. Steve must have outraced her and pretended to have a gun in order to buy me a precious extra second of freedom from Mark's stranglehold.

Despite my haze of pain and panicked struggle to breathe, I managed to look at Linda. She was still wearing her cocktail dress—green silk with a leaf-like uneven hemline. But now she had her service revolver. It was pointed right at Mark.

"Erin. Are you okay?" Steve asked.

I was gasping for air, unable to talk. Mark was staring at a spot on the ground. I followed his gaze and saw a glint—a reflection of the light from the full moon. "Gun!" I managed to say, pointing.

"Don't try it!" Linda growled at Mark. "You don't want to tempt me!"

Detective O'Reilly came running up the path, his revolver drawn but pointed at the ground in front of him. Within seconds, Linda was reading Mark his rights while O'Reilly was putting handcuffs on him.

"Michelle told us about Mark," Steve explained to me. "She'd seen the waiter pointing this way, and she guessed that Mark could have been luring you out here. So we asked the waiter, and he admitted he'd lied about who wanted you to come out here. The whole thing about the DVD was a setup to trick Mark into doing something stupid! She fooled him into thinking it was a recording of him killing Drew. She didn't actually have a surveillance camera on the porch."

"What—" I couldn't talk. Even though pressing my hand to my throat helped a little, it was too painful. I wanted to ask what he was talking about. Why would she pull a stunt like that on me with no warning?

"Let's get you to a doctor," Steve said. "Can you walk, or should I carry you?"

"Walk," I managed reply. While he was helping me to my feet, Michelle emerged and ran up to us. "Erin. Oh, thank God. We got to you in time."

"What the hell were you thinking!" Steve yelled at her. "How could you set her up like this? She was almost killed!"

"I didn't know how else to get him to confess, Stevie! Like I said before, I didn't *have* any actual evidence. So when he told me about killing Fitz on our drive home from your party, I knew I had to do *something*. But I couldn't even goad him into hitting me, or talking about killing Fitz again, once I'd set up a couple of cameras inside. So I made up a bogus story about my having a video of him killing Drew."

Steve didn't reply, his features set in an angry glare.

"He told me he'd made Amelia look guilty by buying the cyanide under her name…on her computer while she was babysitting. I was trying to protect our sister from getting arrested. Plus he's my husband. I can't testify against him. Then when I knew he'd killed Drew, I couldn't cope with my bad luck at not setting up a camera on the front porch. So I bluffed…and he never called me on it. But then *Aunt Bea* got arrested for his crime. I was desperate. Don't you see? This was the only way I could stop him."

"Are you ready to go?" Steve asked me gently, studiously ignoring Michelle.

I shook my head a little. My neck hurt like mad. I looked down. I seemed to have cuts and bruises over my entire body.

My gown was no longer ever going to be suitable to hand down to a daughter.

Linda and O'Reilly each grabbed one of Mark's arms and began escorting him toward the back parking lot, where I could see red flashes of light on the horizon. O'Reilly must have radioed ahead for backup patrol cars to surround the area. Linda paused and said, "Michelle, we're going to need a full statement from you. Wait here for an officer."

She groaned, tears streaming down her cheeks. "I did my best, Stevie. I was just trying to keep Zoey and myself safe from Mark. To make the best life possible, considering my hideous mistake in marrying him." She grabbed his arm with both of her hands.

"Get a lawyer," Steve growled at her. He jerked his arm free from her grip.

"*You* understand, don't you, Erin?" Michelle pleaded. "I'm so, so sorry. I knew he would panic and incriminate himself. And I couldn't figure out any better way to trick him into proving he was guilty. But I didn't know he had a handgun. In my wildest dreams, I didn't believe he'd try to kill you."

She'd used poor judgment, but for a noble reason. "I *do* understand," I whispered, and Steve looked at me, his eyes wide with surprise. Someday, I was sure, he too would understand, and both of us would forgive Michelle. Just not today.

Steve returned his attention to his sister. "Don't talk to Erin. She was nearly killed. You put my wife's life at risk! You don't deserve to be her sister-in-law!"

We started down the path.

"I didn't know what else to do," Michelle cried, sobbing audibly. "I didn't know *how* to warn you guys about my tricking him with the DVD I gave you."

Michelle could have found dozens of better ways to get Mark under arrest. She'd chosen this one—to fool him into thinking she was giving me an incriminating video. But it didn't really matter whether or not the ends justified the means; either way, it was over. Aunt Bea would be vindicated; Mark would go to prison, quite possibly for the rest of his life.

"We'll be okay," I said to Steve in as loud a voice as I could muster. I wanted to say more, but talking was too painful. I wanted to tell Steve that, even if it turned out to be just him and me against the entire world, this was still where I always wanted to be—right by his side, as his wife.

Bride and groom.

ABOUT THE AUTHOR

Leslie Caine was once taken hostage and gunpoint and finds that writing about crimes is infinitely more enjoyable than taking part in them.

She is author of three cozy mystery series: the Molly Masters Mysteries, writing as Leslie O'Kane, featuring Leslie's alter ego: a mother of two cartoonist who creates eCards; the Allie Babcock Mysteries, writing as Leslie O'Kane, featuring a dog therapist; and the Domestic Bliss Mysteries, writing as Leslie Caine, featuring interior designers Erin Gilbert and Steve Sullivan.

To learn more about her series and learn about new releases, please visit: www.leslieokane.com

DISCOVER LESLIE CAINE

Allie Babcock Mysteries
Play Dead
Ruff Way to Go
Allie Babcock Box Set (Books 1 & 2)
Give the Dog a Bone
Woof at the Door
A Dog-Gone Christmas Novella

Domestic Bliss Mysteries
Death by Inferior Design
False Premises
Manor of Death
Killed by Clutter
Fatal Feng Shui
Poisoned by Gilt
Holly and Homicide

Molly Masters Mysteries
Death Comes to the PTA
Death at a Talent Show
Death on a School Board

Death Comes to a Retreat
Death of a Gardener
Death Comes to Suburbia

Rhoads Memorial Library
103 S.W. 2nd Street
Dimmitt, Texas 79027
(phone: 806-647-3532)

66677936R00173

Made in the USA
San Bernardino, CA
14 January 2018